Preview Excerpt

Dom glanced at the door, which Nikolai had left slightly ajar. Suddenly, he was fumbling the cigar. It nearly fell to the floor and burned a hole through the massive, fifteen-thousand dollar area rug.

"Are you all right, Dom?" Yuri asked. "You look like you've seen a ghost."

Dom squashed the end of the cigar against the platter on his father's desk, set it down, and stepped out into the hallway. Her back was turned to him, and although she wore a silky, high-necked, long-sleeved blouse and wide-leg black pants—another requirement set in place by Ekaterina—he knew that body. Her hair was tucked into a bun, but he knew that hair. That scent, that jawline, those fingers...he'd dreamed about them.

He walked up behind her, wrapped his fingers around her neck, and pushed her face-first against the wall.

Prince of the Brotherhood

A Mafia Romance

The International Mafia Series
Book 1

K. Alex Walker

Sage Hill Romance

To all the lovely authors and readers I had a chance to meet at IRAE. Thank you for helping a girl genetically predisposed to awkwardness feel like she fit in somewhere.

I'd like to especially thank Phoenix, S.K., Kassanna and Olivia. Phoenix, I adore your personality, and you called me your sister. S.K., you are sweet and beautiful and gave me the most genuine and wonderful welcome. Kassanna, you called me "baby" and made me feel loved. And Olivia, you called me "punkin" and made me feel cherished.

I went back to my hotel room and cried (good tears!!) because there's a little, lonely girl I often keep hidden inside who's waited her entire life for moments just like these.

Chapter One

"Your eyes are poisonous."

Dominik Sokolov tore his attention away from the reflection in the stacked glasses on the bar's tile countertop to find the woman behind it staring at him.

"Excuse me?" he asked.

"Your eyes." She swirled a rag inside a stem glass with a deep bowl. "They remind me of mercury, which is poisonous."

He'd been on the island of Grenada for the last three months and didn't think he would ever get used to that accent. Everyone who spoke, it was like a melody as opposed to the rougher, more abrasive Russian spoken in his home country.

"Oh."

He returned his attention to the glasses.

His father, at least, hadn't deviated from the type of goons he usually kept around. The minute he'd walked into the small beach hut overlooking the Atlantic, he'd known these two men were there for him. Though he'd left Moscow to live with his aunt in the U.S. when he was sixteen, he still knew his people, and he especially knew Yuri Sokolov's people. But it wasn't like he could stay away forever. He was the son of the head of the Bratva. Russia would always find him and bring him home.

"You are in a tropical paradise." The bartender leaned over the bar counter, her already decent-sized breasts swelling larger in the bikini top. "Maybe try to look like you're having a good time? You're too handsome to be sulking, friend."

Dom studied her. *Really* studied her. She worked at the resort. He'd seen her before, on multiple occasions. She was the one who'd come in to make sure his room was to his liking his first day there, and when she wasn't tending bar, she walked around in crisp white collared shirts, black pencil skirts, and low-heels to ensure all the guests were satisfied with their accommodations. The one thing that had remained constant between both roles was the bright red lipstick that stretched and accentuated her pretty white teeth when she smiled.

"Look, I appreciate the compliment, but I'm not really up for...you know."

She cocked her head to the side. "Up for what?"

"I mean, you're a beautiful woman." Very beautiful, in fact. "But I'm here to relax."

"Hmm." She leaned back and folded her arms across those plump breasts. "Well, no offense, but I work here, and you've only ordered one drink since you sat down. It's either I flirt with you to get you to order more, or I boot you from my bar so a paying customer can have a seat."

A smile played at the corner of his mouth. "Fine. I'll order something else. What do you recommend?"

"Do you like fruity drinks?"

He tipped up his left brow. "Do I look like a man who likes fruity drinks?"

"You look like a man with poisonous eyes."

"Rum." He tapped the bottom of his empty glass on the bar top. "Give me something with lots of rum."

She nodded, turned around, and her taut arms flailed as she mixed. For someone who worked in administration and bar-keeping, she had an excellent back. Then again, since he'd been here, he'd walked most places. Every once in a while, he took a taxi or a minibus, but most of what he needed had been within walking distance of the resort.

When she worked inside, she kept her hair pulled back in a tight bun.

Today, it was out.

Free.

Wild.

Curls and coils sprung from her scalp, with splashes of chocolate and golden highlights spread throughout. The curls and coils framed her face, a crinkled set of bangs falling slightly over her forehead, and the colors popped against her complexion.

"One of sour," she turned around and placed the drink in front of him, "two of sweet, three of strong, and four of weak."

He stared at the pink-orange concoction. "What is it?"

"Rum punch, Grenada-style. Try it."

He took a sip, and the alcohol slapped him across the face.

"Damn. That's...is it always this strong?"

"You said lots of rum."

"Caribbean rum isn't normal rum."

She smiled and looked behind his head at the water.

Since she was distracted, he followed the trail of her brown skin down to those full breasts, her stomach with a sprinkle of sweat that created an enticing sheen, and the colorful wrap she'd tied at the hip.

He took another sip. "You have a beautiful accent, by the way."

"Don't get me wrong," she met his eyes, "you're a good-looking man, but—"

"All right. I deserved that." Laughing, he held out his hand. "Andrei."

She shook his hand, studying him through narrowed eyes. "You don't look like an Andrei."

"Well, what's your name?"

"Emerald."

He studied her the same way. "You don't look like an Emerald."

"Maybe it's not my name, but a girl can never be too careful."

Not that he believed anybody on the island knew what the name Dominik Sokolov meant, and those who had been sent to collect him thought he was someone who'd betrayed Yuri. Why make things easier on the Bratva, Interpol, or any other organization that either wanted to abduct him or had a red dot on the back of his skull?

She tipped her chin at the drink. "You like it?"

"It's pretty good."

"Well, I didn't get this job because I know how to tie my shoelaces."

"You've...got a mouth on you." He drew a longer sip, eyes never leaving hers, and glanced at her mouth for reference. Her lips were full, and there was a dimple high on her chin, to the left of her mouth, when she smiled.

The number of beautiful women he'd seen or come across meant he should have been fucking his entire time on the island, but knowing his father was looking for him, it was hard to trust anyone. The more beautiful they were, the more dangerous they could be.

A customer walked up, and she left him to take their order. It was one of the men Yuri had sent. One clothed in scars. He had his fair share, but they looked like they could have come from fighting, childhood, or the military. With his head tattoos and marked-up face, this man screamed organized crime.

"You've got a set of tits on you," the man said with an accent so pronounced, he wasn't sure whether the man had spoken in Russian or English. "What are you doing later? Me, I hope."

Emerald turned away from the man without a response.

"Hey," the man rapped on the countertop using his knuckles, "I'm talking to you."

"Leave her alone," Dom warned. "There are beautiful women everywhere. Find somebody else to fuck with."

Their eyes met, and a message was silently exchanged: *"Make this easy so no one dies."*

Someone would die, but it wouldn't be him.

"Emerald" finished preparing the drink and slid it toward the scarred Russian. The man tipped the glass at her, shot Dom one last look, and left.

She scanned the beachfront and, spotting no new customer requests, returned to stand in front of him.

"Thanks, Andrei."

"No problem."

"Feel like another drink?"

"Yes." He tipped his head in a firm nod. "But not here."

The confident smile she'd worn since he noticed her faltered. "Where, then?"

"Out." He tossed back the rest of the rum punch and cleared his throat to ease some of the burn. "Just the two of us."

"What did I put in that drink that made you go from not being interested in anything to wanting to go out, just the two of us? Are you a killer?"

Now *that* made him smile.

"Do I look like a killer?"

"No, but you don't look like an Andrei either. The name, is it American?"

"I have no idea. My mother was one of those eccentric types. If the mood had struck her, she would have given me a Korean name."

She laughed.

Like her accent, it carried a melody.

"Now," he leaned toward her, "how do you pronounce *your* name?"

She did the same, folding her arms on the bar top, dropping her voice to a whisper. "What do you mean?"

"I'm staying at this resort. I'm sure this isn't the first time you've seen me? It's not the first time I've seen you."

Her eyes made slight movements as she scanned his face. "No. It's not. I make it a point to know all our guests."

"I've wanted to know how it's pronounced since I got here."

"Where did you see my name?"

"You wrote it on a napkin for a man I've been jealous of ever since."

Red hair, beard, tall. The kind of man she didn't need to waste her time fucking.

"And you have been with us for how long?" she asked.

"Three months, but I didn't want to ask at the time and make you think I'm hitting on you."

One thing was clear—the woman had no issues with eye contact. If she hadn't gone into resort management, she would have made a hell of a detective.

Her voice lowered even further. "And now?"

"Oh, I'm definitely hitting on you now." He grinned. "So...dinner?"

"I thought it was drinks."

"The more you talk, the more I like you."

She looked away again, over his shoulder, at the beachfront. "On one condition."

"Name it."

"I take you to see my Grenada, not the watered-down beach resort version."

"I'm down for that."

A large, loud group of customers approached, and her chest and shoulders moved with a deep sigh. "Meet me in the lobby at eight tonight," she said. "And it's pronounced 'Asia.'"

He slid off the bar stool. "Pretty. I'll see you tonight, *Eija.*"

Chapter Two

Eija Barrett tightened the sarong wrap draped around her waist. She had exactly one hour to shower, dress, and meet the man from the bar downstairs. Her hair alone would take a half-hour, so the fact that she wasn't anywhere near her room didn't help.

But she couldn't waste this opportunity.

All their intel had pointed to the prince of the Bratva, Dominik Sokolov, hiding out in the Caribbean. Luckily for her, he'd chosen to hide out on the island where her parents had been born and where she'd spent seventeen years of her life.

No one knew what Dominik looked like, but they knew what his father, Yuri Sokolov, looked like. They knew what Yuri's wife, Ekaterina, and their other children looked like. They'd used the information to compile a profile that perfectly matched the golden-haired companion of the tattooed piece of shit who'd hit on her at the bar. But Mr. Head Tatts wouldn't be a problem as she'd laced his drink with enough sedative to leave him comatose on a lounge chair on the beach.

She sauntered down the corridor leading to Dominik's suite with a stack of towels on her palm and stopped in front of the door. Just as she was getting ready to call out, the door opened. Although she was holding towels, she kept them low to frame her breasts. Dominik's dark eyes immediately fell to them, and he tucked his blond hair behind one ear.

Up close, he looked younger. Intel had put the Bratva protégé between twenty-five and thirty-two years of age, and she'd been expecting the older side of the spectrum. Twenty-five seemed too young to lead an entire criminal organization, but Yuri was getting ready to pass the torch. A transition of power was often a country, organization, or nation's most vulnerable period.

"You requested fresh towels, sir?" She played up her accent and smiled. "I'm sorry. I also tend bar to help out, and I didn't get a chance to change before I came up. Please excuse my unprofessionalism."

His accent seeped from his mouth like tar. "It's okay. I remember you from downstairs."

She held out the towels. "Here you are."

"You want to put them inside? You can put them wherever you like."

"Of course, sir."

The room had been registered under the name Yevgeny Arbenin, a character from a Russian play from the mid-1800s. It was why their team believed Sokolov knew they were watching him and closing in—Yuri could have used a traditional name, but he'd chosen one from a play reminiscent of Othello. They just weren't sure who, in Yuri's mind, played the role of Iago.

Eija stepped inside, stopped in the middle of the room, and turned around. "Where would you like them?"

"Anywhere is fine." He pointed to the other side of the suite. "In the bathroom closet, maybe? That would make the most sense."

She sent him another smile, deposited the towels, and returned to find him leaning against a wall, staring at the doorway.

"Where is your friend? The one with all the..." She drew a circle around her head.

He laughed. "The tattoos on his scalp? Passed out drunk on the beach. He thinks he's a Viking."

"His tattoos, they look painful."

"Do you like them?"

"Oh, no." She covered her mouth, giggling. "It isn't my type."

"What is your type, then? Maybe tall, blond hair, and with a Russian accent?"

"What do you..." She giggled again. "Oh. I get it. Well, compared to your friend, you are more my type. Russia certainly has some good-looking men."

"The women here are so beautiful," he said. "*You* are so beautiful. How can you stand it?"

"Stand what?"

"Not being able to walk two steps without a marriage proposal?"

She dropped her gaze to his mouth. "If all the women here are beautiful, doesn't that make me average?"

His long legs had to stretch only twice before he was in front of her. He bent, both hands gripping her ass as he picked her up and walked to the bedroom, their mouths colliding.

She went through a series of practiced moans, fiddling with the bracelet on her wrist. The primary objective had been to confirm the identity of the mysterious Bratva prince. Still, the quicker they brought him in, the quicker they could use him as leverage against Yuri. What would be the point of knowing who he was only to walk away? With a man like this, returning later to finish the job was unlikely.

Dominik lowered her onto the bed and climbed over her, trailing kisses from her neck down the middle of her chest. He started to pull aside the bikini top, but she pushed at his chest and coaxed him until he was on his back.

"Oh, you like to be in control?" he asked.

She straddled his middle. "Are you surprised?"

"Surprised and pleased."

She reached back and tugged at the straps holding the top up around her neck. It fell, and his eyes went almost as dark as her areolas and nipples. The number of men who'd seen her breasts for the sake of the job...if there'd been an easier way, she would have taken it, but if she'd had a brand, it would be efficiency. They were just breasts, anyhow.

"Fuck." He massaged her breasts. "You have the most beautiful color, *lapushka.*"

Darling.

It was kind of sweet and unexpected of him to choose that endearment, especially when he had no idea she'd understand it.

"What was that you called me?"

"My darling."

"Oh." She covered her face. "You're sweet."

He pulled her hands apart. "No, lapushka. Let me see your beautiful face."

She nodded and let her hands fall.

He sat up, cupped her left breast, and bent, leading with his mouth. When his lips were inches from her deceptively taut nipple, she flipped the latch on her bracelet and pressed the point against his neck.

"Fuck!" He slapped his neck. "What was..." His eyelids drooped. "What did you..."

He slumped.

Target acquired.

She left his lap, retied her bikini top, and picked up the phone in the room. "Hello, Mr. Redd? This is Miss Brown. Can you send a maid to Mr. Arbenin's suite, please?"

She waited for the affirmative, hung up, and sprinted to the suite's front door. When she opened it, the companion with the head tattoos and scars stumbled through, his eyes hazy. With the amount of drugs she'd dropped in his drink, the man had to have the metabolism of a horse to have burned through any part of it that quickly.

"W-what's this?" he asked, in Russian, his words slurred. "Why are you here?"

Eija glanced back at the bedroom. If Head Tatts stumbled even a few feet to the left, he'd spot his unconscious friend.

"For fun," she said.

"Fun?" Head Tatts looked around the room. "Oh, I see. So, you don't have time for me, but you have time for my friend and the pretty boy at the bar. What, am I not your type? Am I too Russian for you?"

He lunged for her, and the momentum from his lunge forced his thighs into a small table next to the front door. The porcelain vase that had sat atop crashed to the floor but remained intact.

"You will not leave this room without sucking my cock. Is this understood?"

She waited until he'd scrambled and struggled back onto his feet. She then picked up the vase and swiped it across his head. His body dropped to the floor and twitched briefly before going still.

Red hair appeared in the doorway, and Colin Favreau, her partner of four years, stepped into the suite. His matching brows were low on his forehead, and his hand hovered near the service weapon he kept tucked on the right side of his hip.

"E, what happened?" He crouched and pressed two fingers against Head Tatts' neck. "What the hell happened in here?"

She slipped past him to the doorway. "I got them both. That

one's probably got a bit of head trauma. Sokolov's in the other room, drugged."

"That wasn't the objective, E. Randy is going to foam at the mouth when he finds out. And where are you going?"

She raced down the hallway. Now, she had forty minutes to meet Andrei.

Their organization would handle the rest, silently retrieving both men to transport them back to headquarters in Lyon, France. Once everything was wrapped up here, she would head out, debrief with the team, and take the lead on interrogating Dominik and his companion. With any luck, they'd have access to Yuri before the end of the year.

Tonight, however, she would drink, have fun, most likely have sex, and then get on a flight in the morning. Returning to the island after so long had been nice, but she missed her life.

She was only eight minutes late meeting up with Andrei, and she found him sitting by the resort's indoor swimming pool at the edge of a lounge chair. He sported a denim jacket with the sleeves pulled back, a black shirt, and white jeans. A silver necklace hung around his neck. His dark hair, which he'd worn in a ponytail at the bar, graced the tops of his shoulders in gentle waves, and even before she smelled him, she knew he'd be spicy and sweet. The only thing she didn't like was the cigar he put out as she drew nearer, but the smoky-cherry scent didn't linger.

She leaned up to hug him around the neck. "You clean up nice."

"I would say the same about you," he bit his bottom lip and slightly shook his head, "but you looked good earlier too."

They released, but he let his hands rest at her hips and smoothed his palms over the fabric of her mustard-yellow, high-slit, spaghetti-strap dress. She'd paired the dress with flat sandals to add more inches to their height difference. If she could get him to feel like either her champion, warrior, protector, or all three, she could get him to do the things she needed to be done to her tonight.

"Can you spin for me?" he asked.

She obliged him.

"This color on you is amazing." He spun her himself. "You look gorgeous, Eija."

Somehow, he'd seen her write her name somewhere. She only used it when exchanging notes with Colin, aka Mr. Redd, but it wasn't like Andrei could look her up and see what she did for a living. She had fake social media profiles and listed phone numbers. Still, she would have to do better in the future not to be observed, even by mercurial eyes.

"Ready?" she asked.

He scanned her face.

"Andrei?"

"Yeah." He ran his fingers through his hair, and it fell perfectly back into place. "Yeah, I'm ready. Where's our first stop?"

* * *

She took him to her favorite restaurant in St. Georges, one of the few eating spots where she was confident no family would recognize her. It was primarily extended family left on the island as she'd taken her grandparents with her when she moved to the U.S. and again when she moved to Lyon for the Interpol job.

Many of those extended family members wouldn't have been able to pick her out of a lineup, anyhow. Those who she had seen thought she was "home" taking a break from her teaching job in France.

Stars scattered the dark sky. Steelpan music hummed around them from the restaurant's live band. Green, red, and yellow triangle flags hung from the restaurant's ceiling, and aromas she'd miss once she left filled the air.

She and Andrei were seated on the dock, and the patio lights above them picked up on the more chocolate notes of his hair. The sound of trade winds stirring the waves fused with the music, the ocean, and the band playing in tandem.

He'd suggested she order for him, so they had codfish and green fig salad for their appetizer. His main entrée was braised lamb with macaroni pie, and she had fresh mussels with linguini pasta. They shared a bottle of white wine, held long gazes, and she touched him with every chance she got.

She twirled her pasta with a fork. "So, you had really strict parents, then," she said. "Or, you were so bad, they had to send you away?"

"I wasn't *that* bad, now." He craned his neck to show off a scar and extended his hand so she could see the ones on his fingers, lightly visible around a skull tattoo that started above his wrist. "I might have gotten into a few fights. A few scuffles."

"I got into a few fights too. Nobody sent me anywhere."

"You grew up with your grandparents. They probably spoiled you rotten."

She grinned. "Well, yeah."

"Hey, at least you're repaying the favor by caring for them. I respect that."

Her grandmother, Rose, would eventually need around-the-clock care, her condition deteriorating even quicker than her doctor had initially speculated. Even for his age, her grandfather, Simon, was the picture of good health, but she suspected Nana would still outlive him.

Andrei swirled the wine in his glass, worrying his bottom lip with his teeth. "You don't seem like the type to get into a lot of fights. I can't imagine anybody trying to bruise or scar any part of your beautiful body."

She'd been playing roles for so long, it surprised her when there was an actual tug in her stomach.

"Cocoa butter," she said. "I put it on every night."

"You've already put some on tonight?"

"Yep."

"Damn." He took a sip of his wine, eyes never leaving hers. "Missed my chance."

"If you're good," she leaned forward and lowered her voice, "I'll let you put it on for me tomorrow morning."

The way his expression changed, for a split second, she wondered if she'd forgotten and told him she was leaving. Dominik and his companion had already been cleaned up. She hadn't received the all-clear yet to leave, but receiving a plane ticket in the middle of the night after everything had been confirmed wasn't unusual.

The steel pans drowned out, giving way to a live band. Tourists flocked to the open area in front of the performers, beers in hand, dancing and swaying beneath the lights. The band started with a song she vaguely remembered from her childhood, warming up the crowd, but they would eventually segue into Caribbean versions of pop songs.

"What made you change your mind?" he asked. "About having drinks with me, I mean."

Eija swallowed a bite of pasta. "If I remember correctly, you were the one who wasn't interested in anything."

"You knew I was lying."

"How was I supposed to know that?"

"Look at you."

"I noticed you first." She twirled pasta around her fork and held it up toward his mouth. "Here. Eat some of mine."

He looked from the fork to her face. "You are *such* a fucking flirt."

She burst out laughing, nearly dropping the fork.

"How many men have you brought here to seduce?" He finished his wine and refilled the glass. "Are all their bones out back?"

"What do you mean?" She batted her lashes. "You're the first."

"Uh, huh. Sure. That dress, those red lips, your hair, the way you look at me and touch on my sleeve." He softened his voice and did a pretty convincing accent. "'*Andrei, you're so funny.' 'Oh, Andrei.'* God, Eija, you're terrible for my ego."

"I thought that would be great for your ego!"

"Not when I'm supposed to be *convincingly* wooing you. I brought out the expensive cologne, the designer jeans, the hair. I've been waiting all night for you to mention my hair, but no. Nothing."

"Aww, boo-boo." She stroked his middle finger with her thumb. "Your hair is gorgeous."

"I even planned to *discreetly* drop my Black Card," he mimed the motion, "on the table."

She stopped laughing. "Like an Amex Black Card? Well, you didn't say all that, now."

He rolled his eyes, a broad grin on his face. She wasn't sure if he usually had facial hair, but the way the shadow of a beard outlined his jaw, it would be nice to see him with some. It would be prickly underneath her fingers, against her palm, and along the insides of her thighs.

She held out her glass for him to top off. "So, does Andrei have a last name?"

"Falcone. Why?"

Italian. That dark hair and olive skin now made sense.

"I have a thing about sleeping with men without at least knowing their last names."

"You're..." He set the bottle back inside its ice bowl. "I like how direct you are, but you're assuming we'll sleep together tonight."

"You don't want to?"

"Maybe I want to take you out for breakfast. Lunch. Dinner again. See if you have any more dresses in colors that kiss your skin. Underneath these lights," he glanced up at the ceiling, "you are breathtaking, Eija."

They finished the bottle, and he did end up trying some of her pasta. Eating from the same fork was a move she'd used many times before, but it usually never worked on her. Yet, watching her fork slip between Andrei's lips had made her pulse from head to toe, sending the wine quicker through her bloodstream.

When their plates were empty, with nothing else to distract them, they stared at each other. Smiled at each other. There was no way she wouldn't be riding his dick later, and she could already tell it would be the perfect ending to close out her Sokolov case.

"What about you?" He broke their stare and studied the tourists who'd flocked to the dance floor. "Is your last name as unique as your first?"

"Nope. It's Brown."

He blinked and was suddenly looking at her again, eyes creating a fiery path that started at the arch of her neck.

"Brown," he echoed. "I like brown."

The wait staff removed their plates from the table. Andrei asked her to choose their desserts, so she went with sweet potato pudding, which was more like a pone, and nutmeg ice cream. While they ate, the live band switched from contemporary music to older songs. The performer began a rendition of "Is

This Love" by Bob Marley, and she swayed in her seat, eyes closed with her fork in her mouth.

Fingers tapped her shoulder, and she opened her eyes to Andrei standing, his hand outstretched. She took it, and he pulled her up, flush against his body. The tourists had packed the dance floor, but they had their own little spot there near the water's edge. Underneath the lights, he was magnificent and one of the best-looking, if not the most good-looking man she'd ever spent an evening with.

She tightened her arms around him and pressed her cheek against his chest, drowning out the low buzz of chatter around them. There was only the music, the waves, his warmth, and his scent.

The song ended, but he didn't release her.

She didn't release him.

"What time is it?" she asked.

He tipped up the face of his watch. "A little past eleven."

"Really?" She looked up at him, her chin pressed into his chest. "That went by kind of fast."

"Do you have to get up early tomorrow? Considering you have a million jobs at the resort."

"I have one main job, unlike some people with Amex Black Cards and three-month stays at expensive resorts."

He brushed a curl aside. "You were just helping out today, then?"

"Yes."

"So, if I go back to the bar tomorrow, you might not be there?"

22

"I don't know." She shrugged. "I could be, but it's not like you'll have to go looking for me. Not after tonight."

"No?"

She shook her head. "No, Andrei Falcone."

His expression went neutral.

Somber, almost.

"I'm not ready to leave yet, though," she added. "We can go back to the resort and walk around."

"You're not afraid of your coworkers seeing you with me?"

"With you?" She blew air between her lips. "I *want* them to see me with you. They'll be so jealous."

"I should probably hold your hand, too, then."

"You should."

He paid the bill, and he actually did have a Black Card, and they took a cab back to the resort.

From his clothes, hair, and how he carried himself, it was obvious he'd come from money. He'd told her his mother died when he was young, and he was estranged from his father. It sounded like the classic case of a wealthy man seducing a middle-class or lower woman who'd expected the wealthy man to give her things the man had never truly been capable of.

She wasn't looking for marriage, a long-term commitment, or kids, so she'd take this wealthy man to bed, fuck him senseless, and return to her average yet wonderful life.

The resort was beautiful during the day, but at night, it *breathed*. There was still a sense of awe whenever she looked at it all lit up, tall palm trees billowing in the wind, the beach only a few paces away. Tiki candles cast their orange glow along the paved walkways, and there was something about the smell of the islands.

She would miss it.

Andrei slipped their hands together, and she took off her sandals, the ground warm beneath her feet.

"Need me to hold them?" he asked. "Since you have your purse and everything."

"Seriously?"

He opened his hand, and she handed them over. As they walked, the straps of her sandals hung from his hooked fingers.

At five-foot-seven, she wasn't the shortest person in the world, but he still had those long legs. Yet, he kept his gait slow as they shuffled along, flirtatiously bumping into each other. The wine had her head clear and her body warm. The breezes blowing through tossed her hair around, strands caressing the back of her neck like fingertips.

"So, Andrei Falcone, what brings a man, with your means, to a resort on an island with a little over one-hundred thousand people? And for three months at that?"

"Ah, I was waiting for that question." He glanced down at her. "I...had a hard year. The aunt I told you about? The one I went to live with when I was sixteen? She died last year."

"Oh. I'm so sorry." She squeezed his hand. "That must have been hard."

"I'm not close to my father, so, for years, she was the only family I had. So when I lost her, I lost a good chunk of my world."

"Can I ask why you and your father are estranged, or is that too personal for a first date?"

He grinned. "Hmm...*first* date?"

She didn't realize it until the words left her mouth. Now, she had to run with it.

"You don't want a second date with me?"

"I do, but I figured getting one with you would be like winning the lottery after playing for a *while*."

Her skin tingled, followed by another pull in her belly.

"I was a troublemaker," he said. "My father and I, we butt heads a lot. He wanted me to follow the career path he chose for me, but I wanted to branch out on my own."

"And what career path is that?"

He sucked in a breath and let it out slowly. "International Business."

"Gag."

"Exactly."

They walked past the pool where a few vacationers lounged, some wading on the surface while others' fingers scraped the bottom.

"What did you end up doing that affords you the ability to have a Black card, then?"

He looked her up and down. "Guess."

They stopped walking, and she stepped away from him, squinting and cupping her chin while she scrutinized. This was a man people would give money to just to say they'd breathed the same air as he did.

"Well, based on the size of your package," she let her gaze fall, "I'd say porn star."

"I knew these jeans were too damn tight." He covered his crotch. "Stop looking."

Laughter tore through her. "I'm not!"

"Yes, you are." He closed an imaginary robe and tossed his hair. "You're undressing me with your eyes."

"Real talk? I've been doing that all night."

With a grin on his handsome face, he walked toward her, and she floated to him, and he held her against his body for a few heartbeats before they returned to their stroll.

"Venture capital," he revealed, their fingers slipping back together. To her surprise, he kissed the back of her hand. "Specifically, clean technology. I may not look it, but I did go to Stanford."

"I'm genuinely impressed. It's not often you get beauty and brains all wrapped in a...nice package."

He bumped her side.

"What about you?" he asked. "Is resort management in your family?"

"Not even close. My mother was a stay-at-home mother, and my father was a physician. He went to medical school right here at home. I was born in Illinois, but they moved back when I was a little over a year old."

"You said your grandparents raised you. Does that mean...?"

She nodded. "When I was three."

"How'd it happen?"

"A car accident." It didn't matter that she'd been acting her entire time at the resort. These memories and the feelings that came with them were real. "The other driver had epilepsy. Interestingly enough, he was a patient of my father's."

He squeezed her hand like she'd done his. "I'm sorry, Eija. That's a hard thing to go through, especially at three. Do you have siblings?"

"A sister, but we're not close. She married my college boyfriend, and they started sleeping together when we were still dating."

"Ouch." His lips grazed the back of her hand a second time. "Don't worry. I won't do that to you."

She tossed her head back and laughed.

"I'm a little hurt you laughed that hard."

"You're funny, Andrei. Really funny. I'm having a great time, and I'm not just saying that to get into your pants."

They passed an empty pavilion, and she pulled him inside, letting him sit first before settling on his lap. He wrapped his arms around her, and she leaned against his shoulder. Like this, he felt even better than when they'd danced.

"Can I be honest with you about something?" he asked. "I was thinking about leaving tomorrow."

She stiffened. "Oh?"

"What if I stayed?"

She reached up and passed her fingers through his hair, and it was like chasing them across silk. "What if you did?"

"It would give me time to take you out again."

"Andrei, I don't know—"

"I'm not asking you for forever, Eija." He looked down at

her, his face brilliant in the firelight from the torches. "But I've been here three months, and this is the best night I've had so far. Maybe in my life. I'd like to have more like it. I'd like to talk to you again, see you again...even if it's just for one more day. One more week."

Her heart raced.

That, too, was new.

It wasn't like it hadn't ever raced before, but it certainly hadn't in a while. Her heart was often never involved in these situations. It was always be flirty, attentive, get hers, and then return to work. Go back to the world of espionage, covert intelligence, and organized crime.

However, if it was just for one more day or one more week, she wanted to see this man again. On at least two of those days, she wanted to wake up, naked, in his arms.

"I'd like that too," she said.

"So, tomorrow, can I take you to lunch on your lunch break?" he asked. "We can eat around here, so you don't have to go far."

"Yes." She touched her palm to the side of his face. "But, what about tonight?"

She knew the kiss was coming—he was moving in, she was moving in. Still, she sighed when their lips connected.

His were tart, sweet, and soft, and he didn't immediately slip his tongue into her mouth. Instead, he let his breath warm her lips and nibbled on the flesh, taking her from ripe to bursting open. The fingers on her other hand wound around the thick fabric of his jacket.

She leaned forward, offering more of her mouth. He ran his tongue around the entire circle, kissing the corners and tasting the smooth pink just inside. This man had done this to the point that he had the shit down to a science.

"You have the most beautiful lips," he whispered, raising his thumb to the center of her bottom lip. "A man could get drunk on these."

She gripped the back of his head and plunged her tongue into his mouth. A low, thick groan rumbled in his throat, and he pulled her tight against him. She moaned, their tongues sweeping almost timidly. When her head tilted, so did his. When he pulled her so close he crushed her against his chest, she wrapped her arms around his neck. This was what people meant when they said they felt like they were floating. She was in the middle of the ocean, feet dangling and her body a buoy against gravity.

"Andrei," her voice was raw, dripping with need, "make love to me tonight."

Another groan thundered in his throat, lower than the first, pulsing against the palm on his chest.

"I want to," he said.

"Then let's do it."

"Not tonight."

She nodded. "Okay."

Kissing him was so good, she would be fine with just this. Plus, anticipation was the best kind of foreplay. By the time they made love, she would crave him. Eat, drink, and sleep him.

They parted when their lungs were empty. His eyes

sparkled, almost in awe, and she was certain she looked at him the same way. He'd come from somewhere, a place she'd never looked. A place she hadn't even known existed.

"Oh, no." She swiped her thumb over his lips. "I got my lipstick all over you. I guess they lied about it not rubbing off."

"Is it my color?" he asked.

"You are working it, honey."

He laughed and kissed her.

She laughed and kissed him.

"Why couldn't I have met you earlier?" His gaze roamed her face, and he wrapped a curl around his finger. "At least at the beginning of my stay here."

If they'd met earlier, she wasn't sure she wouldn't have, at some point, compromised part of her mission in some way. And she'd never so much as considered compromising an op before.

"What would have been different, you think?" she asked, genuinely curious.

"I don't know, but I know it would have been good."

"This is good too."

"You're right." He kissed her cheek. "This is good too."

They sat, holding each other and kissing and talking until it was a little past one in the morning.

He walked her to her room, their fingers locked, and it was hard to let him leave. Then, to make matters worse, he gave her the sweetest, most tender kiss she'd ever experienced in her life right before stepping back and wishing her a good night.

"Lunch tomorrow," he said. "Don't forget."

"I'm looking forward to it." She opened the door. "I

really am."

"Goodnight, Eija."

"Goodnight, Andrei."

She closed the door, leaned against it, and took a moment to collect herself before checking her phone. As expected, with the op closed out, the agency emailed her ticket. While she usually went home immediately, there were two weeks between now and the debriefing at headquarters. She could afford to give Andrei at least one of them.

Someone knocked on her door.

Through the peephole, she saw it was him.

The minute she opened the door, his mouth latched onto hers. She kissed him back with the same fierce, borderline savage hunger.

When he finally released her, she plastered herself to the door. He backed up to the other end of the corridor. A thick bulge tented his zipper, and her nipples tried to push through the fabric of the dress.

An imprint of his kiss remained on her lips.

"Good night," he said again, clearly trying not to look down at the overeager buds. "I mean it this time."

He watched her go inside.

She listened for his retreating footsteps.

Once confident he wasn't coming back, she went straight to the shower, stripped, and stepped underneath the stream. Eyes closed and back against the tiled wall, she relived the night— from flirting to laughing to kissing—and lowered the spray between her legs.

Chapter Three

Dom approached the front desk just in time to see Eija's face light up as she read the card attached to the blue roses he'd sent. The other staff at the front tried to grab it from her hand, but she dodged them, laughing and lighting up the room with that lipstick and that smile.

He wasn't in love.

Love was ambitious after knowing anyone for one week that had turned into two, no matter how warm the Caribbean air, how sultry the music, and how clear the ocean waters. Yet, if they'd had a little more time, he would definitely fall for her.

Yuri's goons had disappeared, and so far, he hadn't spotted anyone else trying to blend in like water in an oil factory, which wasn't exactly a good thing. It was more like a tsunami pulling water from the shore because a massive flood was about to follow.

One of the girls at the front looked up and spotted him, and she whispered something to Eija. Eija turned around, and when their gazes connected, her smile grew wider.

He leaned on the desktop. "Hey, pretty lady. You ready?"

She nodded. "Let me get my bag from the back, and I'll be right with you."

The pencil skirt hugged her hips and stole his attention as she walked away. When she was out of sight, he realized the other two women at the front were staring at him with coy smiles.

"Good evening, ladies," he greeted.

One, whose complexion was like looking at honey through a glass jar, blushed. The other, whose complexion was closer to mocha and entirely even from the tip of her forehead to her chest, spoke up.

"Where are you taking her?"

"She's been the captain of all our dates so far," he informed them. "I think she said we're going to Gouyave for Fish Friday?"

The blushing woman's eyes widened. "Oh, that's nice. You'll really like it. They have some of the best lambi in the Caribbean."

"What's lambi?"

They looked at each other.

"You probably know it as conch," the second woman said. "If you don't eat conch, though, they have fish, lobster...all kinds of seafood."

That accent.

Fuck, it was such a turn-on.

It was like God had ordered a shipment of beautiful parts, but the shipper had accidentally sent him a duplicate. So, He'd dumped them all in the Caribbean, from the waters to the people, the buildings to the music.

"Then I'm looking forward to it." He glanced at the door Eija had walked through. He wanted to see her. He'd just seen her less than a minute ago, but he wanted to see her *again*.

She emerged, and he had to stop himself from scooping her into his arms. Since he knew he was leaving at some point, he didn't want to make love to her. The way his luck was set up, they would have a nice night together, and that would be the moment the Bratva descended, taking him and leaving her dead body behind.

It wasn't like the organization was known for being considerate. They'd drag him away with half of his dick still inside her. And while he could handle himself better than most, he was only one man against a Slavic army.

"Do you mind if I go upstairs to change?" She motioned to her clothes. "I want to be more comfortable."

Higher-level staff had housing at the resort. It essentially guaranteed they would never be late clocking in, which was a plus for the company, and the staff could relax in the lap of luxury on their days off. According to Eija, they rarely did so at the resort—for them, it was their workplace—but they enjoyed the perks that came with the position.

"Of course," he said. "I'll wait down here."

"No, it's okay." She took his hand. "You can wait for me upstairs."

35

Eija was a weapon—gorgeous and seductive, cute and sexy.

She didn't hide that she wanted them to sleep together, but she didn't fuss when he kept putting it off. She *did* ask him if he was married, so there appeared to be some concern about his reluctance to do to her what he did to her in his dreams every single night.

She walked ahead of him to her room, and he hypnotized himself with the sway of her hips and the curve of her behind. Every so often, she turned around and caught him staring, and all she did was shake her head.

He followed her into a studio apartment whose decor was in line with the rest of the resort—white, blue, and wood. Because of Eija's personality, he'd expected Bohemian prints, colorful area rugs, floor pillows, and plants all over.

"Have a seat while I get ready," she instructed, starting on the buttons on her shirt. "If you're thirsty, help yourself to whatever's in the fridge. I promise I won't take long."

He shook his head. "Please don't. I enjoy looking at you."

That smile of hers was going to be his undoing.

She disappeared into the bathroom and shut the door.

He walked around, one part curiosity and the second part checking for anything that looked less than innocuous. Another thing the "family" was good at was surveillance.

A digital panel on the wall appeared to control different items around the room. He pressed a button, and the sheer curtains surrounding the bed parted, opening up the view from the bed to the balcony and trees surrounding the property. The windows faced east, so Eija always woke with the sunrise, and he wondered what she looked like—brown skin bathed in golden-orange light, wrapped in white sheets, hair untamed.

He adjusted himself in the dark jeans he'd paired with a white button-down, sat on the sofa, and turned on the TV. Eija popped her head out of the bathroom, her right shoulder glistening. Steam from the shower billowed behind her.

"Doing okay?" she asked.

"For now," he said. "Hurry up."

"I'm hurrying, I'm hurrying."

She shut the door.

He leaned back against the sofa cushions and tried to pay attention to the TV. Some crime documentary was showing, but all he saw was his mind's image of Eija in bed. With any luck, he'd end up smelling like smoke, fish, and char tonight, and she would make zero attempts to come on to him. The last string of his patience was thinner than a hair. If she so much as hinted at it, he would fuck her.

She emerged from the bathroom in purple panties.

No bra—just lacy purple panties.

Her dusky-tipped breasts and nipples bounced as she walked to her closet and pulled out two pieces of an outfit, both red. A strapless top went over her head, stopping just above her belly button, and she stepped into wide-leg pants before sitting on the bed to slip on a pair of sandals.

She'd gathered her hair into a curly ponytail on top of her head. Large hoops in her ears swayed with each of her movements. She didn't wear red lipstick, probably on account of the color of her outfit, but her lips were glossy, emphasizing their natural tone.

"Do I look ready?" She hopped up and spun for him to see every angle of her outfit.

He walked over and set his hands on her waist. "You look gorgeous."

"Thank you, Andrei."

He wanted her to call him Dom. He wanted to tell her tonight that his real name was Dominik, so *that* was the name she cried out when...*if* he made her come.

However, telling her was a risk.

Eija didn't come across as dangerous, but knowing his name could be dangerous for her. His one consolation was that Andrei was one of his given names on a long list, making his birth certificate unnecessarily jumbled.

She took his hand, turned off the TV, and they went downstairs to take a cab.

The event started at six, so by the time they arrived, it was already in full swing. The food smelled so good, he wanted to eat the air around them. More steelpan music provided the ambiance, and Eija moved her body like a snake as they walked down an aisle of tents with different food vendors already serving customers or getting set up.

All this she did without releasing his hand.

They watched the steel pan band play for a while, and she explained that they were a group of high schoolers from around the town of Gouyave. While they watched, she hugged him from behind, danced in front of him, or stood with her arms wrapped around him and her head on his chest.

It made him feel like a king.

He had the full attention of the prettiest woman there, as well as the pleasure of seeing how truly sweet and caring she could be.

It was obvious she was used to taking men around Grenada, flirting and drinking and fucking, and that had certainly been an option with them. But his desire to keep her as far away from his family shit as possible had inadvertently added a layer of nonsexual intimacy to their short-term relationship.

She chose his dinner, a mini tradition they seemed to have developed. For him, she found lobster tails and breadfruit while she had fried fish and French fries. For drinks, she picked something called VitaMalt, which was sweet with a hint of hops flavor.

He shared his lobster, she fed him fries, and he toyed with the idea of asking her to run away with him. They would likely have to move every six months to a year, going from islands to states to countries, but he could find a way to make it worth her while.

It was crazy thinking, but it brought an odd sort of comfort.

After dinner, they danced to reggae and calypso. She kissed him while standing between locals and tourists bustling about, some walking around them and others whistling, but they kept it chaste as children were around.

Three hours.

Proudly, he made it three hours before he leaned down near her ear and said, in a voice he could almost feel, "I need you."

They found the first cab back.

She all but climbed on top of him in the backseat, hands cradling both sides of his jaw. He probed her mouth with his tongue and gripped the soft swells of her ass. The cab driver muttered a half-hearted dissent but then spent the rest of the drive peering at them from the rearview mirror.

He left the driver all the cash in his pocket, swept Eija up into his arms, and headed to her room. If they'd had to go to his suite all the way on the other side of the resort, he would have ended up fucking her in the bushes. By the time he kicked in her door, half his buttons were undone.

While pulling her top off over her head, he thoroughly acquainted his teeth, lips, tongue, and mouth with those breasts. They were soft, full, and made for sucking, her nipples made for his pleasure.

Each bite trapped a shaky breath in her throat. He slipped one hand into her panties and stroked her clit while his mouth on her breasts tore cries from her throat.

"Andrei..." She gripped his shoulders, hips moving in a similar motion to how she'd danced earlier. "How am I...how am I coming already?"

Because they'd been putting this off for two weeks.

He didn't know how he wasn't.

A soft cry left her lips.

His fingers grew wetter, and she shuddered, her chest pushing high. Then, he brought his fingers to his mouth.

She reached for him, pulled his mouth to hers, and kissed him until the skin on his lips threatened to bruise. They were still in the small entryway, so he walked them back toward the bed.

Eija tore at his shirt, popping buttons with a sexy little grunt, tugged off his belt, and tossed it. He didn't know how his mind functioned well enough to remember the zipper at the back of her pants, but he dragged them down, and as she stepped out of the pants, he crouched and tore her panties off with his teeth.

It was easy.

They were lace and string.

Still, she whispered a quiet, "Oh my God," right before he helped himself to a mouthful of her pussy.

"Why are you like this?" she asked, part moan and part whisper.

"Like," he swept his tongue from her clit to her entrance and back, "what?"

"A pussy monster."

He laughed.

A smile broke out on her beautiful face, but the smile morphed into a grimace when he slipped his tongue inside her.

It wouldn't be his first time between a woman's legs, and it wouldn't be his last, but Eija was something different. She was something new. He'd never experienced wanting to come from sucking a woman's clit alone. Tiny drops of fluid spilled from the tip of his dick each time his lips wrapped around the slick bud.

"Andrei..." She gripped his shoulder. *"Fuck,* Andrei."

She raised her right leg and lost her balance, but he caught her before she fell.

"I've got you weak in the knees?" he teased, carrying her over to the bed.

"Arrogant much?"

"Did you not *just now* need my rescue?"

He set her on the bed and dove right back between her legs, enjoying how she squirmed and cursed at him. She was smooth down below, her clit firm. Then, as he slid two fingers inside her, her pussy sucked them the rest of the way in.

Jesus.

More fluid spilled from his head, and he slid his hand inside his jeans to grip the base of his dick, stroking the hot, angry length while he feasted.

Each flick of his tongue and thrust of his fingers forced her hips up off the mattress, and she clutched his hair, moaning and crying out his name until she came a second time, bucking and arching, creaming against his lips and chin.

"Eija," he licked his lips, "we're doing this again."

"Uh-huh, baby, but please," she motioned for him to come to her, "fuck me. Now."

His dick twitched.

He discarded his jeans and underwear and fumbled through slipping on a condom, harder than a fucking glacier. She watched him the entire time, and when he was ready for her, she spread her legs wide, baring her glistening sex. He almost went down on her a third time, but his dick would probably find a gun and shoot him if he did.

He climbed over her and pushed his way home.

Home.

His father always said there was no home like Russia.

That was a fucking lie.

He had more inches than she had depth, but he sank into her as if he could completely lose himself inside her body. He told himself to go slow, but she'd fucked with his head. The entire time they were together, this was what they'd both wanted. It was what they'd pretended they could put off.

Now that they were here, he couldn't fuck her easily.

He couldn't fuck her quickly.

His mind had been gone since their first date in St. Georges. Now, she was going to have to take this dick straight.

Chapter Four

Eija's fingers slid along the sheets, searching for a grip.

Finding none, she reached for Andrei, needing to sink her fingernails into his skin. She needed to lick, suck, and bite his neck, brand him so, no matter how hard he tried, she would never completely disappear from his memories.

He moved just out of the reach of her arms, pulled out, and cupped her knees to spread her legs wider. Then he entered her again, burying deep before once more pulling out, this time leaving only the thick head of his dick just inside. Of all the torture techniques she'd used in her line of work, *this* was the one that would have her giving up international secrets.

"Andrei, don't tease me."

He surged forward.

She sucked her bottom lip and looked down at where their

bodies met. Then, she let her gaze trail up over his hard abs and defined chest, ending at that face of his, those eyes.

Of course, he'd be smiling.

It was one thing to fuck a good-looking man.

It was another thing entirely to fuck *this* good-looking man.

"Faster, Andrei." She rolled her hips, but his hands on her knees kept her in place. "Don't do this to me, baby."

Their bodies completely separated, and he bent, drawing a long lick over her clit before he entered her again. Over and over, he sank deep until she was so full with him, each time she tried to cry out, only air left her throat. He thrust so hard that the wet sounds of their bodies fitting together rose above the din of the air conditioner.

A steady pace like this, along with his wicked tongue, wrenched the third climax from her. It was the only way to describe it, a feeling that started somewhere deep inside her that grew tighter and tighter until she exploded.

And she screamed.

She never screamed.

"Didn't peg you for a screamer," he said, restraint sharpening his voice.

"Neither did I." She motioned to him. "Come here."

Without pulling out, he eased down and hovered over her, his fallen hair creating a canopy around their faces. She locked her ankles behind his back and angled her hips, and the very next stroke right after she did made his eyes roll back in his head.

Good.

He deserved it for not telling her what he was capable of.

She kissed his jaw. "God, you're so attractive."

"You think?" he asked, eyes searching hers.

"Yes. You're the most attractive man out of the four-hundred thousand I've had the pleasure of sleeping with."

He rolled his eyes. "I'm already inside you. All that means is that I'm four hundred thousand and one."

She laughed and threaded her fingers through his hair.

The majority of the scars he possessed, he'd gotten from his "rougher" younger years, which was how he'd put it. Most were hidden by tattoos, but she could still feel them. She could still feel them and bend her body to kiss one on his shoulder and the one he'd shown her on his neck. Whenever her lips connected with his skin, his eyelids shut.

"Eija, run away with me."

"Where?" she asked.

"Panama." He buried himself deep, waited a beat, pulled out. "Antarctica. Neptune."

She licked the length of the scar on his neck before kissing the marbled skin. "Okay."

He groaned a quiet "Fuck," and drove into her so hard, she slid on the sheets. If his dick was the thief, her climax was the priceless, forbidden jewel. Each stroke took and took, no matter how much she tried to rein it in or restrain the feeling so it lasted long into the night. They wouldn't make it that far; he was so hard, he would explode soon, and she waited for it like a birthday present.

An unexpected yet sweet, hot climax burst through her

body, ripping her in two. She fell back, letting it take her, warmth and pleasure winding together.

Andrei pulled out, breathing hard, his sweat dripping onto her breasts. After a few seconds, he entered her again, thrust his hips, and pulled out a second time.

"Fuck, fuck, fuck."

She reached between them and guided him back inside her. "Might as well keep going," she said. "This is a battle you won't win."

"You feel so good, I wanted to stay a little longer."

"Don't hold out, Andrei."

He groaned.

"You *want* to come." She licked the sweat from his neck. "You *need* to come all up inside this pussy. Tonight, right now, it's all yours."

He crashed his hips into hers.

"Come for me, Andrei." Her tongue flicked his chin. "Let me feel you come inside me."

After a few more hard strokes, he succumbed to his release, rewarding her with a deep groan and quiet curses of defeat.

God, she loved the sound of a man climaxing.

She locked him in on top of her, not caring about his weight, and he took in snatches of air while kissing the space between her breasts.

"So, was it worth the wait?" she asked.

"Yes." He looked up. "It was worth its 'wait' in gold."

"Oh, my God."

"You liked that one, didn't you?"

"Not even a little bit."

She liked him. She honestly, truly liked him, and it was a shame that it was at this point in her life she felt something for someone that didn't solely come from the organ between her legs.

"I've never had fun with someone the way I've had fun with you," she confessed.

"I was thinking the same thing." He brushed his lips over the inside rise of her right breast. "Feels like we've known each other longer."

"Can you stay tonight?"

A smile lit up his face, handsome, flirtatious, and innocent all at the same time.

He nodded once.

She wanted to wake up in his arms to see what he looked like in bed next to her, wrapped in her puffy white sheets with his silky hair all over her pillow. And she wanted to make love to him again, a few times, at least once in the daylight so she could watch his face as he came.

Because, by one o'clock tomorrow, she'd be on a flight to France, and she and Andrei Falcone would never, ever see each other again.

Chapter Five

Dom woke up to Eija's warm body snuggled against his. It was the middle of the night, so they only had moonlight for illumination, but she'd kept the curtains drawn so it filtered unimpeded through the glass onto them.

Onto her.

Moonlit Eija, he decided, had to be just as exquisite as Eija in the morning sun—something he would prove in a few hours. The silver glow against the white sheets emphasized the curves of her silhouette. One of her breasts poked from the top of the covers, and he reached out, gently rolling her nipple between his thumb and forefinger. She didn't stir, so he leaned forward, lips headed for her neck. A deep voice rang out, and the person spoke in Russian.

"Hello, Prince."

He took a moment to push down his irritation and looked

up, barely making out a man's face, light brown hair, and dark eyes. The man had made no attempt to whisper, so he slid his hand, still beneath the covers, down to Eija's stomach. Thankfully, she was breathing.

"You have a name?" Dom asked, covering her up to her chin.

"I'm called Fadd."

"Yuri sent you?"

"Yes. It's time for the prodigal son to return home."

Dom glanced behind Fadd's head, where a shadow played along the glass sliding door, revealing a second intruder in the kitchen. Whether or not the two unwelcome guests realized it, their deaths were marked. Yuri letting them know Dominik Sokolov was his son was code—only a tight few had the privilege, and these two were definitely not part of Yuri's inner circle. Not even Yuri's daughters knew the "cousin" they'd met, only a few times, was their half-brother.

He ticked his head toward the kitchen. "What's your friend's name?"

Surprise moved over Fadd's face. "Kuz."

"Did you drug her?"

Fadd flicked his wrist. "She'll be fine in the morning. Yuri said killing her would only make you belligerent."

One of the few real things Yuri knew about him.

He searched the side of the bed for his underwear and tugged them on, followed by his jeans. As he played with the button at the waist, he searched the floor for the rest of his clothes.

"By the door." Fadd smirked all the way up to his eyes. "Looks like you had a good night."

"Step outside to give me a minute."

"Is she for sharing?" Kuz asked.

Dom glared at him. "Ask me that again."

"I was just curious. From here," Kuz raised his nose in the air, "her pussy smells divine."

"Out."

Both men left.

Dom moved about the room, dressing with each article of clothing he found. Eija had destroyed the buttons on his shirt, so he left it open.

This wasn't how he'd wanted their time together to end, him sneaking away in the middle of the night after making love to her. He knew how it would look, but what choice did he have? The Bratva wasn't a family from a nineties sitcom. If he didn't go, Yuri would have Eija executed to prove a point, and she didn't deserve to lose her life for being caught up in shit she knew nothing about.

He crouched next to the bed and pressed the last kiss he would ever give her to those lips of hers. He then searched the room, found a card with the hotel's logo on the front, and wrote on the blank space at the back.

Eija,

I'm sorry to leave you like this. Thank you for the best two weeks I've ever had in my life. I wish we had more time. If we'd had more time, I would have been able to tell you, face to face, that my real name isn't Andrei Falcone.

Don't forget me.

Love, Dom

He set the card on the kitchen counter, took one last eyeful of her silhouette, and stepped out into the corridor where Kuz and Fadd waited, passing a cigarette between them.

The men tailed him to the end of the hallway, and just as Fadd began to relay where they were headed, Dom grabbed Fadd's pistol and released two slugs in Kuz's chest. The shots forced Kuz up against the wall, where he slumped, twitching until he was motionless.

Fadd lowered to his knees, arms raised. Behind them, someone called out.

A familiar someone.

"Just as impressive as the day you left," Yuri said, walking toward them.

Dom faced his father. It was funny how much they didn't look alike; he'd gotten all his mother's darker features. Yuri, before his entire head had gone silver, had sported blond hair. His eyes remained golden brown, irises surrounded by dark rings that drew attention to the shallowness of his pupils. Endless, shallow pupils.

Yuri snapped.

On command, Pavel Volkov, Yuri's right-hand man, released two shots into Fadd's chest.

"Do we need to clean any messes in the woman's room?" Yuri asked.

Dom handed the gun to Pavel. "Stay far away from the woman's room."

They headed to the front of the resort, not a soul outside. Yuri had more than likely had the resort grounds cleared in preparation for his arrival, and it wasn't the first time Dom realized just how far Yuri's influence carried. It had been difficult remaining under the radar all these years outside Russia, though not impossible.

Once inside one of the many cars lining the front of the resort, Yuri spoke again.

"Do you love her?"

Dom leaned back against the seat. "No."

"Who is she?"

"Doesn't concern you."

"Pretty?"

He closed his eyes, said nothing.

Yuri, smiling, tapped on the window, and the car pulled off.

Chapter Six

Eija sensed the emptiness before she turned around to confirm it. Still, she didn't want to jump to conclusions, and she ignored the way it felt like a winged hippopotamus flopped around in her chest.

"Andrei?" She sat up, slightly groggy from a night of amazing sex, the covers pooled around her. "Andrei? Are you in the bathroom?"

The hippopotamus plumped up another few thousand pounds and grew a trunk and floppy ears. By the time she'd pulled on a robe and checked every nook and cranny of the bathroom, living area, and balcony, she could no longer lie to herself.

Pain.

It was pain she felt.

Pain she'd tried, for years, to avoid feeling, but she should have seen this coming. He was too attractive. Too funny. With men like him, she was *supposed* to act, but she'd let up the curtain.

Because she liked him.

In her head, she'd already worked out how their last day together would have gone—she'd tell him she'd gotten an emergency call and had to leave the island. Since she would be gone for a while, they would come to the mutual agreement that things would have to end. After one last passionate romp, she'd go to the airport and never forget her time with the incredible Mr. Andrei Falcone.

She started for the kitchen, but a voice called out from the other side of the door.

"E? E, it's me."

"Colin?" She hurried over and tugged the door open. "What are you doing here?"

Colin looked fresh-faced and stubble-free, which hadn't been the case for the majority of the time they'd worked on the Bratva operation. He'd gelled his fiery hair back away from his forehead, his eyes always a bright, expressive blue, even in the middle of gunfire. He wore the traditional "tourist in the Caribbean" outfit—a colorful button-up, khakis, and thong slippers.

A gray head peeked from behind him.

"Hi, Lourdes," Eija greeted and stepped aside. "Come on in."

"Good morning, Miss Brown," the resort's oldest housekeeper said, her voice raspy and melodic. "I have breakfast for you and," she glanced at Colin, "a friend."

Lourdes came every morning to bring her breakfast. The resort knew she was leaving today, but they'd had food sent up anyhow.

"What about me?" Colin asked, grinning wide.

She waved him inside. "Get in here. Randy sent you back, didn't he?"

He stepped inside, the door shutting behind him. "He wanted to know why you stayed two weeks over."

She motioned around. "I'm in paradise."

"Miss Brown," Lourdes called. "Do you need this?"

She squinted to see what Lourdes held up—a card with the resort's logo and contact information on the front. However, after today, she wouldn't need anything with the resort's logo.

"No, you can toss it."

Lourdes glanced at the back, nodded, and dropped it into the trash before removing the bag and tying the end.

Colin looked from the bed to her hair. "Hmm."

"Yes," she said. "Whenever am I not?"

"When you're working."

"Well, there were times I wasn't."

He made himself comfortable on the sofa.

Lourdes let them know she'd be back later to finish cleaning up, pinched Eija's cheek, and quietly shut the door behind her as she left.

"So, who was he?" Colin crossed his right ankle over his left knee. "Or has your sexual prowess evolved since you left Lyon, and it's now either a she or a full-on furry orgy?"

"Nobody," she said, walking to the bathroom.

"They can't be a nobody." Colin hopped up and followed her. "They slept here."

"And?"

"They really slept here? E, not even I get to sleep over at your place anymore."

"That's because you snore, eat all my food, and your hair gets everywhere." She shooed him. "Get out so I can pee, shower, and get ready for the airport. I don't know why Randy sent you. I don't need a handler."

"He thought it might have been difficult for you to leave. After all, this is your parents' birthplace, and you did spend your 'formative' years here."

She stood with her hands on her hips, facing the mirror, and ran through options of what to do with her hair to leave it the least tangled until she got home. To get it into a ponytail in its current state, she would need a lot of water and copious amounts of gel. Not even a beanie would work. Until wash day, it was frozen in this curly 'fro.

"I barely have any family left here." She ruffled the right side of a squashed combination of highlighted curls, kinks, and coils. "I'll be fine to leave. Why are you really here?"

"I swear to God that's the reason," he said.

She looked back at him over her shoulder. "Truthfully?"

"Of course. I'm your partner. You gave me your blood when I had six bullets in me. I was worried about you and wanted to make sure I saw you because if I called, you'd lie to me about how you really are. And...Randy wants to meet tomorrow."

Her brows narrowed. "He wants to debrief *tomorrow?* I won't even be finished going through protocol by then."

"He said it's urgent."

It always was with their head of organized crime, Randy Almas. Everything was urgent. The man was a walking, talking CNN breaking news headline.

"Is Sokolov talking?" she asked.

"The kid still won't cop to the name." Colin stood next to her, eyes meeting hers in the mirror. "But we're working him."

"What about head tatts guy?"

"He's not talking at all."

The elephant left her chest, the vacancy replaced by a blue whale. She'd come on to Andrei the entire time, and the entire time, he'd turned her down. Then, when he finally got what he wanted, he dipped?

Why?

It was good sex!

Granted, she'd been too caught up to remember to go down on him. Was that why he'd left? Did he believe she "didn't do that" when she would have sucked—

"E?"

Her gaze flicked to Colin's. "Um, Lourdes always brings food for two. Help yourself."

"Why does she always bring food for two?"

"A girl gets lonely."

"Damn, E." He eyed her. "Save some scraps for the rest of us. Do you know when's the last time I got some pussy?"

"Christmas." She faced him and cupped the rounded ends of his shoulders. "And I think it's because you want the same pussy."

"I'm not having this conversation."

"Am I wrong?"

Colin backed out of the bathroom. "Pee, take your shower, and come eat breakfast. Then, let's go home."

Chapter Seven

Eija tossed a manila folder on the table in front of her. Dominik Sokolov no longer looked as young as he had at the resort. His wheat-colored hair hung in dirtied strings tinged with blood. Bruises, both fresh and healing, covered his face. Caked dirt blackened his cuticles and nail beds, his nails jagged with some completely missing. Both he and his tattooed partner had been put through hell. While Dominik did speak, the information he gave them was either useless or a flat-out lie. They'd given up on Head Tatts. All they'd gotten from him was his name—Sergei.

She pulled out a chair, sat, and crossed her arms over her chest.

"You look different." Dominik smiled and switched to Russian. "You're the pretty woman from the beach."

Colin entered the room and took the seat next to her. Dominik didn't so much as glance at him.

"That's me," Eija replied. "You can call me Officer Barrett."

"You speak Russian?"

She motioned to herself and Colin. "We both do, but you already know about him."

"With you, it's unexpected because of your color," Dominik went on. "And because of that, it's incredibly sexy."

"Thanks. Let's talk."

"Just the two of us."

"That's not the agreement."

Dominik leaned back in his chair, raised his bound hands, and made a motion that his lips were sealed. Eija looked over at Colin, who shook his head.

"Go." She nodded. "I'm fine."

Colin pushed his chair back, stood, and stormed out of the room. Dominik stared at the door until it shut, then turned back to Eija.

"You want to talk to me," she said. "So talk."

"Will you show me your breasts again?"

"You've lost that privilege."

He frowned. "It doesn't matter. I have a picture of them in my head. I should have sucked them before you poisoned me."

"If I'd poisoned you, you'd be dead."

Dominik ticked his head in agreement and leaned forward, his elbows on the tabletop. He dragged his gaze over her, and although she was sitting, he looked at her like he could see through her gray pants, black shirt, and black blazer. If he felt special then good on him, but she used whatever assets she needed to use to get her target. Some of those happened to be attached to her body.

"What do you want to know?" he asked.

"First, confirm your identity. Your name is Dominik Sokolov."

"It is not."

She opened the folder. "Do you know this man?"

"I don't know. You should have gotten your cameraman to focus a little better."

"His name is Yuri Sokolov, and he's the head of the Bratva." She showed him a second photo. "This is Ekaterina Sokolov, his wife. She has red hair and green eyes. Yuri is blond with brown eyes," she pointed at him, "like you. You have the same bone structure, the same face shape, and a striking resemblance."

Dominik squinted at the picture of Yuri. "You're right. I've never noticed that before."

"This process would go so much easier if you'd just come clean, Dominik." She pushed both photos toward him. "You might have noticed that we operate a little differently here. You lost your rights the minute they brought you into this building. Here, there's no due process, no courts or trials. Here, you're tipped backward in a chair. Your head is covered with cloth, and a bucket of water is drenched over your face until you come so close to drowning, one of your lungs shuts down."

He shrugged a single shoulder. "It's not so bad. It's like kindergarten in Russia."

Eija sighed and shook her head. They knew they would have met pushback, but she wasn't expecting this much. From what they knew, Yuri loved his son. Treasured his son. They believed that was part of the reason no one knew what Dominik looked like, and Interpol hadn't even known he'd existed until *she'd* discovered him a little over four years ago. What better way to protect your child from enemies than to camouflage them in plain sight?

"You work for who?" he asked, staring at her chest.

"I.C.P.O."

"Interpol doesn't have officers."

"Oh, did you read that on Wikipedia?"

He stared a bit longer and then let his head fall, stringy hair all but peeling from the strands matted to his scalp. Rocking side to side, he sang, *"King Henry VIII, to six wives he was wedded. One died, one survived, two divorced, two beheaded.* Do you know your history, lapushka? Do you know about King Henry the Eighth?"

"He's the prick with all the wives who he killed because his Y-chromosome carrying sperm were all slow as shit."

Dominik raised his head. "He tried and tried for a son, but his wives kept giving him daughters."

"In the end, he had two. What's your point?"

His gaze fell to her mouth. In this room and building, she didn't use wiles or whatever it was that made men wilt as soon as she showed a little flesh. This was work. The most he would get from her in this windowless box was an eye-roll and a boat-load of fake smiles.

"If I'm here with you, then the Prince of the Bratva exists," he said, nostrils flaring slightly. "And you don't know what he looks like."

She grunted. "I'm looking right at him."

"Lapushka, my name is Vasily, not Dominik. Yes, I would have the same grandfather as Dominik. My grandfather had one son and three daughters. One of the daughters was my mother."

"So you do know Yuri is what you're saying."

Watching him, for the first time in a long time, Eija got a sinking feeling in her gut. He was too relaxed. His eyes were clear as he spoke, and they rolled around in his skull like he was pulling up memories from long ago. But he was Bratva. The organization had taught him to lie if captured. What the Bratva would do to him if he snitched was much worse than what they ever could.

"Lapushka," his tone softened, "you're looking for a face you have never seen. You're looking for a face *I* have never seen. But, even though I have not, I'm positive you don't know what Dominik looks like."

"And how's that?"

"Because you are here with me."

This man had been in the same place where they'd learned Dominik was hiding out. He looked too much like Yuri, but that could be explained through the fact that he'd admitted to being Yuri's nephew. She'd met her niece exactly three times, and even though it was her sister and ex's child, Analeigh looked like she could be hers.

"Yuri has six daughters." Vasily held up six fingers. "But

rumor is, he has a son." He lowered all his fingers except for the middle. "And that son is not me."

The door to the room opened, and Colin poked his head inside. "Randy wants to see us."

Eija left the chair, the heat of Vasily's gaze on her ass, and followed Colin out the door into a long, narrow hallway. At the end of the hallway, they climbed a flight of stairs and pushed through a door. Bright lights blinded them as they were thrust into an open area filled with junior analysts either seated at computers or flitting about. The low buzz of clicking keyboard keys and chatter followed her and Colin around desks, the analysts scurrying from one side of the room to the other.

They took the elevator to the top floor of the building. Their building was several blocks from the actual Interpol headquarters, and it was more on the modern side, stood four stories high, and had been designed by the same architect who'd conceptualized the Musee des Confluences. It didn't look like a government agency building which, she figured, was the point.

If she'd had to describe, in a few words, what her job was like, she would say it was a combination between the intelligence and clandestine work of the CIA and the law enforcement aspects of the FBI. Because she'd excelled as an officer in the CIA, her old supervisor had nominated her for this position, and she'd fit in almost immediately.

"E, you don't look so good."

Eija looked up to find Colin staring at her. "It's my stomach."

"Something you ate?"

"No. Something I did."

"Like...what?"

"Jump the gun." She lowered her voice. "Fuck, Colin. I don't think he's lying."

"Who?"

"Vasily."

The elevator doors opened, and the walk to Randy's office felt like the green mile. She knew the reason he'd pulled her out of the interrogation. They had something. They'd found something that would prove Vasily really was who he said he was, and Randy would use this as the moment to prove that her jumping the gun wasn't always going to work out in her favor. In the four years she'd worked for the agency, it would be the first time she'd messed up after disobeying orders, and he'd been waiting all this time to throw something like this back in her face.

Colin opened the door.

She stepped through, and he followed her like the child who wanted to get their licks second because their parent would use up all their strength punishing the first.

"Close it." Randy didn't look up. "Sit."

She and Colin sat in the chairs on the other side of Randy's desk. Colin reached across and squeezed her hand. She sent him a shaky smile.

"I think you've guessed by now why you're up here." Randy raised his head, his salt and pepper hair gelled to perfection and his olive jawline clean shaven. "We just got word that Dominik Sokolov is in Moscow."

How?

How was he in Moscow?

Everything had pointed to him being in Grenada. The odds of him being anywhere else were—

"He wasn't in Grenada," Randy said. "Our information was wrong. He was in Aruba."

"How do we know he was in Aruba?" she asked.

Randy slid a tablet their way. "Recognize anyone?"

It was an image of Yuri Sokolov at a resort standing near a long, black limousine. Ekaterina was on his arm, both of them laughing together like a couple who didn't head one of the most powerful crime syndicates in the world. There wasn't anything remotely hilarious about arms, drug, and human trafficking, thousands of deaths, political interference, and money laundering.

"This was taken the night before you took down Vasily and Sergei," Randy said. "We're pretty certain they were there to retrieve Dominik."

The blue Aruban flag, red star and yellow stripes in high definition, flew in the distance. Again, Sokolov knew they were watching him. He'd all but posed for the picture, the flag in the background a tease. A way to show them how far off they'd been.

"We needed an ID, Barrett."

"And I brought you a human." She held up two fingers. "Two humans."

"The wrong ones."

"We didn't know that until we got them here. What if

Vasily had been Dominik? We'd have just a picture of him. Then what?"

"Then we'd gather more intel!" Randy slammed his fists on the tabletop. "We orchestrate these operations this way for a reason, Barrett. For efficient execution and the safety of our officers. This was your op. We sent you in blind and with minimal backup, and you came back with the wrong target."

She stopped a half-second before she rolled her eyes. It was one mistake. Granted, it was one *huge* mistake considering they'd been working the Sokolov crime family, in some capacity, even before she'd arrived at Interpol. But the reason she'd been given the privileges she had was because she was good at what she did. This slip-up didn't change that. Come hell or high water, she was going back in.

She pushed the tablet away. "So what now?"

"Now?" Randy raised a thick eyebrow. "Now, we put you on a desk."

"I'm not sitting behind a desk."

"Oh, so you run the agency?"

"Randy," she leaned forward, fingers clasped, "I still brought you Sokolov lineage. Vasily is family."

He released a hard sigh, reclined in his leather chair, and picked at the skin on his bottom lip. At least she hadn't driven him back to smoking. His lips might end up sore and cracked because of the stress she brought him daily, but lung cancer was no longer a guarantee.

"Tell me I'm wrong," she goaded.

Randy looked at Colin.

"I have nothing to say," Colin said. "This was all E's op. I just support her the way I always do."

Randy's nostrils flared with another, harder, sigh. "You're still going behind a desk, Barrett."

Eija opened her mouth to protest, but he held up a hand.

"Dominik Sokolov is back in Moscow. That means the transfer of power will happen as planned. Luckily, we still have quite some time before the ceremony, the *Koronatsiya*, but we'll have to start from scratch. Colin will take the lead on this one."

She wanted to vault from her chair and demand the roles be reversed, but they hadn't thrown her out on her ass. Had it not been for the dynamics of her mentor-mentee relationship with Randy, she would have been packing her bags yesterday.

She nodded. "Yes, sir."

"Why do you want this so much, E?" Randy asked, studying her with his head slightly cocked to the side. "The Russians did some dirty shit to you or something?"

Whenever he called her E, that meant he'd transitioned from Randy the hard-ass to Randy the mentor.

"The one that got away," she said, and it was an odd moment to think about Andrei, but she pushed the memory to the side. "The Sokolov Crime Family is my golden egg, and each time I reach out, they move just past the length of my fingers. I want to be the one to put a face to Dominik Sokolov's Red Notice."

Randy smiled. "If every officer here had both you and Favreau's bite, I could retire at the end of the year."

"So, we're back on it?" Colin asked.

Randy hesitated, back to picking his lip. "Yes, and that work starts today. Eija, I want you inside that family unit, in some capacity, before the transition ceremony in eighteen months. I don't care how you do it. Make it happen."

Eija stood.

Randy flitted his fingers at the door. "Go. I'll have someone send Vasily back to his keep."

She turned to leave.

"And remember what I said, Eija. Stick to the objective at hand."

Her jaw pulsed. "I understand, sir."

The door to Randy's office opened. Another agent, Tyrese Janvier, started to enter but pulled up short.

"What is it?" Eija asked.

"Your suspect's dead."

"How?"

Tyrese stuck a finger in his mouth and tapped one of his canines. "He had cyanide hidden in a fake tooth."

Eija closed her eyes and said a quick prayer before she asked the next question. "Is it the blond one or the one with all the tattoos?"

"The blond. The tattoo guy's already dead. Same method."

"Fuck." She wanted to slam her fist against something, but only Tyrese was nearby, and he took a half step backward. "This Sokolov shit can't possibly get worse."

"The moment someone uses that phrase, things get worse," Colin said, squeezing her shoulders from behind. "Shut it. Let's go. We have next to no time to prepare, *and* we have to get a team together."

She left Randy's office and headed directly to hers, to her desk, where she stood with her palms pressed on the wooden surface.

"Where are you, Dom?" The photos of Ekaterina and Yuri stared back at her from their perch on top of a world map. "I want to see your face."

"Hey, E?"

She looked up. "April. Come in."

April Silva was her protege; the slightly younger woman just didn't know it yet. They had a lot in common—island backgrounds, notable achievements and accolades, and a tenuous relationship with authority. Though, April was less inclined to sit topless on a target's lap.

"Before we head to start the Sokolov meeting, I wanted to run something by you," April said, her low, jet black haircut perfectly suited to her oblong face and mahogany skin tone. "Randy believes Nikolai Sokolov will be our in."

"Yuri's grandson?" Eija asked. "Why?"

"He has a nanny who's with him everywhere he goes. However," April handed over an image, "Yuri might be sleeping with the nanny."

The picture clearly indicated *something* was going on. Yuri, the younger woman, and Nikolai were in attendance at Wimbledon, and Yuri's lips were close to the nanny's ears. From the smile on her face, whatever Yuri told her was salacious in a way the woman loved.

"That's going to be difficult as hell to pull off," Eija pointed out. "The nanny's one of the closest roles to the family."

"Me, you, Randy, and Colin can pull this off. I'm sure of it." April looked down when she said Colin's name and then changed the subject, much like Colin did whenever April was mentioned. "On another note, E, how was it to be back in tropics?"

Eija tried not to think of Andrei. If they'd had more time, it made her shudder to think what they could have become. What she could have felt for him.

"It was," she clicked her tongue, "fun."

April cocked her head to the side. "Oh...*fun.*"

"Dinner at my place. I'll tell you all about it. How detailed do you want me to get?"

"Very." April leaned closer to her. "Anyone special?"

"Kind of."

"Aww—"

"Ugh, stop." Eija laughed and stepped from behind her desk. "Let's go. We'll catch up tonight. Should I invite Colin?"

April looked toward an overstuffed bookshelf on the wall that wasn't nearly as interesting as her current expression made it seem. "You can do what you want."

"Aww—"

"Ugh." April followed her out of the office. "Stop."

Chapter Eight

Moscow, Russia
Three months until Koronatsiya

Dominik stared at the woman across the table from him. She wasn't terrible company—she had a pretty face and a nice voice. It was obvious she was educated and the kind of woman who would be happy as a diplomat's wife or something along the same vein. She'd known the restaurant where they'd arranged to have dinner was named after Alexander Pushkin. She'd even known about some of the history and architecture of the building, speaking confidently and eloquently.

They dined in a private hall with ornate columns, a crackling fireplace, and crystal chandeliers. It was the kind of place his father should have taken his mother; she'd deserved to be wined and dined and fawned over. Instead, all Yuri had wanted from her was for her to be on her back when he called and exclusively available until he grew bored.

"And my mother actually helps my father with all the contracts."

Dom looked up into green eyes and long brown hair that flowed past the table's edge, with no recollection of any part of their conversation.

"You could expect that kind of due diligence from me as your wife."

He closed his menu and clasped his fingers on top of the table. "Leila—"

"Leah."

"*Leah,* I have a personal question for you." He motioned to her, himself. "Why are you doing this? What would possess you, a woman with a law degree from Cambridge, to get tied up in something so...archaic?"

Three months to the day, on the same night as the koronatsiya, there was a ceremony known as *Dostavka.* There, he was supposed to present his future wife to the heads of all the major crime syndicates in attendance, including the heads of the different factions of the Bratva. That meant he had three months to choose a wife, and due to the Bratva's longstanding position of power within the realm of organized crime, his choice had to be calculated.

Leah cleared her throat, visibly uncomfortable. "It's my duty, Dominik. Same as you. You know what our union would mean for our families."

It wasn't that she wasn't pretty. She was beautiful, educated, and he supposed if he actually listened to her, she would make good company. But he didn't want a wife. Even if he did, he wouldn't choose one this way, and he would never allow his father to choose one for him.

"Don't you want to marry for love?" he asked. "Isn't that what people want these days, if they want to marry at all?"

"My parents didn't marry for love, but they learned to love each other over time."

"And you think that could happen between you and me?"

She tossed her hair over her shoulder. "Yes. I do."

He had at least a dozen other prospects to choose from, all who looked nearly identical to this one. His father knew absolutely nothing about his tastes if he hadn't so much as attempted to diversify his female companions.

He'd tried finding Eija for several months after their last night together, but then he gave up when he realized he'd left in the middle of the night after having sex with her. Note or not, he was probably the last person she'd want to hear from.

"In addition, we're both attractive." Leah lowered her lashes and ran her fingers through her hair. "If not love, there are other things we can connect on."

That, he hadn't expected, and he liked the hidden twist.

"I'm a lot of man to handle."

Her cheeks pinked. "So I've noticed."

He wanted her to ask him why it was fair that *he* was the one with the right to make the choice. She came from a well-known Italian family. Her grandparents had ties to the Bratva going back decades. She didn't *need* any of this if she truly wanted something else.

Their server entered through a door behind them and asked, in Russian, if they were ready to order.

"What do you think I should have for dinner, Leah?" he asked.

She scrunched her nose. "I don't know you well enough to make that decision."

"I don't mind if you guess."

"In time, if things work out between us, I'd be happy to. Please let her know I'd like the ravioli."

He ordered ravioli for her and a rack of lamb with cherry sauce for him.

They ate in silence, and he found his mind going back to the Fish Friday in Grenada. Fancy restaurants were nice, and he didn't mind a setup like this every once in a while. But, for balance, he wouldn't say no to another evening eating street food while listening to lively music with arms wrapped around him from behind.

After dinner, they returned to his father's penthouse where all the women and their families were currently staying as guests. When the car stopped in the parking deck, Leah kept her head tilted toward the hands she wrung in her lap. Her teeth grated over her bottom lip.

"Everything okay?" Dom asked, turning half of his body her way. "You seem on edge. You didn't have a good time?"

"I did." She chanced a glance at him, cheeks turning the

color of roses. "But, to be honest, when Yuri told me his nephew would be going up for Koronatsiya, I wasn't expecting...you."

He tipped up an eyebrow. "How so?"

"You're," she dared another glance, "very attractive."

"And you're so red, I could cut you open and still wouldn't be able to tell where you bleed."

She choked out a nervous laugh. "I suppose I am. I've never been in a situation like this."

"You want something."

Her head slowly bobbed. "I do."

"Tell me what you want."

"I, uh," she tugged on her fingers, "would like to kiss you good night."

Dom spread his arms wide, extending one behind her head in the back of the Maybach. Heat suffused the cabin, casting a foggy mist over the windows. Her chest rose in a quick tempo.

"What are you waiting for?" he asked.

She sucked in a breath and dove for his mouth. Out of the corner of his eye, he saw a flash of brown.

"Ouch!"

He blinked Leah back into focus and found her rubbing her lip.

"What happened?" He asked the question to the woman in the car, but his eyes searched the penthouse doors for the woman he swore he'd seen standing there seconds ago.

"Teeth," Leah said.

He tore his attention from the doors and let it all fall on

Leah. "To be my wife, you're going to have to learn how to take a little bite, sweetheart."

She replied with a breathy, "Okay."

He tapped on the window and one of the house staff opened Leah's door. She cast a glance back at him but then left without another word. He was about to go home when the door on his side opened and Pavel peered in.

"Yuri needs to see you."

Dom followed Pavel to the far end of the penthouse where Yuri's office was located. Yuri sat at his desk, his headful of wavy silver hair bowed over a short stack of papers. A large framed black and white photo of him, Ekaterina, and their daughters took up most of the office's right wall, a room that had been designed primarily with wooden accents, leafy plants, and olive paint. Dom didn't look at the photos on the left wall where he'd find images of him over the years interspersed with uncles, nephews, and cousins, burying him like a *Where's Waldo?* book. Behind Yuri, views of the sparkling center of Moscow at nighttime glimmered, the lights along the Yauza river, the Kremlin, and Evolution Tower in the distance.

Pavel stood behind Yuri and off to the side at his left hand. The family housecat, a gray, domestic shorthair they'd named Lyubov, prowled around the office as though papers and pens would transform into prey.

Dom sat in the leather guest chair on the other side of the desk. When he'd left, his father's deep voice bellowing objections for him to stay at his back, he'd always anticipated his return. His aunt had warned him that once the Brotherhood sank its fangs into its prey, it locked its jaw. He hadn't expected to love the city again. He didn't like the reason he was there and didn't care for the people he spent time with, but that wasn't the city's fault. It wasn't even the country's fault. Every nation had its waste.

Yuri's hand moved in quick succession, signing papers in a folio on his desk. "Pavel, can you get me a cigar?" he asked. "I want to smoke with my son."

Pavel left the room and came back with a thick Cuban, already cut, on a silver platter.

Smoking cigars wasn't something Dom indulged in much, but it was a good way to unwind. As much acrimony as he'd had toward Yuri over the years, he could admit that it felt good to sit across from his father having a cigar like a son Yuri hadn't spent his life denying.

Pavel held a lighter to the butt of the cigar, and Yuri took two puffs, leaned back, and propped his expensive loafers up on his desk. Lyu strolled over and tangled her claws in his dress socks.

"How was your evening, my son?" Yuri asked. "Leah, she's a member of the Strinati family."

Dom did his best to dance around the question. "What's their family into?"

"Her great-grandfather, Nuncio, is a former Boss of the Sicilian mafia."

"La Cosa Nostra?"

Yuri flicked his wrist, the smoke creating a ring around him. "Nothing so sentimental."

"What if I want a nice, normal girl?" Dom asked. "Maybe a teacher."

Yuri stared at him.

"It's a serious question. What about an opera singer? A concert pianist?" A woman with a passion that consumed so much of her time, they would scarcely see each other. "An actress from America."

Groaning, Yuri took another puff. "You're sending me to an early grave, Dominik."

"Okay, what if she looked different?"

"Different how?"

"Shape, hair, eyes. Skin."

Yuri slid his feet off the desktop, left his chair, and walked around to perch on the edge. Lyu curled up next to him.

"An exotic woman?"

"If that's what you want to call it."

"As a mistress, I highly recommend it." Yuri nodded, the corners of his mouth drawn down. "But not as a wife. You've lived abroad for too long. You do understand how things work for us?"

Dom took a puff. "No. Why don't you explain it to me?"

"The woman from...what's the island called, Pavel?"

"Grenada," Pavel supplied.

"Yes, Grenada. The woman I found you in bed with, what was her background?"

"I don't see why that matters."

"Then, I'll make a guess. She was a local. And her type, they are vixens in the bedroom. Their bodies were made for cock." Yuri slowly shook his head, a corner of his bottom lip between his teeth. "However, it's the optics, my son. I love all women, but there is a way things are done. The Brotherhood would not accept a woman like her on your arm."

Yuri knew more about Eija than he'd claimed, and Dom didn't trust that it had taken over a year for this to become evident to him.

"Got it," Dom said. "Optics."

Yuri spoke to him about more business. Dom listened to half of it. It wasn't until he heard his nephew's name that he found himself once again engaged in the conversation.

"Nikolai has a new nanny? Since when?"

Whenever he and Nikolai spent time together, it was at his apartment or somewhere outside the city. A few times, outside the country. Every trip to the Sokolov penthouse, at least for him, had to be meticulously planned.

"He talks about her all the time, Dominik. Perhaps you should come around more often."

"Miss...Miss..." Dom tried to pull up the name. "Korichnevna."

"Nikolai is really taken with her. He says they're going to be married when he grows up. Maybe, by then, the world will change, and he'll be able to do just that as the head of all this."

Nikolai's mother, Sonya, had died when Nikolai was a year

old. She'd lost the battle against potent pharmaceuticals and illicit substances, which she'd been exposed to because the family had a major hand in their global circulation. Because she'd used while pregnant, the first three years of Nikolai's life had been filled with endless medical specialists. It was part of what Dom had learned since he returned, and he'd bonded rather quickly with his five-year-old nephew.

The door behind them squeaked, and Nikolai came charging into the room.

"Papa!"

"My boy." Yuri grabbed him up in a hug. "Are you all ready for bed?"

Lyu meowed in contempt, hopped to the floor, and left the room.

"Yes, Papa. Miss Korichnevna's going home. Why can't she live with us like my other nannies?"

Because Ekaterina had caught the last nanny naked in bed with Yuri.

Dom glanced at the door, which Nikolai had left slightly ajar. Suddenly, he was fumbling the cigar. It nearly fell to the floor and burned a hole through the massive, fifteen-thousand dollar area rug.

"Are you all right, Dom?" Yuri asked. "You look like you've seen a ghost."

Dom squashed the end of the cigar against the platter on his father's desk, set it down, and stepped out into the hallway. Her back was turned to him, and although she wore a silky, high-necked, long-sleeved blouse and wide-leg black pants—another requirement set in place by Ekaterina—he knew that body. Her hair was tucked into a bun, but he knew that hair. That scent, that jawline, those fingers...he'd dreamed about them.

He walked up behind her, wrapped his fingers around her neck, and pushed her face-first against the wall.

Chapter Nine

Eija extended her elbow into the jaw of whoever had thought it was smart to grab her from behind. It connected and the person, a man, groaned.

He stumbled backward, but he caught himself and tried to pin her arms behind her back. She slammed the back of her head into his chin, elbowed him in the midsection, spun out of his grasp, and pushed him face-first against the wall like he'd done her, her knee in his back.

They couldn't have made her—too much work had gone into this op. Miss *Korichnevna* was an excellent nanny with a background that could have gotten her a job with any president, prime minister, or dictator. Randy had gotten her in as part of the line-up of nannies interviewed by the Sokolovs. The last caregiver, as anticipated, was ousted after her and Yuri's torrid affair was uncovered.

In the middle of the selection process, Colin had found out that Yuri and Ekaterina would be attending the ballet at The Bolshoi Theatre one evening. On the way to their reserved seats, an undercover agent posing as one of the theater staff had apologized profusely to Eija for getting her seating arrangement mixed up, in front of the couple. She'd berated him in flawless Russian and, as she stormed off, "bumped" into one of Sokolov's guards, Gideon Medvedev, who'd caught her in her strapless red gown and silver high heels. As she thanked him, she'd glanced the couple's way, and they'd recognized her from the interviews. She'd avoided Ekaterina's gaze as she apologized, and the couple ended up inviting her to sit with them for the performance.

During the intermission, Ekaterina had requested that she accompany her to the bathroom. There, Ekaterina had asked her if she was at the ballet because Yuri had invited her, to which Eija had nodded, thanking them *both* for the invitation. Ekaterina had then looked her up and down and said, "At least, if he falls in love, he can't threaten to marry *you*."

She'd been there three months so far, and this asshole would not mess things up for her.

"Let me go," the man said, in English.

"Now you want to speak?" She shoved harder. "Why did you grab me?"

He smelled like he'd just come from a cigar house. A smell she loathed. Her Papa had been an avid cigar smoker, and while she'd loved him dearly, she never quite developed a love for his habit.

"Eija, it's me."

"Me, who?"

"Eija..."

She released him. The nature of the job and daily searches had made carrying a weapon difficult but not impossible.

The person turned around.

And she nearly died on the spot.

He'd cut his hair, but the low cut didn't detract from his naturally attractive features. The facial hair she'd wondered about on the island had grown out, which he kept as low as his hair. Then there were those eyes, as dangerous as lead yet as steamy as a heavy downpour on hot concrete.

Andrei Falcone.

She stepped forward, reaching up to touch the side of his face, but he slapped her hand away.

"Who do you work for?"

"Andrei, what are you talking about?" Handsome or not, he wouldn't get her to blow a cover she'd spent over a year developing. "I work for Mr. and Mrs. Sokolov."

"Why are you calling me Andrei?"

"Because that's your name."

He frowned. "Didn't you get my note?"

"Ah, I was hoping to introduce you two." Yuri joined them in the hallway. "Dominik, this is Nikolai's nanny, Miss Brown, aka Korichnevna. Miss K, this is my...son, Dominik Sokolov."

No.

No, no, no.

Fuck, this was bad.

Not only had she bagged and tagged the wrong men in

Grenada, she'd *fucked* the right one. She'd spent months thinking about him and, on her own time, trying to find him. He'd left so abruptly, it was like he'd never existed.

Now she knew why.

Those noxious eyes locked with hers. "So, is it Brown or Korichnevna?"

Yuri chuckled and patted Dominik's shoulder. "When she first came, she and Nikolai worked on patronymics. Nikolai insisted he come up with a name for her."

And *korichnevyy* meant brown.

They'd settled on Miss K.

Eija kept her voice level through the use of brute strength and brute strength alone. "Dominik. It's nice to meet you."

Nikolai talked about his "Uncle Dominik" all the time. She'd known, sooner or later, she'd see the face of the man she wanted to lock away, if not bury six feet under. This wasn't the face she'd been expecting. This was the last face she'd expected to see. Yet, he looked at her like *she* was the one who'd hidden her identity their entire time together. At least, the only one who had.

"*Miss K,*" Dominik said, dragging out the name. She wanted to look away, but she wouldn't be first. "Nice to meet you as well."

Yuri stepped forward and kissed Eija's cheek. "Miss K taught in Moscow years ago, fell in love with the city, and returned to teach after her grandfather's death."

"I'm sorry to hear that. Was he sick for a while?"

"It was sudden." In Grenada, she'd confided in him that her

grandmother had been ill, but she'd always known her grandfather would pass before her nana.

She stroked the fabric she'd had to button all the way up the column of her neck. With the initial shock gone, the memory of their last night together played, on a reel, through her mind. Dominik's eyes fell to where she could feel her nipples trying to poke through, and she covered them with folded arms. She prayed that he simply assumed she was a crazy stalker who'd infiltrated his family's home to get closer to him. At worst, he'd soon figure out she worked in espionage for an international law enforcement agency.

"Miss K!" Nikolai ran up and hugged her around the legs. "Can I walk you out?"

She smoothed his hair. He was such a lovely child, it made this part of the job much easier. With his large glasses frames and blond hair, he was the spitting image of the kid from Jerry Maguire.

"Yes, you may, but only if you ask me in English."

The space between his brows wrinkled. "May...I...walk you?"

"May I walk you...to the car? Try it with me."

She recited, and he repeated.

After a few attempts, he could say the entire sentence.

Ekaterina and Yuri spoke English well enough to get a point across, but they wanted Nikolai to speak English with as close to a neutral accent as possible. Teaching English in Moscow had been another tick on her fake résumé.

Dominik stooped to his nephew's eye level. "Nikolai, you should be in bed. I'll walk Miss K to her car."

"No." Nikolai grabbed Eija's hand. "I want to do it."

"Nikolai..."

"Dominik, let the boy walk her out," Yuri said.

She bid the two men goodnight.

Dominik followed and stood watching Nikolai help her into the car as though he expected her to run off with his nephew.

Eija smiled, waved, and didn't breathe until they'd left the property.

This couldn't be happening.

Had she really had sex with one of the most dangerous men in the world?

She sank into the car's backseat across from Gideon, her private security. The Sokolovs had, at length, explained to her the necessity of privacy and confidentiality in their work as well as why she would need to go everywhere with a bodyguard and security detail. She'd eased their concerns by telling them that if she'd worked at Buckingham Palace, it would have been the same thing, and Yuri had enjoyed being thought of as royalty.

Tchaikovsky filtered throughout the car, Gideon tapping his fingers in time to the stringed instruments. At night, Moscow lit up like any other major city, the difference so stark, it appeared to be otherwise asleep during the day. They passed Evolution Tower with its dancing lights and double-helix design, and there was still a little blue to the sky—a purple night instead of a dark, starless sheet of nothingness.

Instead of living at the penthouse, the Sokolovs had set her up in an expensive Moscow apartment a short drive away. Her apartment was one of their properties, a modern flat with four bedrooms that overlooked the Moskva River. It was more luxury than she would ever see again in her lifetime, with its expensive marble countertops and glossy travertine floors. The concierge desk fulfilled any request she had, and when she wasn't with Nikolai, Colin, or April, she swam, played tennis, and wore herself out at the gym.

The rest of the staff, who'd warmed up to her quicker than she'd expected, had revealed what she already knew—Yuri and the former nanny had been having sex in the penthouse while Ekaterina slept. They'd warned her against doing the same, but as much as she liked to get hers, Yuri wouldn't be on her radar any time soon.

Or his son.

His *son*.

A shiver tickled her vertebrae.

"Are you okay, Miss K?" Gideon asked. "Are you cold? I can have Mikhail turn the heat up."

Their driver peered at her through the rearview mirror.

She waved off the suggestion. "I'm all right. Nice and toasty."

Colin and April had secured an apartment in the same building, through Interpol, where they posed as a young married couple. Colin worked in "technology" while April's cover was that of an introverted author. Their place was homier than hers, with its exposed brick and wood floors. It had two bedrooms, one big enough for a Command Center, but they didn't do any of their work onsite. Colin going to "work" was him going to the undisclosed location where all their equipment had been set up on the outskirts of Moscow.

Initially, April hadn't been part of the undercover lineup, but extenuating circumstances had changed that last minute. Circumstances not even Randy knew about. And it wasn't that she didn't trust Randy; however, his behavior in the months leading up to her assignment had convinced her that some things were best left secret.

Gideon lightly touched Eija's wrist. For a gang of killers, weapons dealers, and drug pushers, their touches were always gentle. They squeezed her hands and kissed her cheeks. Had she not known any better, she would have assumed they were the family-oriented businessmen they claimed to be.

"Miss K, we're here."

She yawned. "I'll make it through one of these car rides awake one day, Gideon. I swear."

"Nikolai keeps you on your toes all day," he pointed out, chuckling. "It's normal to be tired by the end."

She smiled at him with his enormous frame, muscular neck, and arms clothed in tattoos. "Yes, but I adore him."

"He's a lovely child, but don't forget to pace yourself."

"I won't. Thank you." She leaned forward and touched Mikhail on the shoulder. "*Spasibo*, Mikhail. Dobroy nochi. Dobroy nochi, Gideon."

She hurried inside the building out of the cold, greeted the doorman, and stepped into the first available elevator.

The apartment's warmth enveloped her the second she

stepped over the threshold. She headed past the floor-to-ceiling windows, straight to the bedroom to change. Ekaterina had requested that she cover herself up from chin to ankles. While she'd obliged the matriarch, clothes could only do so much to curb Yuri's curiosity. More than once, she'd caught him studying what curves he could see.

Eija stripped down to her bra and panties, went to the living room, and took a moment to compose herself before she called Colin and April on a secure line to check in.

"Nothing today?" Colin greeted, slurping on something. It was probably Borscht, his new favorite food.

"No," she said. "Nothing."

It wasn't until the words left her mouth that she realized she was going to withhold the Andrei-Dominik paradox from her partner. It was embarrassing to know Dominik had been right there, in her face, *and* she'd slept with him. Granted, he didn't look anything like the profiles they'd created, but how was it that she'd never suspected Andrei? How hadn't he even crossed her...

Wait.

Sokolov.

It came from the Russian worked *sokol* which meant falcon. He'd told her his name was Andrei *Falcone*. If she'd bothered to think with her brain instead of her clit every once in a while, maybe she would have picked up on it.

"Eija, you there?"

"Yeah, yeah." She cleared her throat. "Look, Colin, Dominik is going to show his face. If not before Koronatsiya, we at least know he's definitely going to be there. I'll be ready."

"And what does 'ready' mean, babe?"

"Don't call me babe."

He laughed. "I only do it because you hate it."

She knew what he wanted to hear. Considering the sacrifices both he and April had made for her, especially with Colin's loyalty to the job, he deserved the truth. She wouldn't give him the truth, but it was nice to acknowledge that he deserved it.

"It means I'll stick to what we agreed on," she said. "ID, isolation, and backup. When we leave Moscow, Sokolov will be with us."

The doorbell buzzed, and it was unusual that the doorman hadn't called to ask her to confirm her guest.

She walked to the panel on the wall near the door and pulled up the image. "Shit, Colin. It's Yuri."

"Yuri? It's," he paused, "almost ten. What the fuck does he want this late?"

"I think I know, but I'm hoping I'm wrong."

"E, don't let him in."

Eija pushed the button on the panel, let Yuri know she would be there shortly, and returned to her conversation with Colin.

"I can take him, if anything."

"Don't fuck him."

She sucked her teeth. "Really? You think I want to?"

Through the phone speaker, she heard chair legs scraping a

hard surface. "I don't think you want to, but you'll do anything to avoid having your cover blown."

He was right.

And wrong.

No one ever accused *him* of wanting to sleep with everyone that walked into his path. It was only recently he'd slowed down because one night with April had put him in an obsessive brain fog.

Eija ended the call, tied a robe around her body, and opened the door.

Yuri didn't look as dangerous as his title. It was the thing that had surprised her most, meeting him in person for the first time. He was in his late sixties, but he was one of those men whose silver hair made them look younger somehow. More refined and distinguished. Even this late, he still wore a full gray suit with a purple collared shirt underneath, the first button undone.

"I'm sorry for the intrusion," he said. "May I come in?"

She stepped aside. "Of course."

It was his property. He paid the doorman's salary. Saying no wasn't an option.

He strolled to the center of the room, hands in his pockets, and looked around. "You haven't added any personal touches."

"I'm not good at that sort of thing."

"Really? I see you as someone good at many things."

Here we go.

"Would you like something to drink?" she asked.

His mouth stretched into a wide smile. "Vodka."

She went to the kitchen, and he made himself comfortable on the living room sofa. This was a situation she wanted to be completely sober for, so she poured his vodka, filled a glass with water for herself, and joined him on the sofa, leaving enough space to appear friendly but not fearful.

They raised their glasses in a silent toast, and he took a sip.

"Very good vodka, Miss K."

"Thank you."

"Miss K?" He held the glass in both hands, thumb tracing the rim. "How is Nikolai doing, really? I worry about him. I don't like to show it, but I do. His beginning life was...so difficult."

Eija leaned forward. "He's doing well. Honestly, he is. There are places where he struggles, but I'll help him through it all. It's what you hired me to do, and what I was trained to do."

Yuri's gaze fell to her chest.

She leaned back until her bra went back into hiding inside the robe.

"You're very interesting, Miss K." His Adam's apple bobbed with another sip. "Most of Nikolai's nannies have been just as intelligent and worldly, but there's something more about you. You make him try harder. You make him relaxed. Hell, you make *me* relaxed."

"What happened to his last nanny?" she asked, hoping her face didn't give away what she already knew.

"I slept with her." Yuri drained the remaining liquor in one gulp. "Kat didn't like that very much. Not the sleeping with her part. The falling in love part."

"Are you a man who falls in love easily?"

"Yes."

"Well, kudos to you." She raised her glass. "I've had my heart broken so many times, I'm not sure if I have the capacity to love anymore."

She'd never truly had her heart broken, but it wasn't like she'd ever put it on the line.

His voice softened. "Really? Why?"

"It's," she looked down, making paths in the condensation on the side of her glass, "complicated."

"That's because most men make false promises. Me, I make no promises I can't keep. You want this place, you can have it. You want sapphires and diamonds, they're yours. Since I can't marry you or give you children, everything else...I offer it. If *you* had to think of something, Miss K," he edged closer, "what would you ask for?"

"I—"

Banging on the door startled them both.

Dom's voice carried across the room, through the steel. "Open up or not, Yuri, I'm coming in."

Chapter Ten

Dom squeezed his pounding forehead and stared at the building where Gideon and Mikhail had dropped Eija off. It also happened to be the same building he lived in, and he'd never spotted her before today. Not even a glimpse. Eija was one of the most attractive women he'd ever met. In his life. It was laughable he hadn't seen her even once in the three months since she'd signed on as Nikolai's new nanny.

Was she a stalker?

Was this just a fortunate coincidence?

She hadn't known his name wasn't Andrei, the shock on her face genuine, so she obviously hadn't gotten his note. Without that note, it looked like he'd gotten the pussy he'd been chasing and skipped out. Though Eija owned her sex appeal, that didn't make her inhuman. It would have hurt him—pissed him off, really—if she'd skipped out on him after the unforgettable couple of weeks they'd spent together.

If she wasn't a stalker and this wasn't a coincidence, there was one last option—Yuri had orchestrated the entire thing.

But why bring Eija to Russia?

For now, he'd let the dust settle. Then, he'd try to find out if this was all part of Yuri Sokolov's game, or if there was more to the woman, who'd somehow become even more gorgeous since he'd last seen her, than met the eye. Hearing her speak Russian had nearly made his dick hard in front of his father.

A familiar black car pulled up to the building's entrance. Yuri stepped out, unfastening the top button on his shirt.

Dom stepped out of his.

Eija wasn't his woman. Technically, she'd never been. But this wasn't going to fucking happen.

He waited until the car pulled off before entering the building. The doorman, Paul, a transplant from Edinburgh, perked up when he spotted him.

"Ya just missed your uncle, son."

Dom nodded. "Yeah, we're supposed to meet up about something. Thank you."

Yuri had buried his little gray-eyed nephew's true relationship to the *Pakhan*, the Bratva Boss, so well, Dom was hard pressed to believe anyone would believe he was his son when the time came.

"People want to kill me," Yuri had told him. *"I don't want them knowing who you are until you control the Brotherhood."*

Dom took the elevator to the floor where it indicated his

father had stopped and watched as Yuri preened outside Eija's door.

She opened it and welcomed Yuri inside.

He gave them five minutes, then walked to the door and knocked.

"Open up or not, Yuri, I'm coming in."

The lock clicked, and Eija slowly appeared as the door opened. She wore a robe, but he knew, just fucking knew either she was naked or barely wearing anything underneath. The woman was so damn *pretty*. He'd just had dinner with a pretty woman, but Eija radiated beauty, even in moonlight.

"Where's Yuri?"

She opened the door further, bringing his father into view on her sofa.

Dom stepped inside. "Why are you here?"

"To talk to Miss K," Yuri asserted, rising to his feet.

"Bullshit. Get out."

Yuri cocked his head to the side. "Dominik, do you know who you're talking to?"

"I left all my fucks back at the penthouse. I've got none to give you."

Yuri looked behind him at Eija.

Dom stepped into Yuri's line of sight, blocking her from view. "You don't need to look at her. I'm the one talking to you. Yuri, you said yourself that Nikolai loves Miss K. What do you think will happen if your wife finds out you're here right now?"

While he didn't think Eija would have sex with his *father*, she would have had sex with Yuri Sokolov. The woman was very confident in what she wanted, and dick happened to be one of those things if memory served him correctly. He hadn't even considered that they might have already had sex, and this was a normal meetup for them.

"You're right, my son. My apologies for stopping by so late, Miss K."

Yuri attempted to bid Eija goodnight, but Dom didn't shift, so he simply let her know he'd see her in the morning. The door automatically locked after Yuri left, but Dom still checked it. When he turned around, Eija was in the kitchen.

"Eija, did you fuck my father?"

She shot him a look, rolled her eyes to Mars, fished a pan from one of the bottom cabinets, and set it on the gas stovetop.

Damn it.

He wanted to smile.

He couldn't believe he was looking at her again, even if it was his father's doing.

"Eija?"

She went to the refrigerator. "What?"

"You didn't answer my question."

"Because it's a dumb ass question." She waved a covered glass dish at him. "Are you hungry?"

"I had dinner earlier."

"Fancy. Was it a date?"

"No."

She dumped half the dish's contents into the pan, returned the rest to the refrigerator, and started the fire under the pan, her back turned to him.

He joined her in the kitchen and stood behind her. "Tell me the truth. Did you really not know who I was?"

"Nope." She shook her head. "I thought your name was Andrei Falcone."

A savory aroma lifted around them.

"Smells good. What is it?"

"It's part of a dish. This is the curried chicken and potatoes to go inside the roti." She motioned to a flat tortilla on the countertop. "Which is that part."

"We didn't eat roti together in Grenada, did we?"

"No, we didn't."

He stepped back, giving her space to warm the dough in the oven, and her robe opened enough for him to see the pink bra underneath cupping those plump breasts of hers. How was it possible to miss someone this much after knowing them only a couple of weeks? The key thing he'd get caught up on those nights his thoughts had revolved around her was what they could have had if they'd had more time.

She closed the oven door.

He hooked her around the waist and spun her away from the stove, up against the kitchen island, less than an inch of space between them. His head lowered, but she leaned back, away from him.

"You're right." He dragged his bottom lip through his teeth. "I'm being presumptuous."

"There you go, using that Stanford degree," she teased, grinning. "No, you smell like cigars."

"So you *do* want to kiss me."

"More or less."

"You just can't kiss me if I might taste like a cigar."

"Makes me feel like I'm kissing somebody's...father."

He rolled his eyes. "You're not funny."

Laughing, she pinched air with her thumb and index finger. "Come on, it was just a little bit funny."

It wasn't like he was addicted to them. Even if he had been, to kiss her, he'd kick the habit.

She stepped around his body, went back to the stove, and grabbed a wooden spoon. Each stir of the pan's contents sent the aroma higher.

He repositioned himself behind her. "It's so crazy that I get to see you again."

"The question is," she glanced over her shoulder at him, and he caught a wave of sadness that quickly disappeared from her face, "what to do now that you have?"

"Take you out."

She stopped stirring, body stiff. "Take me out *how?*"

"You mean *where,*" he corrected. "Get drinks with me. I can show you around Moscow. Or, we can head to St. Pete for a weekend. I have a place out there in the Golden Triangle."

She turned off the burner.

He reached into the cabinet above her head, grabbed a plate, and handed it to her.

"Thanks."

"No problem," he said. "So...dinner?"

As she scooped the curried chicken and potatoes onto the tortilla, a tiny smile woke up the dimple next to the corner of her mouth. "What happened to drinks?" she asked.

"The more you talk, the more I like you." At the penthouse, she'd had her hair in that tight bun. Here, it was out and had a light, fresh scent to it. "Why aren't you more upset with me? You didn't get my note. Shouldn't you hate me?"

"For skipping out on me in the middle of the night after I fucked you so good?"

"That. Exactly that."

She leaned back into his chest and tilted her head, looking up into his eyes. From every angle, this woman was lovely, and it had disappointed him for a long time he hadn't been able to wake up next to her in the sunshine.

"What did your note say?"

"That I enjoyed our time together." He unraveled the strap on her robe. "That my real name isn't Andrei Falcone."

This wasn't about wanting to make love to her. He wanted to feel her skin, feel that she was standing in front of him and not an evil trick up his imagination's sleeve.

She blinked slowly, searching his face. "Did you say what your real name was in the note?"

"I signed it 'Dom.'" One side of the robe fell open, and he slipped his hand inside, her stomach warm against his palm. "I wanted you to know that much, at least."

"Why didn't you tell me before? Why hide your name?"

"I was hiding from my father."

"And I came across as dangerous to you?"

"No, not at all." He slid his thumb over her skin. "But I

didn't know if telling you my name would be dangerous *for* you. Yuri was adamant about me coming home. You wouldn't be the first woman he's scared off."

Something marbled passed beneath his fingertip. She sucked in a breath and pushed his hand away.

"Was that a scar?"

She quickly wrapped her little roti burrito and eased out of his grasp. "Yep."

"You didn't have that before."

"How do you know?" She left the kitchen and took a seat at the oversized dining table. "You can't tell me you paid *that* much attention to my body."

"I can tell you exactly that." He sat in the chair next to hers. "Why does it feel like a knife wound?"

"A knife wound? Really, Andr...Dominik? Where would I get a knife wound? I teach and take care of kids. At times, resorts. I'm not a secret agent."

"Call me Dom."

"Dom." She said the name like she was trying it out. "You should probably go. I really need this job, and I don't want to cause any problems between you and your father."

"Me and my father had problems long before you came along."

Her clear brown eyes lit up. "So, that was true what you told me in Grenada? That you and your father are estranged? What about Ekaterina?"

"Kat's not my mother."

She bit into the roti, and a little of the curry sauce spread at the corner of her mouth. He reached out with his thumb, but she licked it away.

"*Of course,* she's not your mother," she said, looking off to the side. "So freakin' obvious."

"It's why, if you line me up with Yuri, Kat, and their daughters, I look adopted. Why, has that been on your mind or something?"

She nodded and took another bite.

"Can you make one of those for me next time?"

She nodded again.

He sat watching her while she ate, the seconds ticking by in his head. She was right. He had to leave. If Yuri relieved her of her duties, it would limit his access to her.

"What time do you usually show up in the mornings?" he asked, standing.

She swallowed. "Six. A little before Nikolai wakes up."

"Okay. Come to breakfast tomorrow so I can look at you."

She rolled her eyes.

He leaned toward her mouth.

"Dobroy nochi, Dom."

Fuck, that was sexy as shit.

Never again would he touch another cigar if it meant not having his mouth on hers.

"Good night, Eija."

He left the apartment and headed to the other side of the building.

It wasn't until he was in his long entry hallway, slipping off his shoes, that he remembered the reason he'd agreed to join his father for breakfast the next morning—to meet another one of his fiancée prospects. After tomorrow, the taste of cigars would no longer be the main thing between him and his desire to kiss Eija until he sucked her dry.

Cold, sharp steel pressed against his neck. "Hello, Dominik—"

Dom grabbed the wrist holding the blade and drove his head back into the intruder's nose. They stumbled backward, and he turned around to an unfamiliar face. Although this man had threatened him in Russian, it was with an accent and in a dialect he was only vaguely familiar with. A dialect his grandfather had spoken.

"Is it true?" the man asked.

Dom didn't reply. He didn't like to do any unnecessary talking before murder.

The man charged.

Dom grabbed the man's wrist, twisting and bending until the man's fingers went numb. The knife fell from the man's hand and onto his palm, and he wasted no time jamming the blade into the man's neck. He then pulled it out and shoved it through the man's chest wall.

After a ridiculously dramatic period of gasps and gurgling, the man crumbled to the floor.

Dom pulled out his phone, texted Pavel, and headed to the shower. By the time he finished, the body, as well as any trace of it, was gone.

The lights in Dom's unit came on, and Yuri looked down at his watch. "Less than an hour? Unless she followed him to his unit, they couldn't have had sex. If they did, I'm disappointed in my son."

"I'm even more certain it's her," Pavel said. "Dominik's reaction to Miss K only confirmed what we already knew."

The woman from Grenada.

Pavel had been on the island long enough to confirm Dom's infatuation with the brown-skinned beauty. The woman was a cock's dream from top to bottom, head to toe. Her voice took on raspy, sultry notes from time to time, and Yuri was certain bringing her to climax would rival the pleasure the orchestra at the Russian ballet often brought him. It was no wonder his son was smitten. Even for the most unapologetic of philanderers, the right person could still trap a wanderer's heart in a vise grip. If Dom was anything like him, love was the ultimate weakness.

Yuri leaned against the Mercedes SUV's soft leather backseat. "I hope having Miss Brown from Grenada in his bed will keep him entertained. Corrigible."

And distracted.

"Sir," Pavel held out his phone, "Dom needs clean up."

Yuri read the message, brows lowered. Despite Dominik's mother's gentle nature, religion, and background, Dominik was still a Sokolov. He still had Sokolov blood, tainted at birth. The man who'd entered Dominik's apartment likely hadn't lived longer than five minutes.

"I want to know everything about where this person came

from," Yuri ordered. "The only people I've allowed to know who my son is are in this car as well as my wife."

"And Miss K," Pavel added.

"She's no sort of threat. To a cock, maybe, but not to the Bratva." Yuri brushed the air. "Find out who I can't trust, Pavel. Find out who I have to kill."

With a nod, Pavel left the vehicle.

Chapter Eleven

Eija passed by the hallway mirror at Colin and April's and noticed the button at the top of her shirt had come undone. She'd had no idea shirts with this high of a neck existed anywhere outside a convent. Ekaterina was clueless if she believed Yuri would heel as long as he didn't have to stare at exposed breasts all day. She still had a face, a shape. No amount of high-necks or loose-fitting slacks would fix that, his late-night visit evidence of that.

"I still don't know if I want you risking this, E," Colin said from the sofa, his hair disheveled.

She sighed, puffing up her mouth so he could see exactly how frustrated she was. "What's with the handholding and babysitting all of a sudden, Colin? I said I'd get into Yuri's study. I've connected you to their system, and the hallway cameras will only need to be down for about five minutes. Are you telling me not to trust you?"

"Don't hand me that BS, babe."

"Don't call me—"

"I know." He yawned. "I know."

"Don't be mad at me because April has you sleeping on the sofa."

His reddish-brown eyebrows drooped. Any lower, and he'd inhale brow hairs. "First of all, keep your voice down," he whispered. "Second...ouch."

Gideon and Mikhail would be there in a couple of minutes to pick her up, but she sat beside him anyway.

"Why *do* you still sleep out here?" she grilled, fully invested in his lack of a love life. "You're into her. She's into you. Have neither of you communicated this yet?"

Colin fell backward onto his pillow with a loud groan, despite just now telling her to keep quiet. "I don't want to do anything to ruin the relationship I have with her, right now. I like her, E. You wouldn't know anything about th—*ouch!*"

She released his toe. "What's with this idea that I don't have feelings? Because I like dick? What's wrong with liking dick?"

"It's not just that." He pulled his leg toward his midsection and massaged his toe. "You're scared of letting people get close to you."

"You're close to me."

"We're not fucking. Unless—"

"Even if you were the last man on earth, I'd screw a porcupine before I touched you."

A laugh rumbled in his chest, and he pushed his fingers through his hair, only for the strands to fall back onto his forehead.

"Look, E, if I'm wrong, tell me why you stopped looking for you-know-who? He's the one you needed to find. In my opinion, you shouldn't have stopped looking. Andrei Falcone from Grenada's the only guy I've heard you talk about."

She had stopped looking.

Destiny, however, had kept Dom in its search bar.

"Know what would be funny?" Colin tittered a laugh, gearing up for his own joke. "If, when you finally meet Dominik Sokolov, he's hot."

Oh, the irony.

"Why would that be funny?" she asked.

"The ethical quandary it would present."

"You think I have sex with guys just because they're good-looking?"

"Don't you?"

True, her desire to have sex with Andrei-Dominik had initially been because he was good-looking. Still, she'd found herself liking him. Genuinely. They'd interacted like they'd known each other longer than two weeks. He didn't take things, or himself, too seriously. Seeing his tall frame and dark hair headed to the front desk had been the highlight of her day, and the man had sent her roses. The last time she'd gotten flowers from a man, they'd been attached to a corsage at senior prom.

"What do you think, E?" Colin asked, breaking through her thoughts. "Would you risk our entire operation for cock?"

Apparently.

"We're still meeting up later, right?" she asked, dancing around the landmine of a question. "Do we have any new information I should be aware of?"

"Ahh, yes." Colin hopped up, retrieved his tablet, and returned to his seat next to her. "Randy let me know that there's two parts to Koronatsiya. The first part's called *Dostavka*."

Her phone chimed—Gideon letting her know he was downstairs.

"'Presentation'?" she asked. "Of what?"

"It's some kind of engagement ceremony."

Eija slung her Ekaterina-approved crochet tote bag over her shoulder and rose onto suddenly shaky legs. "The Sokolovs have several guests staying with them. They're all..."

Women.

They were all young, beautiful women. With their mothers.

"All what?" Colin asked.

"Women."

"Probably there for Dominik?"

She swallowed. "Probably."

"So, they're there, and he isn't? What the fuck? None of this makes sense. If they're there for him, when does he see them?"

"They leave during the day." She headed to the front door. "I'm guessing it's to meet up with him somewhere, outside of the penthouse, probably for privacy. Anyway, I'll talk to you later. Keep me updated. You know I enjoy the messages and pictures I get throughout the day. Keeps my head on straight, you know?"

He smiled. "Of course. We'll see you later, E."

Eija took the elevator to the first floor and allowed herself to wallow in a little bit of disappointment. Just like Dom had his duty, she had a job to do. What they'd had in Grenada was in the past, and her thinking otherwise only made her look like a fool when she'd dedicated her life to looking just the opposite. Even the slightest notion that there could be something more between them needed to remain in her head or between the pages of a book written by the Brothers Grimm.

Gideon stood next to the open back driver's side door.

She greeted him with a wave. It was still dark out, a typical early spring morning in Moscow, and she closed her coat tighter against a gust of wind that numbed the tips of her ears.

"Good morning," Gideon said, helping her into the car and sliding in beside her. "I have tea. It should warm you right up."

"Sweet." She took the warm, covered paper cup from his hand. "And good morning. Your English is getting good."

"Spasibo."

"You're welcome." She raised the cup to her lips. "Oh, I almost forgot! Updates, please. The last thing I saw was that Natasha had something huge to tell Oleg. I'm assuming it's about her affair with Igor?"

Gideon shook his head. "No...it's a secret baby."

Eija's eyes opened wide. "Oleg's?"

"Igor's."

"But I thought Igor was sterile from the explosion!"

As he went through all that had happened in a Russian

drama they both watched, Mikhail pulled away from the building.

Chapter Twelve

"*I* want children."

"I *don't* want children."

Eija pretended to be occupied with her food, but her ears absorbed every word of one of the oddest exchanges she'd ever come across. First, the auburn-haired woman with the blue eyes sitting next to Dom had introduced herself as his wife. Then, when he corrected her, the woman smiled and said her name was Mila.

Mila's father was a Czech business tycoon, also in the business of international crime. Interpol knew of Mila's father, so if Mila became Yuri's daughter-in-law, it would be a significant power play for both men's legitimate *and* illegitimate businesses.

Mila set down her fork and turned to Dom. "You don't want children?"

Dom, this morning looking more like Yuri in a tailored navy

blue suit and white shirt, avoided looking Eija's way. He'd avoided looking at her the entire morning, treating eye contact with her like looking directly into an eclipse. With Nikolai at school, it was only five of them—her, Mila, Dom, Ekaterina, and Yuri.

"No," Dom said, his tone firm. "I don't want children."

"Don't you want an heir?" Mila prodded.

Dom closed his eyes, letting a groan fully make its way through his body. "What century is this? An *heir?*"

"Well, I want children. I don't understand why anyone wouldn't."

"They're expensive," Eija offered. "They require a lot of emotional support. In my opinion, if you're on the fence about having one, don't. Not until you're sure. And, if you're not sure, take extra...intimate precautions. It's necessary to be on the same page about children before marrying someone."

Dom stuffed his face with eggs and sliced sausages.

"Eija's right," Yuri said, waving his fork at Dom. "I'll make sure Pavel adds this question to the list of things I would like you to speak about on your dates, Dominik."

"I'd still marry you," Mila insisted. "You'll change your mind once my clothes are off."

Dom and Yuri choked.

Ekaterina's groan matched Dom's from earlier.

Amused, Eija dug into her stack of *blini*. The cook, Ludmila, had topped her pancakes with jam just the way she liked them. She and Ludmila had taken to each other the quickest. Ludmila loved to gossip, and gossip was simply a different form of intel. When she got another chance, she'd swing by the kitchen for another "debriefing" session.

Mila swung her spoon through the air, her semolina porridge virtually untouched. "How many more girls are there? What's my competition like?"

"There are several more." Ekaterina lasered Mila with a sharp look. "Consider that the next time you think about what happens once your clothes are off."

Eija, stifling a giggle, spoke again. "Forgive me for my ignorance, but I'm unfamiliar with this process. Is it one date, and then a decision is made, or is it multiple dates? Do the couples have to remain chaste?"

Yuri set down his fork. "Dominik?"

Dom took a gulp of coffee, and his food went down his throat in a thick lump. Then, finally, their eyes connected. "It's called *Dostavka*," he barely said, the food still tightly making its way down. "The presentation of the newly engaged...anyhow, the process is a little like...are you familiar with the show, *The Bachelor?*"

Eija tipped her head. "Um, no. Can you explain it to me? In detail?"

His jaw ticked.

She licked her lips to hide a smile.

"We go on one date," he explained. "After that date, those of us who connect go on to a round two of sorts."

Mila added, "Those Dominik chooses."

"So, you make the choice?" Eija pointed her fork at him. "Why do you get to make the choice? Why don't the women?"

A wide smile spread across his face. "I like the way you think, Miss K."

Mila stirred her porridge, her gaze burning a hole in Eija's forehead. "Truthfully, I don't mind it," she insisted. "In some cultures and traditions, it would be an old guy. At least Dom's young and attractive. *Very* attractive."

Eija looked down so Dom wouldn't see the light green her complexion had transformed into.

"What other questions would you propose, Miss K?" Yuri asked. "You seem to have quite the insight."

Eija polished off her blini and dabbed at her mouth with a designer cloth napkin. "Well, what about...personalities? Mila, you seem more of the outgoing type. Dominik, you seem just the opposite."

"Opposites attract," Mila spat. "I can get him to open up."

"Seems like a lot of work for one man."

"Not for this one."

Eija's mouth quirked. "Expectations of monogamy, then."

Ekaterina set down her utensils and gave all her attention to the couple. "That's a good one."

A servant entered the dining hall, and Dom held up his mug, all but begging for more coffee. The way everyone stared at him, Mila with her brows lifted into her hairline, no amount of distraction would get them to deviate from the topic at hand. Even if he tried to change the subject, Eija parted her lips, ready to redirect.

Mug refilled, he drew a long sip.

"Well?" Mila asked.

He swallowed. "I...I don't know."

"You don't know if you want to be monogamous? What would be the point of all of this if we want to be in the arms of someone else?"

Eija felt like she was back at The Bolshoi Theatre. Not even her and Gideon's Russian dramas were this good.

Dom glanced at Eija. "This isn't about love, Mina—"

"Mila," Eija corrected, and the look he gave her had her crossing her arms to hide her tightening nipples.

"Mila, you and I aren't two people in love, so I expect nothing from you."

"I don't intend to fool around on you!"

Eija pushed away her empty plate and feasted on a bowl of berries like popcorn. She didn't expect her and Dom to fall in love or find themselves in a relationship; at the end of all this, she'd have to arrest him. Still, he'd asked her out, knowing he would be married to someone soon. Watching him squirm this morning would be, without a doubt, the best part of her day.

Mila set the folded napkin from her lap on the tabletop. "Thank you, Mr. and Mrs. Sokolov, for your hospitality, but my mother and I will be leaving tonight."

"You are excused," Yuri said.

With a huff, Mila pushed out her chair, straightened her gown, and stormed out of the dining room. The gown was pretty, and it accentuated the girl's lovely shape. The colors, however, reminded Eija of salsa.

Dom cleared his throat.

Eija didn't look at him.

He cleared his throat louder.

"Drink some water, Dominik," Yuri chided. "You're lucky you didn't choke with the way you were eating earlier. Did you skip eating yesterday altogether? Pace yourself."

They finished breakfast, which had primarily been Yuri and Ekaterina talking about their plans for that day. For two people who'd been married for as long as they'd been, to Eija, the conversation seemed shallow. They talked at each other instead of to each other. However, dry conversation or not, she'd paid attention to them to avoid Dominik's stare attempting to add another piercing hole in her ear.

"Oh, I almost forgot," Yuri piped up. "Miss K, you'll accompany me to London next month."

Eija let her guard slip for a second. "London?"

"I have business out there, and I'll need your English-speaking capabilities in some meetings where I won't have Dominik. I also want to bring Nikolai, so having you there will be convenient. We will stay one week."

Shit.

She'd had zero expectations of leaving the country, but what could she do, say no?

"I'm honored, Mr. Sokolov."

"Dominik, this will be important for you as well," Yuri added. "Can you make sure Miss K's accommodations are adequate? We'll stay at the Havre."

"Are you sure you want him to do something so menial?" Eija asked.

"You're a special guest of ours," Dom replied. "It makes more sense to handle this directly instead of handing it off."

From the wicked gleam in Dom's eyes, she felt like he would book her a room where, if she rolled off the bed, she'd fall through the floor and on top of him below. If they were both naked, it could make for an interesting—

Eija.

Her thoughts were correct to scold her.

Each day she spent with this man without telling Colin she'd already ID'd him was another day she compromised the mission. Dom would pose for the damn picture if she asked him. So, why didn't she simply take it and send it in?

After breakfast, Yuri retreated to his office. Ekaterina disappeared to do whatever it was the woman did during the day. Eija went to the library to prepare Nikolai's English lessons for later. She also needed to update Colin. He'd created a website that, at face value, looked like something she would access to find resources and games to use with Nikolai. However, he'd embedded a way for them to send encrypted messages to one another.

Eija: Going to London.
Next month.

Colin: How long?

Eija: One week.

"I'm pissed at you."

Eija yelped and minimized the game window. "Dom. Hey."

"I see you got used to my name."

She made a noncommittal noise.

"What was that earlier?" he asked, arms folded and legs bumping the front edge of the desk. "I should put you over my knee."

"You should."

His confident smirk fell. "Wait, seriously?"

"You need to remember your future wives' names, Sokolov." She closed out the game. "Because of you, Mila and her mother are 'leaving tonight.' Now you won't get to see her with her clothes off."

"I'll," he dragged his gaze over her body, "live. By the way, how do you go from managing a resort to becoming a nanny?"

It was one of the first questions she'd practiced. The caveat was that she couldn't give the same answer each time, only the same reason.

"I needed fulfillment."

"And you've taught in Russia before, too?" he asked.

"For a little over a year."

"Why didn't you tell me?"

"Why would I have, Andrei Falcone?"

If he'd told her he had a Russian background, it could have come up in conversation. Then again, if he'd told her he had a Russian background, she would have done a full workup on him. There would have been no dancing under restaurant lights, no lunch dates, no Fish Friday, kissing, or hand-holding, and none of the best sex she'd ever had in her life.

If she worked hard enough, she'd eventually convince herself that missing out on all of that wouldn't have been bad if the trade-off had been getting the right guy.

He chased his palm over the top of his head. A part of her missed the wavy hair, but, like this, he was ruggedly handsome. Sexy in a "fuck me, but don't fuck with me" kind of way.

"What do you do after you finish Nikolai's plans?" he asked.

"I get two hours for lunch, and today, I have errands to run for Ekaterina," she said. "Then, Gideon and I pick Nikolai up from school, and he's my responsibility for the rest of the afternoon."

"All I heard was two hours for lunch. Have lunch with me."

"My neck hurts looking up at you."

"Let me sit there." He pointed at her chair. "You can sit on my lap."

"Dom, what do you and a sandwich maker have in common?"

The space between his brows wrinkled. Then, he laughed, and the contrast between his dark features and eyes so light they almost looked silver jarred her. He'd been good-looking in Grenada. Extremely good-looking. Now that she knew who he was, how did that make him even more gorgeous?

"We both lay it on real thick," he answered.

"Yep." She grinned. "I'm not sitting on your lap."

She wanted to, but she wouldn't.

He stepped around the desk, crouched next to the chair, and spun her to face him. "Better?"

"How long can you stay like that?"

"Aww, are you worried about me?"

She glanced at the door, which he'd closed when he walked in. The man's potential fiancée was walking around the Sokolov penthouse; she'd definitely get the boot if anyone caught her kissing him, no matter how much she wanted to. What they were doing now was already over the line.

"Eija, since you treated me in Grenada," someone knocked on the door, "I'd like to take you to get some," the person knocked louder, "authentic Russian cuisine."

She leaned toward him, hands over his ears.

"What are you doing?" he whispered.

She mouthed, "Can you hear me?"

"You're not saying anything, but I can read your lips."

It would be so easy to lean closer.

Kiss him until his mouth hurt.

A third knock sounded, more insistent. "Did you hear *that?*" she asked, removing her hands. "One more knock and it'll be suspicious. They'll think we're in here...fucking."

A streak of lightning flashed across those stormy irises.

Groaning, he stood, went to the door, and dragged it open. "What? I'm busy."

"I was wondering where we were going for lunch," a nause-atingly petite voice said. "My mother told me that I should seek you out instead of waiting. Take the initiative."

Eija tried to peer around him to see which "debutante" it was, but Dom's large frame blocked her view.

"I'll be right back," he told her. Then he stepped outside, pulling the door closed behind him.

Eija left the desk and walked over to one of the floor-to-ceiling bookcases in the moderately sized space. The Sokolovs called it a library.

To her, it was a museum.

The shiny tile floors, walls, and bookshelves were all white, which fit with the modern theme of the penthouse. Artifacts hung on the walls, from ancient axes, spears, and arrowheads to colorful medallions. A statue of a man in uniform on a horse towered over her, the horse reared on its hind legs. Ancient masks, framed artwork of varying sizes, and two pieces resembling shields hung behind the man's head.

Like a museum, the unique pieces had their information next to or underneath them in small print. She headed for a large oil painting by an artist named Alban Moreau and searched for hidden cameras. Finding nothing obvious, she went next to a medallion, red with jewels placed around the edge of the circle. Given Yuri's wealth, she knew they were real, old, and priceless. An unlit scented candle sat next to them, its cinnamon and orange aroma extending only as far as the edge of the bookshelf.

Dom grabbed her wrist.

She knew it was Dom who grabbed her wrist, but her instincts screamed *unexpected intruder*.

She slipped out of his grasp and stepped around him to spin

his wrist behind his back, but he flipped his arm. Her grip slackened, and she found herself pressed against a bookcase with both wrists locked in one of his hands, his feet on either side of her body.

"You won't get me twice." His mouth was so close to her ear, his breath felt like a kiss. Instead of cherry cigar smoke, he smelled like mint. "Self-defense? Judo?"

Her chest pushed into the wooden shelf in front of her. "Basic grappling. Before I had a place at the resort, I used to walk home."

"And?"

"I was grabbed."

It was, of course, a spy's nature to lie.

"Did they hurt you?" he asked, as though speaking through a jaw wired shut.

"No." She tugged on her hands. "You should probably let me go. I don't think we'd be able to convince the cameras that this isn't something more than it looks like."

"There are no cameras in here."

Her ears perked up. That information could be useful later.

"Yuri doesn't place cameras in any of the rooms where he does business. The man will put a camera in a bathroom before he opens up the possibility of anyone eyeing his business doings when he's not around."

"So there are cameras in the bathrooms?"

"No," his lips grazed her neck, "what I'm saying is, if you're looking for places to seduce me, you have here, his office, and there's a meeting room on the top floor."

Goosebumps dotted her skin.

"Dom."

He released her and stepped back.

She faced him, nursing her sore wrists, and the fact that they were sore was a slight turn-on. A few times, she'd done the light bondage thing, but she hadn't enjoyed the lack of control.

He raised his brows. "Lunch?"

"I think you already have lunch plans." She brushed past him and headed for the desk. "So, rain check."

"I canceled. I want to have lunch with you."

"Dom—"

"I want you, Eija." He reached for her elbow, but she pulled away.

"Dom, think about it. There's more at stake for me than you in this situation. I really like this job. I adore Nikolai. Your fiancée is somewhere in this house. And look, I know how I came off in Grenada, like a woman only concerned with good times, attractive men, and orgasms. In truth, I *am* that. Usually. I liked you, though." She clasped her hands in front of her face. "It was only two weeks, I know. Still, in those two weeks, I learned that you're a really good guy. I mean, you sent me roses, asked me to dance, took me to lunch. You're sweet, Dom."

Amazing.

The kind of guy who, even if she'd wanted to forget, circumstances now made it impossible.

"However, at the end of the day, you're going to do your duty, aren't you?" she asked, a sliver of her hoping he answered with a *no*. "I don't know exactly what Yuri does, but whatever it is, he's good at it. I don't ask because I'm not here for that. I'm here to ensure Nikolai hits all his goals and milestones and gets good care. Whatever it is, it's something he wants to pass on to you. For him to do that, you have to take a wife, and I'm pretty sure she's not supposed to look like me."

His focus didn't deviate from her face the entire time she spoke. "So, what are you saying then?" he asked.

"That there are too many men in this world for me to be preoccupied or concerned with one who belongs to someone else."

Although, technically, she'd licked him first. That should mean she had dibs, but perhaps dibs didn't translate the same way in Russia.

A tiny smile played at the corners of his lips. "I liked you too. And yes, it was a couple of weeks, but I had such a great time with you that I wanted to do it again. And again. I wanted to know, with more time, what you could mean to me. What we could mean to each other."

Had there never been an Andrei, there wouldn't have been an inherent pull low in her belly to give in. It *had* been a while since she'd so much as felt a man's arms around her, primarily because of the demands of family and this latest undercover operation. Being with him wouldn't be like being with anyone else. The sample he'd given her on the islands would forever remain with her.

She was already lying to her partner and their entire agency about having identified him. And for what? Because he wasn't what she'd thought he was?

Yuri seemed nice, but they had mountains upon mountains of evidence of his terror. Their entire team had spoken, ad nauseam, about the Bratva's influence in Russia and the rest of the world. Yuri's reign went back to the fall of the Soviet Union. Now, he controlled markets and entire segments of the country. For all his cheek kisses and love for his grandson, his goons left bloodied bodies in their wake. They sold international secrets and supplied guns to extremist groups. Yuri didn't abide by any code, not even the most renowned one that had governed the earliest mobsters—*ponyatiya*. He was so far removed from his "craft," he looked like a legitimate businessman in the pictures on his walls, shaking the Russian president's hand.

Stopping Yuri wouldn't stop the organization, but it would deal them a massive blow. It would also prevent him from selling information they'd learned the Bratva had obtained that could compromise MI6, the CIA, the DGSE, and more allied intelligence agencies. It was unclear whether he wanted to sell the information or hold on to it to exercise power over one or all the agencies, but it didn't matter at this point.

"Dom, let me ask you again," she said. "At the end of the day, will Dominik Sokolov do his duty? If I left right now, went to your place, and made love to you, at the end of it, will Dominik Sokolov still take a wife at his father's request?"

"Eija—"

"Yes or no, Dom."

He scrubbed at his face until it turned red.

"Yes."

"Then there's your answer."

She'd never been much of a sharer, wanting whoever she preoccupied herself with at the time to be concerned with her orgasms only. Until then, she hadn't the need to care; her relationships never lasted long enough for jealousy or possessiveness.

There was more than one reason this man stood out, but she kept one of those reasons hidden in the deepest parts of her mind.

She grabbed her things from the desk and started for the door. Dom reached out and pulled her back, up against him. She breathed his name, and he groaned, tightening his arms around her.

From what she remembered, his kisses were a lot like his personality—gentle at first, allowing her to get used to the movement and synchronicity of their lips. Once they had the coordination down, the kiss deepened. Instead of kissing, they tasted, swallowed, and savored. Yet, Dom and the taste of his kisses would have to remain a memory.

Kissing him would mean making love to him, but the secrets they hid from one another were already bursting through seams that had started unraveling in the penthouse hallway. Tossing passion on top was a lit match in pure oxygen. Regardless, she didn't want to see him like she'd seen Vasily with matted, stringy hair, jaundiced skin, hollow eyes, and a bloodied face.

"Dom...please."

He released her for the second time and crouched to pick up items she didn't realize she'd dropped. When he stood, she noticed the necklace around his neck. It was the same one he'd worn in Grenada.

"You still wear this." She slid her thumb over the silver pendant. "It's beautiful."

He looked down. "It was my mother's. My aunt gave it to me. Even when you can't see it, I'm always wearing it."

A game of tug-of-war initiated in her stomach. He never took it off. If he never took it off, that meant wherever the necklace was, he would be.

"Do you want it?" he asked.

Her gaze flicked up to his. "What? No. You just told me it was your mother's."

"I don't think she wanted me to keep it forever. Plus, I like the idea of you wearing something important to me. One day, you might leave this lowly job for bluer waters. My ego wants it to be that you take a part of me with you."

"I already do."

He slipped it off his neck, took her hand, and pressed it into her palm. "Here. Wear it for a day or two. If it doesn't make you think of me, give it back. If it does, let me know. Either way, it guarantees we'll see each other again. Okay?"

She smiled. "Yes. Will do."

He kissed her forehead, a subdued version of the tender kiss he'd given her outside her door at the hotel resort. She'd been right all along. She didn't deserve a kiss this sweet, regardless of who either of them was. Biblically, there wasn't much difference between a liar and a killer.

They walked to the door.

He opened it, and she stepped through.

When she turned to look back at him, he did the same.

They both took their last eyefuls and headed off in different directions, him presumably to have lunch with the petite princesses whose mothers followed them around like duennas.

She had lunch with Colin in an hour, and she wanted to at least observe the situation surrounding getting into Yuri's office before meeting him. Even if she didn't get inside, they at least had some progress with Dom's mother's necklace.

Eija walked down the hallway toward a second set of stairs, fighting the urge to look back over her shoulder. Without realizing it, Dom had imparted significant information about the cameras Yuri kept hidden.

As far as she knew, she was the first agent or officer of any kind to enter the Sokolov household. Rumor was, he'd taken in former KGB as security, carrying on their domestic tasks in a more private function.

It was possible Dom's information could be incorrect or intentionally meant to lead her astray, but she would step out on faith. She could finagle her way out of a sticky situation should anyone catch her; she just had to play the entire scenario as if there *were* cameras watching.

When she turned to start up the stairs, a housekeeper made her way down, a laundry basket tucked against her side.

"Dobroy utro," Eija greeted, ducking her head slightly. "How are you this morning, Manya?"

Manya returned the greeting. "Wonderful, Miss K. Are you

headed up to Nikolai's room? I've just come from there. It's clean, but let me know if it's not to your liking."

Eija rummaged around in the tote and pulled out a chocolate bar.

Manya's eyes lit up, and her face flushed. "Miss K, don't you spoil me!"

"We're chocolate buddies, Manya," Eija said, leaning in. "I picked one up for myself the other day, so I had to make sure I got one for you."

Manya's face flushed even deeper. "Sweet girl."

Manya was closer in age to Ekaterina, so Ekaterina didn't worry that the other woman slept under the same roof. She still worked Manya to the bone, Manya's tasks often keeping her from society for weeks. A loyal servant to the end, Manya never once lifted her tongue to complain about her circumstances, but when Eija started at the house, she'd seen the need for alliances. Manya and Ludmila interacted with the Sokolovs the most frequently. With them on her side, history could tell her what basic espionage couldn't.

Manya gave Eija's forearm a quick squeeze and continued down the stairs. Eija slowed her steps, and when Manya was no longer in sight, she made a left to head toward Yuri's office instead of the right that would take her to Nikolai's room.

Luck was on her side when she saw a striped, gray tail disappear through the slightly ajar door. As she couldn't wait outside to verify there were no voices inside, little Miss Lyu would make the perfect excuse if Yuri happened to be sitting quietly behind his desk.

"Lyu," she called, picking up her steps. "Lyu, come here."

She pushed in the office door.

No one was inside.

Lyu had walked directly to the sofa Yuri kept inside, hopped onto it, and curled into a ball. Eija crouched in front of the sofa and stroked the top of the cat's head.

"Yeah, you like that, don't you? That's it. Get comfortable. Miss K feels better than that chair, doesn't she? Yes, she does."

After a few more strokes, she slid her hands under Lyu's warm body and lifted. The cat, enraptured by the attention, came willingly. Almost overeagerly. And, cat in hand, Eija walked around the office. If cameras were indeed watching, they'd pick up on a nosy yet animal-loving nanny singing Lyu to sleep. While she sang, she scanned the room and desktop for any files Yuri might have left lying out.

Russia had never really fallen off the map since the Cold War, though North Korea and extremist Islam, over time, had bottlenecked global surveillance efforts. But United States election tampering had pushed it back into the top five.

Randy liaised with the CIA more than he did any of the other major intelligence organizations. They'd had money tossed their way since it was a matter of global security to find out what Yuri had. That meant first getting to Dom. According to Randy, Yuri would do anything for them to spare the life of his solitary heir.

Eija leaned over Yuri's desk and fiddled with the stud earring in her ear. Then, with a quick twist of the earring and a slight tilt of her head, she snapped an image.

Laid out on his desk were plans of some sort, but it was unclear of what. Right now, they looked like the scribblings and sketches of a power-hungry madman, but Colin could probably make sense of them.

Lyu meowed.

Eija resumed stroking. "So needy," she gently scolded. "Now, can you tell me what these are, Lyu?"

She took several more photos, did a quick final sweep of the room, and headed for the door.

It swung open.

She shrieked.

The shriek startled Lyu, who bit her on the wrist.

Pain swelled at her wrist, but the skin remained unbroken. However, the pain forced her to drop the cat. Instead of running for the door, Lyu darted for Eija's ankles. And, before Eija realized it, she was on the floor with the cat underneath her, Lyu's body indistinguishable from that of a crepe.

When she finally got a good look at who'd entered the office, she swallowed a groan.

"I'm Leah," the young woman introduced. "You're Miss K."

Eija eased up off the cat. "Go get help."

Leah walked over and knelt in front of Eija. "I've wanted to meet you, officially, for a while."

"Leah, go get hel—"

Pavel stepped into the office, followed by Yuri and Dom. When they saw her still half on top of Lyu—who was making a sound she'd only heard humans make—Pavel's eyes widened. Yuri's glazed over. Dom's locked onto hers. Eija glanced down and noticed a few of her shirt buttons had popped off, and the way Leah was perched, it looked like the other woman had been diving for her breasts. Hopefully, this current predicament wouldn't make lunch later with Colin, a man, stand out as odd.

"I fell on the cat," Eija said.

Pavel helped her up. "Are you all right?"

Had she spoken English? Farsi? Did no one see that at least two of Lyu's whiskers were bent?

"I fell on the cat," she repeated.

Finally back from his fantasy, Yuri walked over and picked Lyu up from the floor. "She's been in worse scuffles, I assure you."

"I fell on the cat." She felt stuck on repeat. "Dom?"

"Pavel," Yuri extended Lyu in Pavel's direction, "please take Lyu to the vet. Miss K, you go along with him. I have a meeting this morning with Gideon. There are some *questions* I would like to ask him regarding an incident that happened last night."

Leah asked the question Eija couldn't. "What incident? Dominik, are you okay?"

Dom spared her a glance. "I'm fine. Thanks for asking."

Leah beamed, face crimson.

Yuri squeezed Leah's shoulder, smiling with the depth of a kiddie pool. "It's nothing to worry your pretty little head about, my dear."

With the issue settled, Yuri's attention returned to Eija's chest. Even when she didn't want them to be, her breasts always seemed to end up exposed. This, she wouldn't tell Colin. He was a gossip, and all her stories made it back to the agency, turning her into a walking wet pussy.

Speaking of which...

Eija glanced at Lyu, who, thankfully, looked better than she had a minute ago.

"Oh, Miss K!" Leah stepped in front of her. "You'll need to change. I'm so sorry for startling you."

"What were you two doing in here?" Dom questioned. "Miss K, did you need something from me? Maybe you reconsidered my offer?"

It was Eija's face's turn to burn.

"Miss K was already in here," Leah said, uselessly attempting to tug both halves of Eija's shirt together until Eija had to swat her hands away. "I followed her in here."

Though Yuri and Pavel asked the same question, they asked with different undertones: "Why'd you follow her in here alone?"

"I followed the cat," Eija said. "I think I'm about ready to give up on her liking me. Plus, I didn't want her to destroy anything in here. I grew up with a cat. I know how they can be."

Pavel remained skeptical.

Yuri nodded. "Thank you. She's not supposed to be in here without me. How'd she get in?"

"The door was cracked."

Dom and Pavel glanced at each other.

"Gideon must have forgotten to close it when I sent him up here earlier," Yuri said. "I'll make sure he remembers next time. Ladies?"

Eija and Leah left the office, Pavel trailing behind them, holding Lyu like he had no clue what to do with her. They split up at the end of the hallway—Leah went up to the third floor, where the rest of the potential wives were housed. Eija and Pavel headed downstairs.

"We'll stop by your place on the way," Pavel said. "So you can change your top. Then, according to Gideon, you have lunch?"

Eija nodded. "That's right. But can we go to my place *after* the vet? I'd like Lyu to see someone as soon as possible. I have my coat to cover...these."

"Are you sure, Miss K?"

"Ahh, yeah. I nearly killed her."

"If Niko didn't kill her as a toddler, you won't. Trust me. She's been through the wringer." He cracked a rare smile. "Since I'm taking over for Gideon for the afternoon, will I be joining you for lunch, or do you usually eat alone?"

"I usually eat alone. Gideon's joined me a few times, but I usually eat alone."

"Are you meeting someone?"

She paused. "Yes. A man I met the other day while at the gym."

"You know the protocol is for us to check out anyone you intend to build a relationship with," he reminded her. "It wouldn't be the first time someone has tried to use staff to get closer to Yuri."

They stopped at the door for Eija to slip into her coat and then made their way to the parking deck where Gideon stood, the car door open. From the look on his face, she hoped she saw him again after this. It had only been a few months, but she'd grown to like him.

"To be honest, Pavel, this won't be a relationship," she confessed. "I'm not interested in anything with anyone. It'll detract from my focus on Nikolai."

He shot her a look, that look alone calling her bluff. "That's not why this man doesn't interest you, but that's all I will say about that."

Given the circumstances from a few minutes ago, she didn't know if he was implying she and Leah had been carrying on a secret relationship or whether he knew she and Dom "flirted."

Gideon tipped his head. "Miss K, have a lovely lunch."

"Thank you, Gideon." She squeezed his wrist. "I'll see you later?"

Though he nodded, his eyes said something different.

Chapter Thirteen

"How did you find out that Dominik is my son?" Yuri asked, tugging on the trigger of a power drill.

Gideon yanked at the ropes around his wrists, but there would be no escaping. He'd secured Gideon's hands and feet to a wooden chair. They were in the middle of nothing, just outside of Moscow. Not a single residence was near enough to hear his cries.

"Sir, I didn't know," Gideon pleaded. "I swear, I didn't know."

"Then why was Dominik attacked?"

Sweat poured in streams down Gideon's temple. "When was he attacked?"

"Don't do that. Don't feign innocence."

"I swear, sir."

"So what are you saying, then?" Yuri stood over him. "You're saying *I* orchestrated my son's attack?"

"No, sir."

Yuri set the drill bit on Gideon's thigh. "That's what it sounds like. You just called me a snitch. So I'm my own snitch, Gideon?"

"I would never betray you, sir. I swear."

Yuri pressed the trigger and bore down.

Gideon screamed, the muscles in his neck straining.

Yuri let up, and Gideon slumped forward, breathing hard. "I don't enjoy getting my hands dirty anymore, Gideon," he said. "How could you make me do this?"

He moved to the other thigh, drilled again.

Gideon no longer screamed, pain forcing him in and out of consciousness. Even if the man wasn't responsible, someone had to be made a scapegoat until the actual canary was revealed. Gideon's whereabouts were the only ones he hadn't been able to account for at the time of the attack at Dom's apartment.

"You won't survive this." He crouched and looked up into Gideon's face. "So, I suggest you make peace with your God."

Chapter Fourteen

"It belonged to Dominik's mother." Eija stared at the necklace Colin turned, over and over, in his hand. "Yuri told me he's going to give it to Dominik when he arrives."

She felt sick.

But there was no going back now.

Periodically, they looked up and scanned their environment. The cafe where they'd met was far enough from the city center that she didn't expect any of Yuri's thugs to be walking around—other than Pavel, who lingered but kept his distance. They weren't Secret Service. It wasn't like she was such a vulnerability to national security, they had to watch her pee.

"Dominik's mother." Colin released a laugh of disbelief. "We never considered it couldn't be Ekaterina. Do we at least know who she is?"

"No, but I'm thinking it was an affair of some sort."

149

His head bobbed slowly, rhythmically. "How'd you get your hands on the necklace?"

"Chance. But, whatever you have to do to it, you only have tonight. I need to put it back in place before Yuri finds out I took it."

"It's actually quite beautiful. Simple and beautiful. Who do you think the woman engraved on it is?"

"Knowing Yuri?" She shrugged. "I wouldn't be surprised if he engraved Dom's mother on it."

Colin flicked a glance her way. "Dom? Shit, E, you've been doing this too long. You're getting familiar. After this, take an extended vacation."

"I already planned to."

"You forget that I know you. You have a tendency to change your mind."

Work had taken too many things from her already. Despite organizing it, she'd almost missed her grandfather's funeral, showing up at the last minute. But the tension she'd expected between her and her sister hadn't occurred. At the end of the service, she'd even seen an opening, albeit tiny, for reconciliation... if work hadn't been a factor. Even her father, who'd been a physician, had made time for family. These months with Nana were precious and precarious, and she was missing them all the same. Without her sister, if she lost Nana, what else would she have?

Colin tore his attention away from the necklace. "Are you coming by after your shift?"

"As usual."

"You didn't come by last time."

"I ended later than," she sighed, swallowing an unexpected bubble of tears, "anticipated."

"You might think you're incapable of love," he said, "but the fact that you're even taking this big of a risk tells me otherwise. If Randy found out you brought Nana on a top secret, covert op..."

She'd be suspended.

Or worse.

"It wasn't like he gave me a choice," she argued. "You were there when he said what he said. I can't afford to lose everything I've worked for. Not now."

"I know. I'm sorry you have to deal with all of this shit on top of having to take care of family."

"Which is why I'll never stop thanking you and April for stepping in."

"Come on, Eija, me and you, we're family. Plus, I'm trying to make April Mrs. Favreau, so she will be too." He winked and dropped the necklace into his pocket. "Now, about London. What do you know?"

"Very little. It's some sort of business function. Yuri wants me there as part translator and for my usual nanny duties. It'll last one week, and Ludmila told me he goes twice a year. The meetings aren't held in the same city every time, either."

"Do you know where you're staying?"

"The Havre."

Colin whistled. *"Nice.* But, I don't know, E. Are you sure

you want to go out to England cold? It's too risky. Thinking about it makes me all sick and shit. What if they make you?"

"It's a risk I have to take, Colin. I can't just *not* go." She placed her hand on his. "We'll have a way to communicate. I'll be careful. Hell, I might be with Nikolai the entire time, and Yuri won't let anything happen to Nikolai."

Colin hated the plan; his desire to argue against it created lines on his face, and he flexed his forearms, over and over, in restraint. But speaking up wouldn't matter. She had to go. If she didn't, Yuri could fire her, and then what would they have?

"Now," Eija began, "tell me about the photos I took."

He chuffed out something between a laugh and a sigh, head shaking. "I don't know what the fuck it is, E. Shit doesn't make sense. It looks like, on every page, the person started sketching or writing something, got distracted, and never got back to it."

"Have you sent the images to Randy yet?"

"Not yet. I want more time with it first."

She scanned for anyone who might look out of place or too invested in their conversation. "Well, I'll see what else I can get in the meantime."

"These photos and this necklace are huge, E." His phone rang, and a smile spread across his face as he raised it to his ear. "April, what's up?"

While he and April chatted, Eija ran through, in her mind, how she would return the necklace to Dom. After she returned it, she'd then have to tell Colin when Dom, specifically, wore it. She didn't know if they'd seen her with him already and, because she hadn't ID'd him as Dom, they didn't ask her who the tall, gray-eyed man was. If they had, she'd have some explaining to do once that information became known.

Colin ended the call and set his phone on the table. "There's a meeting going down tonight over in St. Petersburg. Word is the Bratva prince might be there."

"St. Pete?" She angled her head. "Could it be that he's been there this entire time?"

"Could be."

"So...what? Late night surveillance?"

"Are you up for that?"

She waved away the question. It had to be her, and he knew it. "I'll be downstairs and ready tonight. Now, you have to go. I see Pavel."

Colin stood, and they exchanged a few words—as though he was trying to get her to go out with him a second time. She politely rejected him, and he left.

She locked eyes with Pavel through the lunch crowd and headed over.

"How was your lunch?" he asked.

She smiled up at him. "Good. I had something called *solyanka*. It wasn't terrible, but it wasn't beef stroganoff."

His hand covered the small of her back, navigating her toward the car. "Some things, like the sweet things, are easier to get used to. Others, they're good because they come with a memory, and the memory is more important than the taste."

She slipped inside the car, Pavel following. He shut the door, and Mikhail pulled off.

Lyu lay in her crate on the front seat, asleep. A white cast covered one of her front paws, and Eija spotted fresh stitches in her ear with each errant twitch. How much damage had she done to the poor cat, and what would that mean for her position?

It was Pavel who'd found Lyu behind a dumpster near the penthouse a couple of years ago. Yuri, against Ekaterina's wishes, had taken the kitten in and nursed it to good health. Usually, he doted on Lyu, and the only reason he'd hesitated to run to Lyu in his office was likely because he'd been picturing her and Leah with their tongues on each other. Now that the haze of lust had cleared, she hoped he could forgive her. She doubly hoped she wouldn't have to convince him to.

"So what you're saying is, there are some foods I'll never get used to?" she asked, one-half of her thoughts on Lyu's ear. The vet had replaced her collar as well.

"Never." Pavel gave an emphatic shake of the head. "But it won't be much. Now, what's first on that list from Kat?"

Chapter Fifteen

"So, this is the mysterious prince..."

Dom scanned the meeting room filled with some of the most clandestinely powerful figureheads around the globe. They'd met in St. Petersburg in a designated space inside the Church of the Savior on Spilled Blood. Yuri believed that, in good faith, nothing violent would happen within church walls. Dom had started to remind him about the church's desecration during Russian Revolution in the early part of the twentieth-century, and the church's role as a temporary morgue during the Second World War, but it had been Yuri's meeting place for over a decade without incident. Perhaps the man knew what he was talking about.

Their meeting room was just as ornate as the rest of the house of worship. Mosaics made up most of the ceiling, images venerating saints, major biblical figures, and religious reenactments. A series of chandeliers provided lighting, but the room still had an ominous, mysterious aura to it. The death that had happened there, Dom felt it in the air. The walls. Too many of them currently sat in a single location, and this group in particular had common enemies.

"I'm not a prince." He locked eyes with Clodagh Ronan, the head of the once defunct Irish Mob. She ran a sect in the United States, buried in Utah instead of the east coast in the New England area where most of the clan was usually found.

"Ya father is the last Sokolov alive, dear," Clodagh insisted. "You, Dominik Sokolov, are the Prince of the Bratva."

The leader of the Yakuza, Moriyama "Mori" Masahiko's dark eyes assessed him. "You still don't look dangerous, kid."

"Neither do you," Dom shot back.

Mori grinned.

Mori's father's assassination had thrust him into the role of the "family boss" of the Japanese crime syndicate, to Mori's chagrin. High on Mori's list were parties, women, alcohol, and the occasional hallucinogenic pill or powder. Leading the Yakuza hadn't made the top one hundred. Dom had known Mori since childhood, but after he left for California, it would be twelve years before they spoke again.

Also in attendance was Igor Kuzmin, the head of the *Avtoritet*, Yuri's intermediary for communicating with the main Bratva cells; Ale Strinati, Consigliere of the Sicilian mafia and Leah's father; and Musa Ujima, whose actual name was John Clarke, a Jamaican drug lord who regularly networked with Colombian and Venezuelan cartels.

Mori was the only one without a spouse, mistress, or lover of any sort in attendance. Dom had more than once found himself considering what pursuing something with Eija could mean for her life in the long run.

"Now that you have met my Dominik," Yuri announced, and Dom tried to ignore the love and pride in the man's voice, but it always proved difficult, "let us move to other business. The dostavka and the koronatsiya."

Clodagh smiled at Dom. "Have ya found yourself a wife?"

Clodagh had a harem of lovers as young as twenty-one to her sixty-seven years. In her youth, she'd lived an austere life-style. Now that she had her business handled, it was time to focus on pleasure—at least, that was the way the older woman had put it. Her mantra was to never make love to fewer than two people at a time.

Dom started to reply, but Yuri squeezed his knee. "There is plenty of time to choose a wife, and the selection is quite...what is the word..."

"Vast," Dom supplied.

"Not too vast, I hope," Ale jumped in. "To not choose my Leah would be a tragedy."

He couldn't see himself, as a father, being so accepting of having his daughter "chosen" by someone rather than the other way around. Leah had much more to offer than it appeared her father believed, or cared to believe. Maybe, had he never met Eija, that would have been enough for him.

Musa craned his neck for one of the ladies he'd brought with him, who'd switched places on his lap all night, to pop a pale-yellow berry into his mouth. "But why marry?" he asked. "Why not have fun?"

"It is tradition," Yuri said.

"And we can expect a peaceful transition afterward?" Mori questioned. "A lot of what the Yakuza does hinges on the Bratva."

"Everything will go smoothly," Dom reassured the table. "Be more concerned about keeping up your agreements with the Bratva."

Yuri squeezed his knee again, this time out of encouragement. Even when he hated the man, Yuri never ceased to see him as some sort of rose growing in a forgotten cemetery.

After discussing each organization's responsibilities in relation to the koronatsiya and dostavka, the meeting concluded. The other members left the church, leaving behind Dom, Yuri, Igor, Pavel, and their security.

Dom clasped his hands on the tabletop, switching to Russian. "Someone was at my place the other day. Now, Igor, you know my name, my face, and understand that I have a list of the few who have this privilege. If I find out you have crossed me or Yuri, I will kill you, your family, and anybody else who could carry on the memory of your existence."

Igor's face paled. "Yes. I understand."

The uneasy feeling that had been building, budding, and stretching in Dom's chest finally snapped. His ears perked up, and he motioned to Pavel and the rest of Yuri's guards, then pointed to the ceiling. With the room quiet, they could hear the footsteps, dozens of them, circling the church.

He, Yuri, Pavel, and Igor outlined a quick strategy. The other three brandished their weapons while Dom removed a semiautomatic pistol from his blazer and started toward the meeting room's main entry.

"Where are you going?" Pavel called.

"We can't all leave the same way and bottleneck ourselves," Dom said. "I'll take the main door."

Someone on the other side of the door kicked it in, and the nozzle of a gun appeared.

Dom waited for the wielder's face to appear, grabbed their head, and bashed it against the wall of brick near the door. Before they had a chance to recover, he lodged a bullet in their abdomen and neck, and propped them up to use as a shield to navigate his way out of the building.

Shots sounded from above, which would pull some of the gunfire out of his path. Apparently, Yuri's faith or luck, which-ever had kept this sanctuary from being breached the last several years, had run out tonight.

Over the shoulder of his "shield," Dom hit two additional shooters in the head and torso. A hairy arm wrapped around his neck from behind, tight against his windpipe. Both Dom's gun and human shield fell to the ground, so he used his forearms to break the hold and ducked a massive fist that would have collapsed his jaw.

Having shoved all his bodyweight into the punch, the man with the hairy arms stumbled forward. Dom used all of *his* bodyweight to topple him to the hard floor, pushed Hairy Arms' head twice into the ground, then finished him the same way he'd done the others. A straight path to hell awaited him for killing at least four men in a sanctuary.

He returned to the corridor, grabbed his gun, and continued to the exit.

The twinkling lights in the sky, a little more plentiful out here than back in Moscow, let him know when he'd left the dark corridor. The minute he stepped outside, a knife went into his bicep. A human tank, this man twice the size of all the others, stepped back and lowered into a fighting stance. It would have been simple to put a bullet in him, having brought a knife to a gunfight. But, from the looks of it, the tank's "armor" had taken several futile hits already.

Dom put away the gun and slipped off his tie.

The hulk took the motion as an opening and charged.

Dom slid out of the way and wrapped the tie around the man's neck, which was damn near a tree trunk, tugging hard.

Massive arms flailed.

Annoyed, he removed the tie, stepped back, and lodged a bullet in the behemoth's skull. Strangulation would have taken forever, and he didn't have time for that.

His phone rang.

"Pavel," he answered.

"Where are you?"

"Northeast corner under the tree."

The car pulled up just as he reached the street. He got in and, before he thought through what he was doing, he scanned Yuri for injuries.

"Ah, you do care," Yuri teased.

He leaned back against the seat. "Whatever."

"Son?" Yuri grabbed his injured arm. "Do you not feel this?"

"Have you seen the scars I already have?"

"A regular man did not make those. Take off the blazer."

Dom groaned but did as he was told.

Pavel looked out the window, searching the darkness. "There was another car here that didn't look to be associated with the group who stormed in tonight. A man and woman were inside."

"Doing what?" Dom asked.

"I think you can probably guess what they were doing. They sped off when I confronted them."

Amateurs. Gunfire wouldn't be enough for him to consider leaving the warmth of Eija's body. Hell, gunfire wouldn't stop him from kissing her, never mind missing out on any opportunity to make her orgasm. She was beautiful when she came. He knew they'd talked about keeping their distance, but he wanted to hear her voice. After a night like this, he craved the sound of her voice.

"Anything on the men's affiliation?" Yuri asked.

"We'll have information before sunset tomorrow," Pavel promised. "Initial speculation is that nobody we met with tonight is involved, but we're still searching."

Yuri finished cleaning and bandaging Dom's wound, then gingerly helped him back into his blazer as if dealing with a three-year-old.

"Are you coming to the penthouse?" Yuri asked.

He wanted to go home, take a shower, and lose himself inside Eija's body.

"No," he replied, eyes closed. "I'm not."

* * *

Eija flipped the switch on her night-vision goggles to increase the range. They knew they were in the right place because they'd spotted Mori Masahiko and Musa Umaji enter the church, of all places, and she pretended not to notice feeling grateful they hadn't spotted Dom go in. Maybe he wasn't even here.

Behind her, Colin crinkled and crunched.

"This is supposed to be a quiet surveillance op, and you bring potato chips."

He extended the bag in her direction. "You want some? It's butter and dill. I've never had anything like it before. It's amazing."

"No, thank you." She lowered the goggles and faced forward in the passenger seat. "Okay, so we have Mori, Musa, and possibly Yuri and Dominik. At *least*. We knew about the Yakuza and the Bratva working together, but I never guessed the Jamaicans would be part of this."

"Why not?" Colin shrugged and sucked on his fingers. "They're like corporations. On the outside, they're competitors, but they know in order to stay afloat, there has to be some sort of interconnectedness or..."

When he added nothing else, she turned to him. "Colin,

162

right now you look like a child someone intentionally lost in a shopping mall."

He folded over the top of the potato chip bag, the noise extra pronounced in the small cabin space, pulled a soda from somewhere near his feet, popped the top, and chugged.

She couldn't remember the last time she'd seen Colin eat chips or drink soda. According to him, high school was the last time he'd drank soda, at least regularly, because he'd struggled with his weight and acne. Chips, he didn't eat because he didn't mess with empty carbs. When he was stressed, however, all his rules shriveled up and died.

"Colin, what's wrong? You're eating like a middle schooler."

He pulled the can away from his mouth and licked his lips. "It's April."

"I figured at least that much. What about April?"

"It's...well, there's something I haven't told you."

There was plenty she hadn't told him, and the jury was still out on *how* and *when* that would happen. The word "if" floated through her mind, like a wisp of smoke from a dancing flame she mentally blew away.

"Me and April, we didn't just sleep together," he said. "We *were* together."

Eija's mouth fell open. "Really? For how long?"

"Seven months." Sorrow pooled in his tired eyes. "The more time we spend together while *not* together, the more I realize how stupid our break-up was. I could have tried harder, E. I could have, but I was so fucking arrogant."

"Why did you break up?"

"We were getting too close, and that freaked me out. Like... talking about moving in together, close." He drew a long sip from the can. "I got cold feet and slept with that one blue-haired intern."

"Aimée?"

"Was that her name?"

Eija faced him, her kneecap brushing the gearshift. "Jesus, Colin. That's...pretty bad. You know April's last serious relationship ended because her ex cheated, right?"

"No, I did *not* know that. See if you can reach my gun and just..." He tapped his temple. "Make it quick."

"You want April back. Just tell her you want her back. If she says no, it's her right, but she could say yes. I thought you two hooked up a few times, but it makes much more sense why she gets all awkward when your name comes up. Why *you* get all awkward when I bring her up."

"I'm in love with her."

She gave his shoulder a squeeze. "I'm sorry."

"For being in love?"

"Yes. I hear it's painful."

He shrugged off her hand. "Anyway, now that I've gone all 'Dear Abby' on you, you owe me a personal question."

She granted his wish.

She already knew what it would be, but she granted his wish anyhow.

"Sex is your thing, E," he began. "You're confident in yourself, you go for what you want, and you get yours. Without a doubt. But then...Grenada. How does that even happen?"

"I'm not in love with him, if that's what you're asking." Though, these days, she wondered if she was simply at the top of the hill while love waited at the bottom, waiting for someone to give her a swift kick in the behind.

"That's not what I'm asking. I already know you're incapable of," Colin hooked his index finger and tapped his chest, "these kinds of feelings."

For a moment, her body went cold. She'd lost her parents young, so she didn't remember them. From what her grandparents had shared, they'd loved each other. Her grandparents had loved each other. One serious relationship that ended with her ex being her niece's father wasn't enough to drive her to close herself off to love. At no point had she ever said she had an aversion to love. Her preference had simply been nonexclusive relationships. That, for some reason, appeared to have made her the Interpol ho when Colin ran through half of the junior analysts during his first two years on the job...which had somehow made him more attractive. She'd even heard some of the analysts call him "swoon-worthy," and though she loved him dearly, she'd gagged.

"Don't say that," she whispered, the hurt in her voice stumbling out, of its own volition.

Colin's face fell. "E, I'm sorry. I didn't mean anything by it. It's just...you don't suffer in love like the rest of us. The closest you came was with that Andrei dude, and I honestly think the only reason you stayed hung up on him afterward is because—"

"Stop."

"Is because of *how* he left you," Colin finished, anyway.

Andrei Falcone had slipped out in the middle of the night. When men did shit like that, they didn't want to be found. Back then, she hadn't known he'd left a note.

The same night she'd accepted that realization, that he was as good as gone, her grandfather had a stroke, reminding her of the fragility of life and how important it was to spend as much time in the present with the ones she loved.

Colin's mouth curved into a dim smile. "What's on your mind, Eija? Talk to me. You can tell me anything. You know that."

Almost anything.

Eija tilted her head back and thought about how to carefully word her response. "Colin, I don't know what to tell you. I just... liked him. I messed up, and I can acknowledge that, but that doesn't change the fact that I really enjoyed being with him."

She still did.

Watching grass grow with Dom would bring her joy.

"But then he left," Colin mumbled.

She nibbled her bottom lip. "Mm-hmm."

"And it's been hard to move on. It's even harder now that you're essentially one half of the closest family you have remaining."

Harder now that she saw his face just about every day.

"I think, deep down, you cared for him more than you realized," Colin added. "That's why that night went the way it did."

She'd tried to hide it, but Colin had seen the hurt. For it to bite as hard as it had, she wondered if that was the real reason she didn't want what, had they been different people, would have been so easy to pursue with Dom. Strong women, those who took down criminal organizations and extremist groups, didn't lament over broken hearts. They didn't create fantasy worlds in their heads while alone in their apartments in France, dreaming about what could have been.

Life was or wasn't.

That was all there was to it.

Colin motioned to their equipment, the church. "Well, look at it this way. This op, the work you put in this past year...E, you birthed a baby. Even Randy pointed out how hard you've been working. And I know it's in part because of what happened in Grenada, but cut yourself a little slack. Maybe it's time mama got back out onto the scene."

She turned back to the church and raised her goggles. "When mama's baby finally learns how to walk, maybe."

"Well, it's only a matter of time before Sokolov—"

"Colin, we've got movement."

His casual demeanor left, and he grabbed his goggles. Emerging from the church was Clodagh Ronan, Mori, Musa, a man she didn't recognize, and each individual's entourage.

"Who's the guy in the gray suit?" she asked.

"Ale Strinati. Sicilian mafia. La Stessa Cosa."

"La Stessa Cosa? Do we have a task force for them?"

"Yeah, but it's latent. They've been quiet."

After each crime leader got into their vehicles and sped off, the night remained quiet for about ten minutes more, and then the first gunshot lifted into the air. More than a dozen bodies dressed in black emerged from the darkness, flooding the church, weapons of all different types raised.

"What the fuck?" Colin whispered. "Where'd they come from?"

Eija recognized Yuri's men firing back at the shooters. "I don't know. Can you pick up any audio?"

"Russian, but it sounds off."

Eija took the earpiece he outstretched. "It's dialect. Southern region. I can't remember from where, which oblast. They're saying what sounds like 'inside' and 'the prince is here.'"

Cold sweat sprouted on her upper lip.

"Dominik?" Colin asked. "He's here? He must still be inside. If we wait, E, we might be able to ID him tonight."

She swallowed, but her esophagus had twisted itself into a bow. "If they're still looking for him, I don't think he's here, Colin."

"We'll wait."

"We don't have the firepower on us to risk being caught up in this level of mafioso shit."

Pavel, swift and efficient as usual, picked off men one by one. He led a crew to one side of the church, all of them crowded around a figure. Once the figure, which she'd already guessed was Yuri, was in the car, Pavel made his way back to the chaos. Then, a familiar face emerged from the belly of the cathedral.

Colin raised his goggles in Dom's direction. "Who—"

Eija grabbed the goggles with one hand, the back of Colin's head with the other, and brought his mouth to hers.

"E, what are you—"

She slipped her tongue between his lips. After a moment of stunned surprise, his tongue tangled with hers, sweet from the orange in the soda and his lips sour from the dill in the chips.

"Pull my shirt up," she whispered.

He hooked his fingers in the hem of her shirt, tugged it up, and when it was over her head, knuckles sounded on the window.

Eija didn't look up.

With her head covered, Pavel wouldn't make out her hair, and her undershirt hid her skin. It wasn't like there were a ton of brown-skinned, curly haired folk in Russia.

"Hey, out of here," Pavel warned.

Colin looked up. "Oh, sorry."

"Go do that somewhere else."

She felt Colin nod, and he pulled out of their surveillance spot, backed up to the end of the street, and sped away from the scene.

Eija, heart racing, fixed her shirt.

She felt sick, could scarcely breathe, and her hands shook. But she didn't feel sick and out of breath and dizzy because she'd just blown their operation, yet again. It was because the last thing she'd seen, right before Pavel had started toward the car, was a large man with an equally large knife headed toward Dom.

"Sorry about that," she said. "I didn't know if he'd believe that we were out here in the dark doing anything other than getting hot and heavy."

Colin rubbed his bottom lip, a slight grin on his face. "No, no. It's...uh, it's fine."

"Come on, just give it to me straight. 'Ugh, E, that was like kissing my sister.'"

"It wasn't...that." He glanced at her. "But I will say this...the guys who stumble and fall all over themselves over you? I get it now. I totally get it now."

She punched his arm.

He burst out laughing.

Chapter Sixteen

Eija opened the door to her apartment, not at all surprised to see Dom standing there. No light shone in his eyes, the usual steely gray replaced by a color that reminded her of a Louisiana bog at midnight. She pictured herself trudging through the muck in search of the man who lived deep within—the Dom she'd known all this time, her Dom, who needed rescue after getting trapped in hanging moss and enchanting willows weeping in the night.

This was him, wasn't it? Dominik Sokolov. The man who Yuri trusted to take over one of the most organized crime families in the world before he turned the age of thirty-five.

Dom's suit, though dark, had visible spots of blood dotted throughout. The white shirt underneath had a quarter-sized stain on the chest, and she mentally soothed herself. If the blood had been his, he would have been in obvious pain.

He blinked.

And, just like that, the darkness began its regression.

"What are you doing here?" She stepped back and motioned for him to come in. "I thought, after our little talk, I wouldn't see you again."

She shut the door.

When she turned around, he was right in front of her.

"We were always going to see each other again," he said, and then he grinned like an android trying to convince a room full of humans that it was *one of them.*

She didn't like him like this, but she'd needed to see it. Even if it was a small peek, the Dom he showed her daily wasn't someone she could see sanctioning the slaughter of entire families or selling guns, women, and children. That was what the Bratva did. Someone like that, no matter how sweet the "yang" to his "yin," was impossible for her to be with.

"Are you hungry?" She scanned his clothes. "I made that extra roti, so while I heat it up, you go get cleaned up. I don't have anything here for you to change into, but I'll throw those in the washing machine if you don't mind walking around in a towel and your underwear for a bit."

He angled his head. "You don't have men's clothes here?"

"Know what? You can go home now."

"I'm good right here, actually."

"We'll see about that." She pointed to the hallway. "The bathroom's that way. You'll see the linen closet right before you hit the door."

He walked off, and she headed to the kitchen to reheat the

roti and pour him a glass of vodka. Because she knew how his night had gone, she knew he needed it. Usually, at this time of night, she would be down at Colin and April's, but after tonight's activities, she'd stayed in just in case someone from Yuri's camp had come looking for her.

Dom returned, a white towel wrapped around his waist and his clothes balled up in one hand. Eija traded him the vodka and roti for the clothes.

"Are these designer?" she asked, searching for a tag. "I don't want to ruin them by tossing them in the washing machine."

He shrugged. "It's okay. I don't care."

"Dom, are you okay? You're...not yourself."

"No." He took a large bite of the roti and studied her face as he chewed.

"Can I help in any way?"

"You already are."

As her nana would say, she and Dom *"pull on too well."* It was why she'd known, the minute their conversation in the penthouse library had ended, they would be back here. She'd never meshed with anyone as quickly as she had with him. Even Colin, when they were first assigned to work together, she'd butted heads with because their personalities were too similar.

Then, in the middle of an unanticipated shootout, Colin had taken several slugs to the torso, arm, and leg, nearly bleeding out on the streets of Thailand. She'd had her arm extended for them to take blood before they could ask, her and Colin one of the few pairs whose personality tests had placed them together *and* their blood types had matched for scenarios like the one in Phuket.

After that, they became inseparable.

With Dom, she'd fallen into a rhythm with him from their very first date, and that was something she found equally intriguing and terrifying.

She flopped down onto the sofa, legs curled underneath her. Before he arrived, she'd been watching an American crime show with Russian subtitles. Dom sat on the floor in front of her, long legs passing through the coffee table, periodically lifting the roti to his mouth.

"Like it?" she asked.

He moaned his approval. "Love it. Perfect amount of heat and perfectly seasoned. You made this just for me?"

"You asked."

"I did. Thank you."

When he was finished, he put the plate and glass in the dishwasher, turned it on, and went to wash his hands.

"Don't scrub too hard," she called after him. "Those curry stains are going to hang around a while."

He returned, and she stopped herself from getting too caught up in his physique. The strategic way he was inked, he'd obviously gotten most of the tattoos to cover his scars. The ones that turned her on the most, for reasons unknown, were the ones on his fingers. Namely, the skull that started on the back of his hand and ended past his knuckles. Underneath all that ink was a body she'd never forget; abs that clenched and triceps that bulged with each thrust of his hips, pushing his dick deep inside her.

Instead of returning to the floor, he lay on the sofa. As though it was instinct, she unfolded her legs, grabbed a pillow, and he laid his head on the pillow, on her lap. She stroked his head, the strands of hair smooth despite the low cut.

"What made you cut it?" she asked.

"You miss my hair?"

"I like you with either, honestly."

"Yuri. He said my hair made me look too pretty. That no one would take me seriously."

"Is that why," she scrubbed the hair on his face, "you grew this out?"

"Yeah. You like that too?"

"I prefer you with it." She scrubbed again. "I like you with any style hair, but I *love* this. God, you're so good looking it's disgusting."

A smile pulled at the right side of his mouth. "Are you flirting?"

"No."

"Sounds like it."

"It's my natural way of interacting. I'm genetically flirtatious."

A deep laugh shook his shoulders. Dom slowly filtered back in, Dominik slipping away and returning to the place where there was no love or light.

They had heated debates over which of the reenactment actors would wind up being the killer. Eija nailed it every single time, and he joked that she would have made a good detective or law enforcement officer.

As another show geared up, he reached for her hand and massaged it with the back of his thumb. "How'd you learn to speak Russian so well?" he asked.

"Classes." That she'd taken way back when she was a runt in the CIA. She'd also learned Farsi and Czech as necessary parts of the job. "I always knew I wanted to teach here, so I enrolled in an immersive program."

"What, were you trying to get a job with the CIA or something?"

She snorted. "Uh...no. Not even."

By the time she'd gotten to Farsi, she'd already been an officer at the agency for a few years.

"I mean, I don't even hear your accent when you speak it," he went on. "You sound like you grew up here."

She raised one shoulder in a shrug. "That's the point, I think. It makes people feel comfortable, and I wanted to charm Yuri and Ekaterina. They had all the prospective nannies meet Nikolai, and I just knew I had to be in his life."

"Honestly, I never pegged you for the caregiver type."

"I was the 'mother' of the resort."

He ticked his head. "I guess so. You do an outstanding job. Nikolai adores you."

"He's a sweet kid."

"Can I make one request thought?" He held up his right index finger. "When we're alone, can you use it for me? Your accent, I mean."

"Didn't you say it was a turn on?"

"*No.*" He dragged out the word. "I don't recall ever mentioning that."

She smoothed the short hairs at his temple with her fingers. "Whatever. I'm not going to do anything that'll have us end up in bed together and break our covenant. I won't share you, Dom, and especially not with a fiancée or wife."

"Eija, I want you more than I want them. Collectively."

She squeaked out a sound of disbelief, but her heart went full crane kick in her chest.

"It would be a marriage in name only," he added.

"It's still *marriage.*"

"I know. I get where you're coming from. But if you don't want us to end up in bed together, you should probably stop rubbing my head."

She kept rubbing his head.

They finished another television show, this one about neighbors who ended up turning violent when minor altercations escalated.

He shared with her an incident with an old neighbor of his aunt's. The man hadn't known his aunt was no longer living alone and had fancied himself a Homeowner's Association enforcer. He'd complained that the blades of grass in Dom's aunt's yard were a half inch too high and knocked on her door one morning to issue a citation it looked like he'd created in Microsoft Paint. When Dom opened the door, the neighbor had faltered and hurried back to his house. Dom then spent the next several months periodically visiting the neighbor's yard with a tape measure, and a clipboard with blank sheets of paper.

"Just to be an asshole," he finished.

"An asshole looking out for your aunt," she justified. "Were your aunt and mother close? Is that why you chose her to live with?"

"For most of their lives, yes."

"How'd your mother and Yuri meet?"

"They met in California. Aani was her name. She was Iranian." He cupped her knee, slowly stroking. "Hey, Eija? Instead of drinks or dinner, what if I took you to a wax—"

"Dom, I swear to God..." She shoved his hand away from her knee. "Yes, let's go to a wax spa. While they work on my *perfectly smooth* legs, I'll ask them to wax off every last bit of this lovely hair."

"Lovely, handsome, gorgeous, beautiful. Why are you so obsessed with me?"

"When did I call you beautiful?"

"I'm pretty sure you did. Don't worry. I'll remember."

They laughed together, back in that comfort bubble it hadn't taken long for them to build. Once their laughter died, she asked the hard question.

"Can I ask how your mother passed?"

It wasn't clear how much of this information she would pass on to Colin, or if she wanted to know because she was looking for something that would absolve him from shouldering the responsibility of his father's crimes.

"Kat's not Yuri's first wife," he explained. "Her name was

Anika. With her, Yuri didn't do the dostavka because he didn't want anyone knowing she existed. According to him, she was smart, quick-witted, sharp. She was also insanely jealous, emphasis on the insane. As you can probably already tell, Yuri's dick wanders from time to time."

"So I've noticed."

"Most of the women, when Anika found out about them, she paid them to leave, but my mother didn't want money. She wanted Yuri. When he found out she was pregnant, he brought her to Russia thinking he could hide us in Krasnodar. Anika eventually found my mother and...sold her."

Eija went still. "Sold her? Trafficking?"

"Yes. Wasn't hard considering the Brat...considering Yuri's influence."

She knew nothing of Anika, but selling a woman was something that had Yuri written all over it. "How did Yuri find out? And was she still pregnant when all of this happened?"

"She was."

"Dom, did she use while she was pregnant with you?"

"At first, unwillingly, but dependency doesn't care how you started. Luckily, I wasn't affected. From what I understand, Yuri looked for us the entire time. When he found us, I was already six, and we were living in Astrakhan, one of the poorest oblasts in Russia. My mother did her best, but..." He shrugged. "Anyhow, Yuri took us back with him to Moscow. He tried to get my mother help, but she died by overdose."

"Why does it seem like no one knows he has a son?" Eija

prodded. "But then Nikolai talks about his 'uncle' Dominik, and Yuri introduced you to me as his son."

While working on something unrelated for her boss at the CIA, she'd discovered a series of trips Yuri had taken to California. She'd also found flight manifests of him traveling with a female companion who went by "Annie," and the large sums of money he'd send to California regularly. She'd tracked the funds to a shell company and then eventually to Dom's aunt. After going through his aunt's bank records, she'd learned a good portion of those funds had gone to tuition.

Eija closed her eyes and mentally cursed.

Tuition at *Stanford.*

He'd told her he'd attended Stanford back in Grenada but, by then, the stars in her eyes had already blinded her.

Not long after that discovery, her boss sent her to France to join Randy's task force. It was from there she'd eventually learned of Dominik Sokolov, but Dom had been so well-buried, it was only because Randy's file on Yuri had included one family member whose lineage had been unclear that they'd pieced everything else together. Then the manhunt for the Bratva prince had taken shape.

Dom stretched his neck, chest flexing with a massive sigh. "Yuri hid me to keep me safe from his enemies. As a boy, and because I had no mother, I was more vulnerable than his daughters. For whatever reason, my father will do anything for me. So, since Anika brought me grief, he had her killed. I'd assumed he'd sent Anika into hiding to protect her from any repercussions for hurting my mother, and I'd hated him for it, so I left

Russia to live with my aunt in Redwood City when I turned sixteen."

"And now that you know the truth?"

"I owe him."

"Does any part of you want to run," now *she'd* nearly slipped up and mentioned the Bratva, "Sokol Incorporated?"

"Nope. If it was up to me, I'd live out my days in a villa in Central America with a certain West Indian goddess."

"Rihanna?"

"Who else?"

A laugh bubbled up and through her, and he smiled in response.

"So, I've told you a lot about me." He turned onto his back and looked up into her face. "Tell me everything that I missed out on learning about Eija."

"There's not much to tell."

"Well, what did you do after you left the resort?"

She ran through the story she'd rehearsed so much, she'd started merging the fake events with her actual life, mixing the memories together.

"I spent time with my grandparents. Then, after my grandfather's death, I needed a...change."

"I really am sorry to hear about your grandfather. What about your grandmother?"

When she didn't respond and instead looked out the window, he took her hand and brought her fingers up to his lips. What she hadn't expected was for her to prefer her grandfather's condition to her grandmother's. One...maybe two days was all he'd had to live with the pain, and he'd been unconscious the entire time. Her grandmother's condition and the gradual way it had stripped the parts of her that had made her who she was had been harder to deal with.

"Anyhow," she cleared the emotion from her throat, "I came to Russia not really expecting much, and now I have one of the best jobs I've ever had. Funny how life works that way." She squeezed his bicep. "Now, are you going to tell me why you're bandaged up here and had blood on your clothes?"

He raised his arm and looked at the wound like he'd never seen it before. "Would you believe me if I said I got into a shootout and knife fight?"

Yes.

"Um...no. Dom, there are other ways to impress me. You don't have to make yourself seem dangerous."

"I *am* dangerous. Look at all my tattoos. I have tatts on my fingers. Only dangerous men have ink on their fingers, Eija."

"Or men trying to hide childhood scars." She took his hand. "I do like this skull tattoo, though. I like how it goes all the way down past your knuckles. It's...making me..."

His pupils grew. "Making you...what?"

She turned her attention to the TV.

"Making you *what*, Eija?"

"Look, Dom, we got one wrong. The wife was the killer the whole time."

He flipped onto his side. "I fucking hate you."

She doubled over laughing and kissed his cheek.

* * *

After a great deal of coaxing, Dom had gotten Eija to lie down on the sofa with him. The fatigue in her eyes had been clear since he walked in, but she'd stayed up to spend time with him despite his unexpected late-night visit. He'd half expected to walk in and find her with a man, and he'd fully expected to throw the man off the balcony if that had happened.

Sometime between a show that interviewed people who'd grown up with killers and another one recounting a detective's past cases, she'd fallen asleep. As tired as he was, he stayed awake to watch her sleep. He wanted to hear her breathe, see her chest moving with each deep inhale and exhale.

He'd never been what some would consider a womanizer. He loved women and enjoyed their company, but he didn't see fucking one—or as many as possible—as some sort of conquest. First love had come in the form of Ivy Lawrence, who he'd met his senior year of high school. Last he'd heard, she'd gone on to work in some genetics lab, dodging the bullet that would have shattered her life if they'd stayed together. While she'd been researching cures, he'd invested money during the day and carried out for-hire contracts at night.

So, he had no problem admitting to himself that he was into Eija. Whenever they spent time together, he walked away feeling better than good, and that she was the same fucking amazing person he'd met in Grenada didn't help how badly he wanted her in every way and position imaginable.

"Eija?" He stroked her arm. "Eija, come on. Let's go to bed."

She grumbled something, folded his hand against her chest, and went back to sleep.

"All right. Fine."

He eased up off the couch, lifted her clean off the cushions, and walked them to her bedroom, the towel falling off on the way. Both their places had the same layout, so he'd known where the bathroom was even before she'd told him.

"Dom." She groaned and let her head fall back. "I've already seen your muscles. Put me down before you hurt yourself."

"You're not heavy." He set her on the bed and climbed over her. "I'll grab my clothes from the dryer and go. I'll lock up, okay?"

"No. Stay. You left me in Grenada, so you owe me a night here. Plus," she yawned and gave his body a quick, sleepy scan, "I don't know the entire story, but you've had a hard night. I can tell. Let me hold you."

"Think that's supposed to be the other way around."

"Not really. Just as much as I like your arms around me," she yawned again, "you like my arms around you. At least, that's what the hundreds of men I've slept with have told me."

He smacked her on the ass. "Keep fucking around and see what happens."

"Okay." She grinned. "I will."

She raised the covers, and he got in beside her. Instantly, the warmth of her body soothed his muscles and loosened the tension that had been docked in his chest all night.

He dragged her up against him.

She cupped the left side of his jaw and stared like she was trying to navigate her way through his soul. "You make this so hard."

"Or you do," he argued. "Eija, you think this is over? Maybe it would have been had fate not conspired to fling us back together. But we're here now and you'll learn, sooner or later, what this is eventually going to be."

She snuggled against him. "I'll fight it."

"And you'll lose."

If it took them lying on the sofa, her stroking his head while they watched television, to show her he was serious, it was what he'd do. Something about her told him that he needed her.

That he could trust her.

No matter what.

Chapter Seventeen

Two months until
Dostavka-Koronatsiya

When Dom showed up, Eija was at the tail end of a five minute mental flagellation session.

But it hadn't started out that way.

It had started with anxiety, regret, and a scoop of self-loathing. She'd sprinkled self-doubt on top, so when she opened the door and found him standing on the other side, it didn't surprise her when his face told her she looked like shit. People usually did when they didn't sleep, had mints and cookies for breakfast, and the past and present collided like a tub full of atoms.

"What are you doing here?" She stepped away from the door, allowing him to enter. At least, she'd blow-dried and flat-ironed her hair the day before, so that was one less thing to worry about.

"Picking you up." He shut the door behind him. "Did you sleep, at all, last night?"

How could she? She'd become one of *those* people who jeopardized secret missions with clandestine government organizations. And because of what? Dick? Cock? Penis? Shimmering eyes, an easygoing personality, and a gorgeous smile? Which one was it? What, exactly, was she risking her career for?

The other thing.

"Eija." He placed himself between her and the window she'd been aimlessly staring through. "What's up? What's going on?"

"Aren't you supposed to be on a plane?"

"Like I said, I'm picking you up. We're taking the same flight."

The man even looked good in a turtleneck, slacks, polished dress shoes, and a long wool coat. She was pretty sure her sweater was on backward or inside out. Both, probably.

"You're flying commercially?" she asked.

He dragged her over to the sofa, sat on the arm, and pulled her between his knees. "I never take my father's jet. Now, talk to me."

"I think I'm coming down with something." She sniffled for effect. "Nikolai had a runny nose the other day."

"Are you sure you can make the trip?"

"Yeah, yeah. Of course."

He smoothed his palms up and down the sides of her arms. "Is that all?"

Tell him!

"Eija."

She blinked a few times. "Yeah, that's all. Why, do I look that bad?"

"I'm actually not sure that's possible for you." He tucked her hair behind her left ear. "You *do* look like something, or someone, broke your heart, and I'm in a weird spot where I'm hoping it's me."

She slipped her finger inside the top of his turtleneck. "You look nice too...even though people stopped wearing turtlenecks in 1999."

"Know what?" He gently nudged her aside, stood, and headed for the door. "I'm not offering you any more comfort. Ever again."

She chased him and wrapped her arms around him from behind.

"Nope." He pulled at her locked hands. "You hurt my feelings."

"But you didn't even let me finish! What I meant was, people stopped wearing turtlenecks in 1999...unless they were models in a JCPenney catalog."

"Let me go, woman. And don't even think about sitting next to me on the plane."

She laughed and squeezed tighter. "I'm kidding. You look cute."

"You're only saying that because you want to sit next to me."

"No, you look good." She released him and formed a square with her thumb and index finger on each hand. "You look perfect. Amazing. Dom, you in all black is...artwork."

They stared at each other until she convinced herself them kissing, at that very moment, would be a bad idea. She didn't know what he told himself to snap out of the trance, but he looked away, grabbed her beanie from on top of her suitcase, and pulled it onto her head.

"Now, how do *I* look?" she asked.

He cracked a grin. "Edible."

"Well," she took a step forward, "maybe you can take those enormous hands of yours and put them...on my...suitcase handle."

He grabbed her suitcase. "You're going to turn yourself on to the point of no return one of these days. Don't come looking for me when you do."

"Why, you'd turn me away?"

"That's the thing." He took her hand. "No. I would not."

While her brain sifted through his answer to find meaning, between her legs understood. Right away.

They headed down to the car.

Dom never took his father's jet, but that didn't mean he flew like a peasant like her and the rest of her constituency. They had plush, first-class seats and, after a big breakfast, she caught up on some of the sleep she'd missed out on the night before. At one point, she woke up to his arm around her and pretended to be asleep until she eventually drifted off again.

The plane's wheels touching the runway jolted her

awake. They exited, her gloved hand tucked in his, and she didn't fully wake up until they came to the airport's bright lights and windows blasting with sunshine, the terminal busy in that way airports always were. It wasn't her first time at Heathrow, but she read the welcome signs and studied the British flags along the corridor as though it was. It *was* her first time walking through where she wasn't so focused on her next task, she could look around and take in the sights. Breathe a little.

Dom squeezed her hand as they meandered through the crowd. The conspiratorial grins and winks she got from other women made her grin and wink back.

They knew.

She knew.

The man holding her hand was *nice*.

"Are we not going to the baggage carousel?" she asked, looking back as they passed it.

"Somebody will get our bags for us." He extended a leather-covered index finger. "There's our car."

A Mercedes sedan waited at the curb, and they relaxed in the warm cabin while the driver retrieved their luggage. Dom tapped the seat between them with his middle finger, and she rolled her eyes but slipped her fingers through his, indulging in the flush that went through her body.

"Ever been to the Havre in London?" he asked, thumb stroking her palm.

Eija let out a small laugh. "Dominik, in what world can I afford a twenty-thousand-dollar per night suite?"

"I don't know." He shrugged. "Figured some rich guy might have wined and dined you."

"Hasn't happened, but it's not a bad idea. We're here for a week. I'll find one."

"Don't look *too* hard now."

Smiling, she turned away from him, giving her attention to the world outside her window.

Even though every time she'd come to London it had been for work, she'd always taken a moment to marvel at how green it was. The sky was gray more often than it was blue, but all the trees looked like they'd been nourished by hand. Certain spots reminded her of visiting Richmond and others of driving through Detroit. None of it, however, reminded her of Grenada. The globe was so vast with different nooks and pockets, and she was part of a team tasked with teasing out some of the seediest criminals known to man from those nooks and pockets. None of those criminals had been like the man sitting across from her, but she couldn't tell if it was jaded thinking or if Dom truly was different.

"Sir, Madam, we have arrived at the Havre," the driver announced.

Parked in front of the hotel were a pair of Ferraris, and the establishment might as well had posted a sign that said, *Poor People Needn't Venture Further.*

She and Dom released their caged fingers.

While the driver retrieved their bags from the trunk, he leaned across and snuck a kiss against her cheek. "This is me being friendly and letting you know I'll be thinking about you this week," he said. "In a purely platonic manner."

She eyed him. "Thinking of me naked doesn't count as platonic."

"What if it's you naked in the middle of a room while I paint you?"

"Are my legs closed or open?"

His eyes rolled upward. "I see your point."

The door on her side opened.

She placed her hand in the driver's and stepped out while Dom got out on the other side.

The hotel entrance swallowed her whole and washed her down with opulence. A beautiful chandelier and matching wall sconces brightened the entryway. The Havre's decor was a collision of the old and the new, antique and contemporary, from the checkered floors to the large windows and dark paneling. She didn't know how she would return to her average life in her flat, barely big enough for two, when this op was over.

"Miss K!" Nikolai raced over and crashed into her legs. "You made it!"

She crouched and wrapped him up in a tight hug. Virtually everything else about Nanny K might be fake, but her adoration for Nikolai was genuine.

"I did. I'm so glad to see you."

"Have you seen your room yet?" he asked.

"No, not yet. I'm excited to see it. How is yours?"

"It's attached to Grandma and Papa's room. It's very big and bright. We can see the river out of the window."

"Big and bright? Hmm..." She tapped her chin, mouth twisting. "How would we say that in English, you think?"

He scrunched his face in that cute way he did whenever he focused. "Big and bite."

"Bright."

"Bright," he echoed.

"Very good."

Yuri and Ekaterina said their hellos before disappearing with Nikolai in a swarm of hotel guests. Just as they walked off, Dom appeared with her room key and slipped it into her hand.

"Does this also open your room?" she asked.

He held out his hand. "No, but I can go fix that for you."

"Kidding." She swatted his coat with the piece of plastic. "Don't tempt me."

"I'm not the one doing the tempting, Eija." Before she could get a step off, he wrapped his fingers around her forearm. "I have a meeting in an hour and then the rest of my day's filled. At some point, however, I'd like for us to have lunch or breakfast. Maybe dinner. A snack, a pretzel stick. Something. I know what we talked about, but heaven help me, Eija, I can't stay away from you."

Her stomach took a tumble, and her heart wanted to follow suit.

"We'll meet up when both our schedules are clear," she promised. "Have you looked at them yet? I'm not sure when sleep's supposed to happen."

He bent, his lips near her ear. "I'll find time."

She turned her head, placing their mouths inches apart. "I'm looking forward to it."

On the first day, she got about an hour's worth of rest, and then she spent the rest of the day as Yuri's unofficial translator. Everyone they met let her know how shocked and impressed they were with her Russian because Americans, as they'd told her repeatedly, barely knew how to speak English.

On the second day, she, Pavel, and Mikhail took Nikolai around Trafalgar Square. Nikolai had attempted to read every sign and plaque they came across, and Pavel had to pick him up to read the ones that had towered above his head. Pavel had replaced Gideon as her personal security, and she figured it had to do with the "keep your enemies closer" adage. Something happened that first night Dom came over to her apartment, and it had placed Gideon high on Yuri's shit list. She hoped, wherever Yuri had reassigned Gideon, the new person loved Russian dramas as much as Gideon did.

They took pictures in front of and on top of the Trafalgar Square lions. By three o'clock in the afternoon, after lunch *and* a tour of the National Gallery, Pavel had to carry Nikolai on his back because he'd nearly fallen asleep standing up.

On the third day, they took the iconic big bus tour, and Nikolai stood the entire time, pointing out structures he recognized from when they'd gone over them that morning, in both English and Russian. The landmark he found most fascinating was Tower Bridge, and the bridge was all he talked about until he fell asleep again, in Pavel's arms, this time a little after four.

The fourth day, she spent the morning in meetings with Yuri and managed to catch a glimpse of Dom walking through the lobby with a group of men in expensive-looking suits. His was slim fit, gray, and he'd worn it with a striped blue silk tie tucked into the vest. When their eyes met, his had lit up. Actually lit up. He'd then smiled and winked before they'd continued walking in separate directions.

That same afternoon, she and Pavel took Nikolai around the playgrounds in Hyde Park. They'd spent so much time doing what his grandparents wanted, they decided to spend the afternoon doing what he wanted. It turned out to be a learning experience for him, as there were children of varying backgrounds present, so he'd had to communicate with them in the only language they all shared—English. Currently, Pavel was pushing him on the swings while the two of them chatted about Tower Bridge. As she watched them, her mind eventually replaced Pavel with Dom and Nikolai with a little curly-haired girl. The image lingered for less than five seconds.

That was even *more* dangerous territory.

Her phone rang, and, smiling, she brought it to her ear. "Who gave you my number?"

"Doesn't matter," Dom said, a grin in his voice. "What are you up to?"

"Me and Pavel are at the park with Nikolai. They're playing. I'm watching. What are *you* up to?"

"I have roughly two minutes between meetings."

"And you called me?"

"I wanted to hear your voice."

Her temperature rose a few degrees.

"But it doesn't look like we'll get snack time in with how much our schedules keep alternating." Someone called his name, and he told them he'd be right there. "What about tonight? I have time tonight."

"I'm working on something for Yuri tonight," she said.

She wasn't.

"Fuck, you've got to be shitting me." The person called out again. "Look, I have to go, but I'll call you later. We'll figure this out."

She'd taken Colin's advice. "Mama" had to get back in the game, put herself out there, so the night before her flight, she'd searched for local singles groups in London around Westminster. Tonight, a few from the group had arranged to meet at a pub off Parliament Street, less than ten minutes from the hotel by car, and she'd chatted pretty heavily with one man in the group all week—Wesley Langstaff.

"We will," she said. "Have a good meeting."

Dom groaned. "It's a meeting, but thank you."

They hung up.

Dom's charm had worn her down, and not sleeping with him was the very last stone holding up her crumbling wall of defense. Crossing that threshold would mean definitively throwing the entire op into the toilet, since sex with Dom wouldn't be like sex with anyone else. Sex with Dom would ruin her, and she would enjoy the ruination.

Pavel headed over, a drowsy Nikolai on his back. When they were in front of her, she smoothed Nikolai's hair until his eyes shut. Things she'd never imagined for herself had begun taking up space in her thoughts. Though it wasn't much space, it was more than she'd ever granted those "things" before.

From what she'd learned by decoding conversations with Ludmila and Manya, Pavel had met Dom on a few occasions. But, like everyone else, it appeared Yuri had led him to believe that Dom was a nephew borne from one of Yuri's father's numerous extramarital affairs. Considering how little Dom resembled Yuri, no one had questioned it, and no one ever questioned Yuri. However, she didn't believe Yuri had let her know, right off the bat, that Dom was his son for absolutely no reason. Right now, she simply wasn't in a position yet to do anything about it.

"We should head back," Pavel said, switching to cradling Nikolai in his arms. "Nikolai's done for the night. If there's any pressure from Yuri or Kat to do any further activities, I'll cover for you."

She nodded.

Pavel dropped Nikolai off at his grandparents' suite. Eija went to hers and checked in with Colin and April. Their video chat took a few hours, so right after it ended, she hurried to the shower. While actively trying to not think of Dom—which the chat had made it ten times harder to avoid—she swiped on some makeup and slipped into a long-sleeved body suit, a skirt, leggings, and thigh-high boots.

Pavel met her downstairs to let her know she wouldn't be

walking or taking public transit, so she allowed Mikhail to drive her the five minutes to the pub.

Only Mikhail left afterward.

"I'll blend in," Pavel said, following her inside. As if the six-foot-four beast of a man wearing all black could blend in anywhere.

"Will you hold my coat, then?" she asked.

He nodded, and she draped it over his forearm.

"Also, whatever you do, don't tell Dominik I'm here."

But also...tell him.

Pavel neither agreed nor disagreed.

Inside the pub, at the bar, she spotted a few familiar faces. The group waved, kissed her cheek, and hugged her like they'd known each other for years. A server announced their table was ready, and they headed over, chatter rising above low pop music.

Eija sipped on all virgin cocktails, having already explained that she watched a rich guy's grandson for a living and had to remain clearheaded. The group was a lovely mix of backgrounds, cultures, and personalities, but someone was missing.

"E?"

He looked exactly like his photos—perfectly coiffed blond hair, warm brown eyes, and a clean-shaven face. Tonight, he wore a tailored designer suit.

"Wesley. Nice to meet in person." She looked him over. "Very nice."

His face flushed. "Thank you. And you are *absolutely*

gorgeous. Your photos and our video chats didn't do you justice."

Wesley sat next to her in the seat the group had deliberately left vacant. They ordered burgers to keep it casual. She had another virgin cocktail, and he had red wine.

"E, you are...I don't even have the words, love. I'm speechless." He reached to tuck her hair behind her ear.

She moved out of the way and pointed to the dance floor. "Want to dance or are you shy?"

"Not shy at all, gorgeous. Lead the way."

He tipped back his glass, and she finished her drink.

They whittled out a spot beneath the lights, and he wrapped one arm around her waist. As the song selections changed, they progressed from dancing with a modest gap between them to grinding against each other. When her ass touched his pelvis and she felt the unmistakable bulge, she knew he was ready.

"Hey," she leaned toward his ear, "you want to get out of here?"

He stared at her, blinking, like he hadn't heard correctly. "What's that, love?"

"Sex, Wesley. Do you want to leave so we can have sex?"

His eyes bugged. "Yes."

They used the crowd as cover to slip through the front door, him probably assuming she was hiding from the group instead of the behemoth's eyes she felt tracking her every movement. She didn't release Wesley until they reached the end of the block where she pushed him into an alcove between two buildings.

"Um, I have a place we can go inste—"

"So Colin really thought I'd need you here with me?" She pushed him against the wall. "Did he think I wouldn't make you?"

He dropped the accent and groaned, eyes squeezing shut. "Fuck."

"Wesley *Langstaff*? Really? Could you have been more obvious? All of you male agents with your dick names. It's like you're obsessed." She jabbed her hand in the direction of the pub. "I have security with me at all times. I'm an asset to the Sokolovs. So, the reason you're here isn't because Colin was concerned about my safety on a different continent. He's concerned I might screw up again."

"Langstaff" leaned his head back against the wall. "I see your point, but that's not how he put it. He said you needed extra eyes. I'm a precaution."

"What's your name?"

"Dan."

Her right brow shot up.

"Daniel Pembroke," he clarified. "I'm new to the field. I used to be an analyst."

"How much do you know about what's going on?"

"Only as much as is necessary."

She studied him. "And you're supposed to watch out for me."

"Yes. That's it. I swear."

"You still want to fuck?"

"What?" The word was airy, and even though she wasn't pressed against him, she stepped back to give him more room to breathe. "Like...sex?"

"Yes, Daniel Pembroke. I'm still trying to fuck. Are you interested?"

His head nearly rocked off his shoulders. "Yes. One-hundred times, yes. Oh my God, you're so hot, Eija. I can't believe this is actually going to happen. *I'm* going to fuck Officer Barrett."

He wasn't, but he'd learn soon enough.

Hands once again tangled, she stepped from between the shadow of the buildings. Daniel suddenly tugged on her arm, and she turned around.

"What's the proble—*oh shit.*"

Chapter Eighteen

Dom dragged off his tie, unbuttoned his blazer, and fell backward on the hotel bed. This shit was exhausting. He'd thought all the crap he'd had to do and learn when he'd first arrived in Moscow was intense, but he couldn't see himself going to this many meetings to talk about virtually nothing more than one week out of the year. According to Yuri, this high up, getting their hands dirty was a rarity. Yet, he would have preferred spending his time trying to make someone talk through various torture mechanisms than hear the words synergy, *biz-ops,* or strategic partnership.

Ever again.

It was a good thing he hadn't made plans with Eija. The meeting had finished four hours later than originally expected. He'd wanted to eat dinner while looking at *her,* not a man forty years older than he was with a twenty-eight-year-old wife who sucked off the bellhop whenever her husband wasn't looking.

Their conversation in the library had happened, and he understood why Eija wanted them to cool things off, but he wasn't getting married—a wife was being tossed at him. *Eija* was who he wanted and who he thought about, all day and every day. *Eija* would find a way to make him laugh to ease the monotony that had imprisoned him for the last twelve hours.

His phone chimed, and it was late for Pavel to be calling him.

"What does Miss K mean to you?" Pavel asked, side-stepping a greeting.

Dom sat up. "I don't understand the question."

"Is she important?"

"We're...friends."

"Will it bother you if she spends the night with this man?"

"*What* man?"

Dom grabbed his tie, his brain processing only snatches of Pavel's reply. Jealous rage had tossed a rope around his neck, dragging him out of his suite all the way down to the lobby. They had a few cars at their disposal at the hotel, and he crushed the ticket in the valet attendant's palm, Pavel still on the phone.

"What's she doing now?"

"Gyrating," Pavel said. "They look stuck together, almost."

He was going to kill her. First, whoever the asshole was, and then Eija. She had every right to go out and drink and dance and sleep with whoever she wanted to but, right now...fuck that.

If she'd simply give in and fuck *him* like it was obvious they both wanted, maybe then she wouldn't be a prisoner to that libido of hers. And he'd be able to take showers again that didn't involve nursing hard-ons that could crack diamonds.

The valet attendant pulled up with a silver Mercedes AMG. The pub wasn't far from the hotel, but he drove like it was on the other side of town, and he only had five minutes to get to Eija before a bomb strapped to her chest went off.

He parked the car in front of the pub, the engine still growling as he hopped out. Pavel met him at the curb.

"Where is she?"

Pavel pointed down the sidewalk. "There, about twelve meters, on the left. Want me to wait?"

"Yes. For spinal fluid clean-up."

He spotted her slipping from an alcove, holding some tall, blond fucker's hand. He plucked the tie from his jacket, crept up behind the blond, and wrapped it around the man's neck. A flick of his wrist yanked the blond backward, fingers scrambling in a futile attempt to dislodge the silk from his trachea.

Eija turned around. "What's the proble—oh shit."

"Oh, shit is right," he growled, forearm flexing. "Eija, *what the fuck* are you doing?"

She bit her lower lip. "Nothing."

"Pull your lip out of your teeth."

It popped out.

"I'm going to kill you. You know that, right?"

"Yes." She nodded, and her eyes darted from him to the man whose windpipe he was crushing. "But just me, okay?"

The blond tapped his forearm.

"Let him go, D—" She squeezed her eyelid. "Please let him go."

Why couldn't she say his name? Had she told this fucker about him? If so, who'd she say he was?

Women like Eija were dynamite. What else could explain why an otherwise levelheaded man, notwithstanding the whole mafia leader and killer bit, would chase a woman down in the middle of the night when she'd turned down every one of his advances since they'd run into each other again?

The blond's taps turned into frantic tugs and scratches.

"Let him go," Eija repeated. "I'm still fucking him tonight."

Dom released. "What the fuck did you just say?"

"It got you to let him go, didn't it?"

The blond stumbled forward, gasping and coughing, and situated himself behind Eija. One of his hands hovered near her elbow, and Dom watched closely to make sure it didn't connect. If so much as a fraction of the man's palm touched her skin, he'd shoot him. Consequences be damned. He was running on little to no sleep with too much shit on his plate and a desire for the woman standing across from him matched only by insanity.

"So you're lying to me now?" he asked her. It was in the form of a question, but he wasn't asking one. "You told me you were working on something for Yuri."

"I was...not," she confessed. "I lied."

"Why?"

She gestured to the man quivering behind her.

"I suggest you get the fuck out of here," Dom warned. "If

you're trying to get pussy tonight, I'll kill you before you get hers."

Eija spoke over her shoulder. *"Wesley...go."*

"Are you sure?" the blond had the nerve to ask.

Dom started forward, but she pushed the other man until he got the hint and scrambled off down the sidewalk. She then had the audacity to watch him go.

Dom grabbed her waist, hoisted her into the air upside down, and headed back to the car. Pavel, who'd been on his way over, pivoted and headed in the same direction.

"Bridge," Dom said. He tossed Eija in the car and got in beside her. "If not Westminster, Lambeth or Vauxhall. Whichever one's got the fewest witnesses."

Pavel nodded, positioned himself behind the wheel, and drove off.

Eija, chest heaving, plastered herself to the seat. "Dom, why are we going to a bridge?"

"To throw you off it, sweetheart," he said.

Her bottom lip snapped back between her teeth. Large pupils darkened her irises, her eyelids lower than usual. When Pavel stopped at Westminster, he pulled her out of the car and she lazily resisted, but he'd already known she would. He'd already figured out why that lip was back in her mouth.

"Eija." He nudged her, backward and stumbling, to the side of the bridge. "This is a turn on for you, isn't it? You'd like it if I fucked you against the side of this bridge, wouldn't you?"

"No." The word barely made it out of her mouth. "I would...not."

"Why then," he grabbed her shoulders and spun her so her stomach pressed against the stone, "are you at London pubs with motherfuckers who can't fuck you like you want me to?"

"Dom, please. Use less aggressive words. I'm on the verge of...bursting."

He reached around her and maneuvered through what felt like seventeen layers of clothing before the palm of his hand met the warmth of her skin. It was cold out, but she'd worn more than enough layers to battle the London weather. The blond would have found Atlantis before he found Eija's pussy. This was what she'd been hoping for, him to show up in the middle of her date, guns blazing and psychotic.

"Eija, I can't do this. I *cannot* stop thinking about you. When you're happy, I'm on a fucking cloud. When you're not, I do mental gymnastics trying to figure out how to make shit better for you."

"Dom—"

"I'll keep busting into pubs and strangling *anybody* who thinks they're going to see even your naked upper arm. I swear to God, I won't stop. I want you, Eija. I don't know what that means, but I don't really care either."

"And I want you too," she said, finding his unoccupied hand and braiding their fingers together.

"I'm not just talking about sex." He extended his middle finger until it landed on her slit. "I want you. Only you."

Now that some of his anger had dissolved, vulnerability returned. He'd never felt this way before, never considered compromising the integrity of an entire organization over a woman. Not a single one from his past had ever crept into his brain, a tapeworm sucking away all his logic and common sense. She was funny, sweet, beautiful...and there was something light about her. Something that told him, underneath all that sex appeal, she desired someone in her life who wouldn't bobble her heart.

"Eija..." He spoke close to her ear, his finger still nowhere near where he knew she ached for it. "Tell me you can be without me."

She turned her head to kiss him, but he pulled back each time she tried.

"Tell me you haven't been thinking about me." He pressed into her from behind, slid two fingers lower. "Tell me you don't want me, and I'll stop. I'll never touch you again. I'll stop daydreaming about," he caught her earlobe between his teeth, licked the shell of her ear, "making you scream again."

Which he did all the time.

All damn day.

"Why does it have to be this way?" she asked, shaking her head. "Honestly, I want to be with you too."

"Then let's be together."

"For how long?"

"However long you want me."

"That's not realistic." She angled her hips, and when the pads of his fingertips brushed her clit, she purred. "It would only be a couple of months with you as mine."

"It can be longer if you want it to be."

It was wishful thinking. He had his orders, so all they really had was the next two months. Two months that he would make count.

He spread her lips with his fingers and stroked her there, against the bridge, underneath the cover of darkness. Instead of moaning, she released a series of quiet gasps as if surprised each time a jolt of pleasure rushed through her. When she tried to rock her hips, to match his rhythm, he held her still. She'd made him lose control, and he wanted it back. This wasn't a climax to share.

She went stiff.

He held her in place.

Warmth became heat on his fingers, his hand. And, as she came back down, he kissed her cheek and temple.

"Dom, can I kiss you now? Please?"

She turned around, and he allowed their lips to connect. He swept his tongue inside her mouth, first reacquainting himself with the taste of her he'd gone without for too long. Then he kissed her fully. Hard. Until she twisted and squirmed and he could tell that she was floating as high as he was. She kissed him back, insistent tongue like she thought *this* was punishment for denying her earlier, and he tasted the words that, had she not said them earlier, he would still know.

"Are you still going to throw me over?" she asked.

He picked her up.

She shrieked, arms locking around him.

"Did you eat?" he asked, lowering her back down to the ground.

"Half of an okay burger."

"Have dinner with me."

"Kiss me again."

He pinched her bottom lip between his teeth and released. "Not until you agree to have dinner with me."

"I agree to have dinner with you, Dominik Sokolov."

They ate at a nearby Japanese restaurant. Eija laughed and smiled more than he'd ever seen her. He ordered their entrees while she picked dessert—a fluffy cheesecake slice with powdered sugar and berries. He only took his eyes off her every once in a while to lock gazes with the man in the back corner that, for right now, he wouldn't give two shits about. Right now, Yuri Sokolov was nothing but a distraction.

Chapter Nineteen

Eija leaned up on her elbow and looked down into Dom's face. Before coming down to his suite, they'd stopped at hers so she could grab her headscarf and toothbrush. He'd let her walk for most of the way but scooped her up into his arms when they stepped off the elevators.

She'd changed into one of his shirts, and he'd stripped down to nothing but his boxer briefs, the band lying flat on his stomach and highlighting the toned muscles in his thighs.

Then they'd climbed into bed.

And promptly fell asleep.

His suite was on the other side of the hotel, so the Thames peeked through the large windows next to the bed. She'd asked him to leave the drapes open so she could watch him like she did now, moonlight streaming onto his profile and emphasizing the hard lines of his face in contrast with the soft hills of his lips.

As the night had progressed, his eyes had gone from cold steel to stormy droplets humming on a galvanized roof. It was a shame they hid behind his eyelids while he slept, but with all the work he'd put in that week, she was grateful he had this chance to rest.

"You're so beautiful, Dom. I hate that you're so beautiful."

They were getting closer.

He deserved to know the truth.

Telling him now could mean that the fallout later *might* not end in her death. Since she'd never compromised a mission to this magnitude, she wasn't sure what the punishment on Randy's end would be. He'd already threatened that if she didn't execute this operation and stick to their objectives as previously agreed upon, he'd strip her of everything she'd ever attained or hoped to attain. With how hard she'd worked for her accolades, her respect, and even her pension...

Had it been even five years ago, the threat would have held less weight. These days, it was everything.

She went to slip out of bed, but Dom hooked his arm around her middle and dragged her back to him.

"You're so beautiful, Eija," he whispered, dropping a full yet too brief kiss on her mouth. "I hate that you're so beautiful."

They woke up an hour before she had to get ready for another day with Nikolai. He had another long day of meetings. Still, they lay in bed together and watched dawn approach, each stretch of sunlight adding more color to the sky. She lay on his chest, her left hand and his right moving together.

"Dom, why do we do this? Get all worked up and then not sleep together."

"We 'slept' together last night," he teased. "But I wanted to take you to dinner. Be with you. That's pretty much where my focus was."

It was what she'd wanted as well.

However, she also wanted to bang his brains out.

"I've been going through my schedule, looking for things I can move around just to find time to spend with you," he added. "I enjoy being with you, Eija. That's the truth. I mean, you can have sex with anybody. Look at Mr. Blond, who you almost got killed last night."

She raised their clasped hands to her face and rubbed the back of his across her cheek. Each pass brought an increasingly intense sensation that steered clear of the region below her belly button. This, she'd never experienced before. Pillow talk. The rumble of a man's deep morning voice. She'd had no plans to sleep with the fake Wesley Langstaff but, for a moment, she imagined what would have happened if she had. What if she'd missed out on this? Dom was somehow warmer before sunrise. The kind of warmth that made people grumble before leaving bed to go to work in the morning.

"You're all talk," she goaded. "You wouldn't have hurt him."

"Try me."

For a split second, she'd forgotten who he was.

"How many times have you done *this?*" He slid his fingers

along hers. "How many times have you spent hours talking over dinner? Falling asleep in the arms of somebody who's satisfied with holding you all night? Somebody who wishes they could hold you every night?"

She'd made sure it never came close to happening. Espionage wasn't glamorous, and it often required lengthy assignments where the only contact she was allowed to have was with designated individuals at specific times. In the recipe for love, secrecy didn't make the cut. It was the CIA where she'd learned, implicitly, the importance of keeping an ice wall around her heart. Over time, she'd mistakenly come to believe she no longer had one.

Flighty, fun, and flirtatious Eija had been borne out of necessity. Without strings attached, there was nothing to trip over. Dom had forced her to see herself as simply *Eija* for the first time in a long time. He'd forced her to slow down, to derive pleasure from good food, laughing, and intimate, nonsexual touches. She'd never known a man tracing her lips could make her heart stop, or that a kiss could both clear and cloud her mind.

"When I'm with you, I feel like a...treasure," she confessed. "And I know how ridiculous that sounds."

He laughed, low and throaty. "It doesn't. It just means I'm doing what I set out to do."

"You're kind of wonderful, Dom."

"Why do you sound surprised?"

"I don't know. I guess I expected you to be charming, but I never expected you to make my heart beat like crazy or be the kind of guy I miss when we're not together. With you, I understand what happy means. I feel it. I think about things that had been pipe dreams eight, twelve months ago. Hell, five years ago."

It took him close to a minute to respond.

"Eija, there's something I have to tell you."

She pushed up off his chest. "This sounds serious."

"It is." He sat back against the headboard and pressed his thumb to his brow. "It's not until right this second that I realized I could lose you after saying this, but I don't feel right not telling you."

She froze.

He wouldn't.

He couldn't.

"Eija, I'm a member of the Bratva. More specifically, I'm known as the 'prince' of the Bratva."

Her secret was worse. So much worse. He thought she'd walk away from him because of who he was? If he found out all what she'd kept from him, she'd be lucky if she walked away with her life. He kept talking about how much he trusted her, how genuine she'd been with him, and with each word the dagger she'd lodged in his back sank deeper.

"What's the Bratva?"

He paused. "The Russian mafia."

"Mafia? Like crime bosses and things like that?"

"For the most part."

"Does that mean Yuri's the king of the, what was it? Bratva?" Now, she was making herself sick.

"Yes, but he thinks it's time for me to take over."

"Why?"

"I'm bound by blood." He let his head fall back. "It's what I have to do. By all means, I don't want to. I'm pretty sure the Bratva's responsible for my mother's death."

"You mean because Yuri's first wife killed Aani?"

A smile drew light to his face. "You remembered her name."

"It's important to you. Of course, I do."

He stared at her, wordless for a moment.

"On the outside, Yuri's a charmer," he explained. "But there's more to the man underneath. Rage. Secrets."

Colin's voice in her head yelled for her to ask Dom what secrets he was referring to. Was it what she'd photographed on Yuri's desk? Was it something else?

If she asked, Dom would tell her more.

He'd tell her everything.

He trusted her.

And, because he trusted her, she asked, "Do you love your father?"

"It's complicated. Deep down, I want to make him proud, but I also want to kill him. I'm convinced he's a narcissist without the ability to truly care about anyone, whether it's me or Nikolai. I've spent years trying to expose the man behind the mask, but it feels like I've gotten nowhere." He slid a hooked finger along her jawline. "Anyway, what do you think? Can you see yourself with the son of a killer? A killer himself?"

"You've...killed people?"

"Yes."

So have I.

I work for Interpol.

I planted a device in your necklace, but I hide it in various places and say it's Yuri.

I'm the m—

"Dom, everyone has skeletons."

His thumb slid along the border of her bottom lip. "I have a whole graveyard, Eija."

"I still want this with you. I want more than this, if I'm being honest. Back in Grenada, it stung when you left. This second chance with you, it's been...unforgettable."

It was one of the few truths she could grant him.

"Yuri came to get me," he said, lying down and coaxing her back to his chest. "I had no choice but to leave with him. If I didn't, I wasn't sure he wouldn't hurt you."

Why would he have protected her from the Bratva if they hadn't even known each other that well back then? And the fact that he'd protected her, essentially saving her life, didn't she owe it to him to do the same?

"You protected me."

He nodded. "Yep."

"Why?"

"Because it stung to leave you too."

She squeezed him. Then, tears came.

"Dom, I'm a terrible person."

"What?" He closed her into his embrace. "No, baby. You're far from it."

"When you left, I thought horrible things about you."

Like how I wanted to find you, toss you in a cell, and leave you there for days without food or water. I'd dream up new and inventive ways to torture you. You weren't human to me, Dom. Not then.

"Eija, are you upset that I left, or are you really upset because you now know who I am?" he asked. "You can tell me. I didn't expect you to take this easily. I mean, part of you probably knew something was amiss when I told you Yuri killed his first wife. Then I showed up bloody at your place. Shit's not normal."

A laugh sputtered between the tears. "I guess."

"I know it's a lot, but you've been honest with me about how you feel and what Dostavka means to you. Everything, Eija. You've been honest with me about everything. I owed it to you to tell you this."

A second, stronger wave of tears came.

"Eija...what would make you feel better? Tell me, and it's yours."

The truth.

She would only feel better once she told him every last bit of the truth.

"Now I know you're really upset." He brushed his lips over the top of her head. "I was expecting you to answer that question with any word or phrase related to cunnilingus."

Another laugh weaved its way through her sadness. "Mr. Sokolov, I don't know how I'm going to let you go."

She didn't mean let him go to another woman. She didn't

know how she was supposed to let him go to Interpol. Let him go to be tortured, knowing he'd never speak out against his father. It was their code, and he felt like he owed Yuri. They'd torture him to death.

"Let's not think about that right now," he said.

She nodded.

Poor Dom.

He had absolutely no idea he was a killer lying in bed with a snake.

Chapter Twenty

Dom's schedule intensified, and Yuri decided he wanted Nikolai to see even more attractions, so he added extra stops to the itinerary. Nikolai had fallen asleep halfway through the day, but Eija and Pavel had gone to the locations Yuri had assigned to avoid going back to the hotel before he expected them.

Later that evening, she'd had dinner with Yuri, Ekaterina, and business associates of theirs in the same room where Dom had sat, a few tables away. Each time she'd looked up, they'd ended up staring at each other. It was hard, them being close enough to touch but unable to.

It felt intentional.

Dinner had ended with Dom at his table. As she'd passed it, she'd overheard the group say they had a lot of work left to do, so they'd have to move the meeting into a conference room. They planned to be there for the rest of the night and maybe into the early morning, and at that point, it had felt like punishment.

Now, it was a little past midnight on their last full day in London. She'd showered, slipped into a nightgown, talked to Colin, and then stayed up, hoping to be awake when Dom was done to at least talk to him on the phone. But her eyelids felt hooked by a fisherman's line. This was a level of exhaustion she'd rarely experienced, and she'd been in a hostage situation where she was sleep-deprived for seventy-two hours.

Her phone buzzed.

Dom: I'm outside your door.
Too tired to knock.

She swung heavy feet over the side of the mattress and dragged herself over to open it. Dom leaned against the jamb, eyes closed.

"Hi."

His lids barely rose. "Hey."

"You didn't have to come tonight."

"Yes, I did. I had to see you."

Instead of the suit she'd last seen him in, he now wore a long-sleeved black T-shirt and gray sweatpants.

And he smelled like soap.

She took his hand and walked him inside, all the way over to the bed where she undressed him, raising his shirt over his head. He stepped out of his shoes but left his socks on. To get him out of the sweatpants, she had him lie on the bed, untied the string at the front, and slid them off over his legs. His neck was damp, and she didn't want to believe he'd rushed through a shower just to come see her.

"Did you eat?" she asked.

He yawned. "You saw me at dinner."

"I mean, after that. Dinner was hours ago."

"I'm not hungry." His eyelids opened to the length of his lashes. "Come here. I've been waiting for this part all day."

"And what part is that?"

"The part where I get to hold you."

Several knots simultaneously tightened in the lowest part of her stomach. "Does your father know this side of you?" she asked, climbing onto the mattress. "You're too sweet to be the head of a crime syndicate."

"It's the difference between business and pleasure. I'm Dom with you. I hope you never have to meet Dominik."

Eventually, she would.

Instead of crawling into his embrace, she tossed one knee over his midsection, her head pointing toward his feet. They were both exhausted, and she wasn't sure if this would even be good or worth it, but she'd left the impression on him back in Grenada that she didn't do *this*.

She lowered the waistband on his underwear.

"Eija, if you suck my dick right now, I'm going to die," he warned, already semi-erect.

"So I shouldn't?"

"I believe it was Nietzsche who said, 'Death is close enough at hand...'"

"Really? You're quoting Nietzsche right now?"

She wrapped her hands around the thick base and first took time to admire his length. She hadn't the chance to appreciate its girth and heft before, as they'd been frantic and crazed from anticipation that had built between them over the course of two weeks. Now, she lightly stroked him with her fingers, tracing the prominent vein that stopped at the base of the swollen tip. Then she squeezed, drawing out a creamy dot. Lowering her head, she licked it away and drew him into her mouth, sucking hard and releasing just in time to catch his thigh muscles relax.

"Are you awake yet?" she asked.

He responded, but she was sure he hadn't used actual words.

With the fingers on her left hand wrapped tight around the thickest part of him, she used her right to cup and massage his sac. When she took him in her mouth again, he dragged out a long moan, sending a tight pulse to her nipples. The corners of her mouth stretched, dribbling as she took him to the back of her throat, going deeper with each pass. The slurping sounds she made, combined with his hisses and curses, drowned out the rest of the noise in the room.

"Eija..." He hooked one hand around her right thigh. "*Fuck, baby.*"

The middle of her panties went from damp to drenched.

"How did I know this would turn you on?" he asked, pushing up her nightgown and chasing his fingers over the wet spot.

She let him slip from her mouth. "The fact that I can hear

how good I'm making you feel makes me want to do this more often."

"Oh, no," he said, voice light with sarcasm. "Please don't."

She laughed and swallowed him again.

He tugged the middle of her panties aside and slid his thumb over her clit. She moaned, which came out as a hum with him deep in her throat. Spurred on by her response, he slipped two fingers inside her. As the pressure of climax built, she increased her pace.

Then her hips were in the air.

When her knees met the bed again, they were on his pillow.

Right.

The pussy monster.

She looked down but had to look away when she saw his tongue between her legs, pink and lapping and licking. Soon it became a competition, who could make the other come first. She gagged and swallowed, but he had her latched to him, arm locked at her lower back. He took his time, dragging his tongue along her slit, sucking at her labia, slipping his tongue inside her, and soothing every spot she ached. Right when her orgasm crashed into her, he stiffened and released in her mouth.

Orgasms, especially when exhausted people had them, usually meant sleep.

Their breaths slowed.

She brought her knee back over his middle, turned, and sat back on her legs, facing him. He reached along the side of the bed for his pants, and she slipped out of the panties.

"I'm going to be tired as hell in all my meetings tomorrow."

She knew the answer, but still asked, "Why?"

He came back with a condom, and she snorted a laugh. Now, instead of *his* hands shaking like they'd done back in Grenada, she had to hide hers under her legs so he didn't see how nervous she was. It had never happened before, so she wasn't sure what to do with them.

The minute the condom was in place, she climbed over him again, positioned the head of his somehow already revived erection, and slid down until she could go no further. He mumbled something in Russian, too low for her to pick up on it.

"How are you still this hard?" She squeezed her thighs, raising and lowering on top of him. "I'm...sorry I...made you...wait."

He pivoted his hips, catching her rhythm, and lapsed into another stream of low, coarse Russian. Those eyes of his, poisonous and addicting, held her in place as firmly as his fingers sinking into her hips. Each strike of their bodies coming together sent a jolt of pleasure through her and made her breasts jump, her nipples rubbing against the smooth fabric of her nightgown.

"Dom, can I have you on top of me?" What she couldn't bring herself to ask was if he could hold her while he was inside her. If he could lock her in, make her feel his hardness, his warmth. Make her feel his trust.

They changed positions.

Another night, she'd ask for fast and hard. This, full and slow, their bodies touching and eyes connected, was what she'd needed for a long time.

"I missed you," he said, his voice quiet and straining.

There it was, the beginning of her heart slowly becoming his to do with it whatever he pleased, even if it was to throw it away once everything was out in the open.

"I missed you too."

There was no sense in holding anything back now. She didn't know how this was going to end, but it would end. It was better that he knew how she felt. One day, when they looked at each other from the other side of a dinky plastic table, he would doubt whether she'd truly felt the way she said. She could only hope, even with that doubt, he'd never forget this moment.

"And Dom, I'm sorry I lied."

"You didn't lie to me, baby." He tucked his hand under her hips, angling them for her to take him deeper. "You never lied to me."

Eija cried out, back arching and grip around him tightening. To draw out her orgasm further, she squeezed his length. A slew of curse words spilled from his lips as he came on a deep stroke, lodged as far as he could go inside her body.

She held him in place.

He didn't try to move.

"Dom, will you really be mine for these next two months?" Then, at the end of it, she'd do her job before Randy or Colin did it for her. At least, if she retained control, she could keep him somewhat safe.

"Will you?" he countered.

For two months.

And possibly longer.

"Yes."

"I'm serious, Eija. I don't want anyone else."

"Neither do I."

He pulled out, disposed of the condom, and fell asleep with her on his chest, both arms wrapped around her.

Chapter Twenty-One

"Gentlemen, I think I'm going to have to skip out on the rest of this meeting."

The men looked up at Dom.

"And those for the rest of the afternoon."

"Do you have somewhere more important to be?" William Thorpe asked, frowning, his silver brows like wolf fur.

On the outside, he was the CEO of one of the largest asset management firms in the world. However, his money was even bloodier than Yuri's. The group of men, all over the age of seventy, probably believed their little cushy set up hid the fact that they were all sociopaths in poorly tailored designer clothes.

Dom nodded. "Yes. I do."

"Yuri wouldn't have left like this."

"Do I look like Yuri?"

"Actually, you don't. I've always wondered if he shouldn't

have done a second paternity test, verified the purity of the Sokolov lineage. Yuri's so eager for a son, he's blinded by your ineptitude."

Dom grabbed a steak knife from the tabletop while William continued to flap his lips.

"Yuri would be better off putting one of his daughters at the head of Sokol Incorporated. We've heard the story. Your mother was some whore. Her father was a junkie. The funny thing is, I never knew Arabs could be whores. That's what she was, wasn't she? One of those Arabs?"

Dom studied the stout, ruddy-faced little man. All of them, every last one, stumbled over their own feet or choked on Yuri's dick for the little bit of power he drizzled their way. But that power didn't give any of them, especially this sweat-soaked motherfucker, the right to talk about his mother any way they pleased. No amount of money in the world would ever grant them the right.

He wrapped his elbow around William's neck and jammed the knife through his hand until the steel tip met wooden tabletop. William cried out and looked around for help, but no one so much as leaned toward him.

"I don't like when people talk about my mother, who's *Persian.*" Dom released him, removed a cigar cutter from his pocket, and grabbed the other hand. Eija didn't like cigars, so he didn't smoke them anymore, but he kept the cutter on him because of a movie he'd watched when he was a kid. "Instead of talking about my mother, you'd be better suited worrying about why your wife is upstairs, right now, sucking the twenty-one-year-old bellhop's dick."

Dom slipped the cutter over the man's middle finger and snapped it shut, taking a couple inches of the digit with it. Yuri entered the room just as he tossed the cutter onto the table with the stub embedded in its jaw.

"Say what the fuck you want about me, but there are two women in this world who, if you say the wrong thing about them, will get you killed. You're right. I'm *not* Yuri Sokolov but, right now, I bet you wish I was." He dipped his bloodied fingers in William's half-full glass of brandy, wiped them off on a hotel napkin, and headed for the exit. Just before he exited, Yuri gripped his forearm.

"Is one of those women Miss K?" Yuri asked. "Careful about how you answer me."

Dom pried Yuri's fingers from his arm. "If I do."

"We have a way of doing things."

"Your point?"

"You have to be strategic about this transition. You can't have a woman like Miss K as your wife. I understand that, as a man, you can't help but find her intriguing."

Dom's teeth ground together.

"And she's an exquisite woman," Yuri went on. "But Leah is the power play. We have the ability to align with one of the most powerful families in Europe. It's all I've wanted for you, ever since you were a boy."

"Then why the whole farce?" Dom asked. "Why the whole

Dostavka bullshit if you've already preordained who I'll end up with? Why not just tell everyone, now, who I really am?"

"Because you still have a choice, and there's a time and place for everything."

"If I really had a choice, I'd be able to pick the woman I want."

Yuri's voice took on a tone Dom had never heard him use. "Listen to me, son. I understand that you have held a chip on your shoulder for me for years because of what happened to your mother. A part of me regrets telling you the truth, but I'd assumed you were man enough to deal with it."

Dom huffed out a laugh. "I was sixteen."

"Do you know what I was doing when I was sixteen?" Yuri flipped up his thumb. "Working my ass off, day and night. Preparing for the role I'd already known I would play being the only male among my sisters. I wasn't sucking my thumb and running to my aunt to take care of me."

Nearly everything that left Yuri's mouth was a lie. There'd been no preparing to head the Bratva; Yuri hadn't even known he would be *in* the Bratva until he was already an adult in his mid-twenties. At sixteen, while Yuri had been lying to him about what had really happened to his mother, who'd *really* forced her into a life of sexual slavery, Dom had been doing his own research. The man could barely talk without a lie spilling from his mouth.

"At least she took care of me," Dom said, stepping forward until he was only a few inches from his father's face. "And, one day, I hope you'll let me do the same."

Then he stepped around Yuri and headed for the exit.

* * *

Dom, tipping back a paper cup of coffee, found Pavel, Eija, and Nikolai once again at Hyde Park. Pavel had gotten Yuri to lighten up and let Nikolai do whatever he wanted on his last day in London, which was to spend the day in the park and eat ice cream for lunch. He was sure Eija hadn't allowed him to only eat ice cream, but she'd definitely granted him the treat. She was the type of person who would, and he'd found himself, more than once, wondering what type of mother she would make. Saying he didn't want children hadn't been a lie, but there was a part of him that wanted to see what their DNA could come up with if it had the chance.

Did that mean he was falling for her?

She smiled at Nikolai waving to her from one of the playground houses, and it caused him to almost miss a step.

Yes.

Definitely.

He dropped the empty cup in a nearby trash bin, crept up behind her, and wrapped his arms around her. She leaned into his embrace, eyes briefly closing.

"What are you doing here?"

"I cut out early to spend time with my woman," he said.

"Okay, caveman." She turned so she could keep one eye on Nikolai while they talked, but Nikolai was with Pavel Volkov. That made him one of the safest kids in the world.

"Me want take woman 'round London." He thumped his chest. "Me want woman with me."

She giggled.

Actually, giggled.

Women only brought out the giggle when they were smitten.

"I can't."

"Actually, you can." He waved to get Pavel's attention. "I've arranged for Nikolai and Pavel to spend the rest of the day together so that you and I can get some time alone."

"And if Yuri finds out?"

"What if he does?" He moved a strand of hair out of her face. It was pretty straightened, and it made the colors stand out even more, but he missed the coils, kinks, and curls. "You have my permission. That's all you need."

"You know Yuri doesn't want us getting close."

"Didn't think you'd picked up on that."

"The all day meetings? The full schedules?" She motioned around. "He probably thinks I'm trying to seduce his sweet, innocent boy with my wicked Caribbean pussy."

Unable to stop himself, he drew her into him and bent to place a kiss on her lips. Surprise moved through him when she wrapped her fingers around the back of his neck and kissed him until propriety made them separate. They were at a park, after all. Had it been an empty park, she would have been in trouble.

"Wicked Caribbean pussy? You know I love it when you recite poetry to me."

Again, she giggled.

Pavel approached, Nikolai on his back. "You're all set, Dominik?"

"Yep. I'll see you back at the hotel."

"You're not coming with us, Miss K?" Nikolai's bottom lip trembled. "You'll be lonely if me and Pavel leave you."

"I'll take care of her," Dom reassured him. "Do you trust me to do that? I know she's important to you."

Nikolai nodded, a wide grin on his face. "I trust you."

The pair walked off, Pavel swinging Nikolai around his body like a figure skater and Nikolai shrieking with delight.

"Does he know?" Eija asked.

"Know what?"

"That Pavel's his father."

She was much more perceptive than he'd given her credit for. Pavel had confided in him that he'd had an affair with Yuri's middle daughter, but Sonya had been seeing another man at the time who she'd told that *he* was Nikolai's father. Like her, that man had succumbed to addiction. Around his first birthday, as Nikolai's face changed, Pavel had secretly had his paternity tested.

"He does not," Dom said. "And Pavel prefers it that way. He feels like, with the secret, he's better able to keep him safe."

"Seems to be a lot of that going around." She looked up at him, shielding her eyes from the sun. "There are photos of you at the penthouse, but nothing about them stands out. I guess it's what Yuri had to do to shelter the mysterious *Bratva* prince."

Damn it.

He loved the way she said the word Bratva now, all confident and with the roughness of his native language. He had a treasure hunt planned for them around the city, but if she kept talking that way, they wouldn't make it through half.

"In this line of work," he looked at where Pavel and Nikolai walked, "it's sometimes necessary to keep family under wraps, especially if that family is vulnerable."

"Like a child?" she asked. "Or maybe...someone elderly or disabled?"

"Precisely."

"So why reveal the prince *now?*"

He took her hand, and they headed in the opposite direction. "If there was one thing I knew, Eija, it was that this life was always going to find me. The funniest part about it is, my father had tried and tried for a son, but when he finally got one, it was with someone he couldn't care less about."

"Did Yuri hate Aani?"

"Not even." Dom glanced over his shoulder, around the park. "Hate is just about as strong as love. You have to care to hate. She was property. Something to be used."

To be bought and sold.

"I know your way of picking a wife is archaic," Eija began, "but if you hadn't come along, couldn't one of Yuri's daughters take over?"

They crossed the street with a large group of people.

"Not now. There are female mafia heads, but the Bratva isn't ready for something like that. Maybe my daughter will be the first."

She wrinkled her brows. "You don't want children. Did you forget your conversation with Mila the Lovely?"

"Not even I remembered her name."

"Her dress reminded me of salsa."

He laughed and leaned down to kiss her, needing to feel her lips on his even for a moment. "I don't want children with her," he said. "But I could be persuaded to have at least one with the right woman."

"Just say it, Dom." She rolled her eyes. "You want me to 'sire' your 'heir.'"

He picked her up and threatened to toss her into a fountain in the middle of the square. She latched onto him and begged him not to, laughing, and he realized he liked her like this. He liked carefree Eija just as much as he liked sultry Eija. To hear her shriek and laugh, especially since she didn't seem like a woman who shrieked unless she was climaxing, brought him a deranged amount of joy.

They started their treasure hunt at the National Portrait Gallery, and she was shocked that he'd been serious about what he'd planned for them for the rest of the afternoon. They were on the hunt for The Red Queen, and it would be three to four hours of them going about London looking for clues that would lead them to the iconic *Alice in Wonderland* character. It was one of the most interesting and creative ways he could think of to make up for all he hadn't had time to experience with her, in one day.

Their first stop was inside the National Portrait Gallery, where they had to get a clue from a random worker. The clue turned out to be a riddle written on the back of a pocket watch cutout.

"Cultures clash, green fields," Eija read. "I might be over three hundred years old, but I'm no L-7."

His brows wrinkled. "Isn't L-7 from the nineties? It means—"

"Square." She paced in front of him and then came to an abrupt stop. "Dom, look up when Leicester Square was founded."

"I know that off the top of my head. Sixteen-seventy."

"Baby, you're as smart as you are handsome." She squeezed him, and he leaned down for a kiss. "Okay, enough loving. Let's go!"

By the time he turned around, she was already through the doors.

They bound from location to location—Westminster Cathedral, Green Park, in front of Buckingham Palace, Princess Di's Memorial Fountain, a random H&M—and her excitement grew each time she found a clue. When someone looked at her like she'd lost her marbles, he looked at them like he would shove those same marbles somewhere only a surgeon could retrieve them.

There was a planned break in the middle of their hunt, so they stopped at a tavern for a burger, fish & chips, and beer. Eija had gone for pineapple juice, and he reminded himself to find out if it had to do with Yuri checking for drugs on a too-frequent basis. Father or not, he wouldn't let him treat Eija like *she* was the criminal in this equation.

She couldn't stop talking about what she thought their next clue would be and, with every word she spoke, Dom realized he was definitely in love with this woman.

"Ready to get back out?" he asked, although the answer was obvious.

"Yes!" She sucked down the rest of her drink. "Dom, this is one of the best days I've ever had in my life. Thank you. I needed this today."

"Your whole life?" He covered his heart with his right hand. "I'm undone, *dorogaya*."

"I've made it all the way to 'darling'? You must really like me."

Little did she know, he'd left "like" back at Buckingham Palace and picked up love at the intersection of Downing and Parliament Street. One day, they would return with their grand-children and tell them the story about how Grandma and Pop fell in love in London.

Maybe.

Hopefully.

Someone walked by, set a petit four on their table, and scurried off. "Eat Me" was written in white icing on the pink top, and Eija looked up at him, wide eyed.

"Dom...it's the cake from *Alice in Wonderland*."

He was *definitely* in trouble.

Hijacking the dostavka had been the dominant theme of his dreams these days, but he wasn't sure how Eija would feel if he asked her to sign on as his wife. They'd only just agreed to see each other, *and* their agreement had come with conditions.

241

Going from "be mine for two months" to "be mine forever" was serious fine print.

"Hey, Sokolov." She tapped the table. "Let's go."

The second part of their hunt took them around Trafalgar Square, to Madame Tussaud's, all the way back to Downing Street, across the Waterloo Bridge, and then back across the Thames via the Westminster Bridge, ending at Big Ben. By the end, they were wiped out, but she was happy. Everything was fine as long as she was happy.

They had dinner in Soho and took a black cab to the hotel, Eija asleep against his shoulder. When they reached the front of the Havre, he woke her up with his lips against her forehead. She released his hand as they walked inside, but he didn't care if anyone saw them. Not holding her hand or kissing her in the middle of the lobby, that was for Eija. Had it been up to him, everyone would know what she meant to him before they returned to Russia.

They stopped in front of his suite's door.

"I'm going to run to my room to get my stuff," she said, her pinky hooked around his. "I'll be right back."

He nodded.

She started toward the elevator, but he tugged her back and crushed her to him, claiming her lips. It wasn't until she was breathless that he let up.

"Let's try this again." She licked her lips. "Five minutes. I swear."

Again, he nodded.

She started off.

He pulled her back, pushed her against the wall, and moved his mouth over hers. One hand slid under her top and the bottom of her bra. When his fingers found her tight right nipple, he plucked, and she nearly melted into the wall.

"Dom."

"Hmm?" He dragged his tongue along her neck. "What's wrong?"

"Five minutes."

"Bring everything. All your stuff."

He plucked.

She hissed, fingers sinking into his shirt, and gave in. "Okay. All my stuff."

He released her.

This time, when he dragged her back, she whined.

"Dom, come on."

"What was that?" he asked. "That noise you made just now."

"Shut it."

He mimicked it, a high-pitched sort of squeal-snort. *"Dom..."*

"Stop it or I won't come back."

"Like I won't just come get you...*Eija.*"

He reached for her, but she ducked out of his grasp and hurried to the elevator.

"It's cute," he called after her. "It's like a flirty, congested pig."

Eija unlocked her hotel room door and entered, tingling all over. She'd told Dom five minutes, but if she could get everything chucked into her luggage in under three, she'd sprint the remaining two to get back to him.

She grabbed her suitcase, raised it toward the bed, and subsequently screamed, nearly dropping it on her toes.

"Leah?"

Leah Strinati, of all people, pulled the bedspread up to cover her naked breasts. "Oh. Hi, Miss K."

"Look," Eija squeezed her forehead, "I'm flattered. Really, I am. But I fulfilled all my curiosities by my junior year of college and verified my appetite for dick, even though it's useless seventy-five percent of time."

Leah's face turned beet red. "Oh! Oh, no, I...I thought this was Dom's room. Yuri had me fly out last night. Or, I guess you'd say, fly in."

"Why would you think this is Dom's room?"

"I saw him come in here late last night, and I didn't see him leave."

"And you thought you'd," Eija motioned to the outline of Leah's body, "surprise him?"

"Yes. With sex."

Jesus, be a fence.

"Leah, how old are you?"

"Twenty-seven."

It was seven years older than she would have guessed.

"Why was Dominik here so late last night?" Leah pressed. "Is...is he choosing you?"

Eija moved about the suite, gathering everything she'd unpacked since they'd arrived in London. Leah could have the room. Even if it hadn't been the last day of the trip, there was no way she'd sleep in the same bed where another woman had likely gotten wet thinking about the man she...

Crap.

Crap, crap, crap.

"I'm not in the running," Eija answered. "I won't be Dominik's wife."

"Why not? Because you work for the Sokolovs?"

"No."

"Because you're Black? That's stupid."

"I'm actually still not sure. I guess it's because my family doesn't come from," she motioned to Leah, "lineage like yours. Old money or whatever."

Leah snorted. "You're a knockout, you're smart, and he likes you. He doesn't look at me, or anyone else, how he looks at you."

"Really?" Eija zipped up the suitcase and draped the tote over her shoulder. "How does he look at me?"

"It's not really a way. It's a frequency. He's pretty much always looking at you."

Which was why she would have to cut this conversation short and hurry back to him.

"Look, Leah..." Eija tapped the mattress and Lyu came sprinting from under the covers. "What the...why is the cat under there with you?"

Leah fumbled for a response.

"Know what? Never mind. Not my business." Eija headed

for the door. "Keep the room. It's yours. And, good luck. Some-thing tells me you'll be Mrs. Dominik Sokolov by the end of the dostavka."

"I was keeping her warm!" Leah yelled, but Eija shut the door and fast-tracked it to the elevator.

* * *

Dom took Eija's bags and held the door open for her to enter his suite. "That was longer than five minutes," he said.

"I had a...situation."

"Yuri?"

"No. Leah."

"Leah Strinati?"

"Yeah. She was naked in my room."

His gaze covered her from head to toe, mind already in director mode.

"We didn't do anything," Eija clarified. "She thought it was your room. She wanted to surprise you, and I quote, 'with sex.' And, get this. That's not the craziest part."

"There was a plot twist, and she really was there for you?" he asked, setting down the bags.

"No, horny. Lyu was under the covers with her."

"Doing *what*?"

"Visiting her cousin? I don't know."

He raised an eyebrow, and when realization of what she meant dawned on him, he laughed. Hard. He laughed so hard, it made her laugh. Even when she tried to get him to stop laughing, he simply kept laughing.

"I'm kidding, obviously," she added.

He cupped her face and found it extra warm. "Yeah, but that was even better than the sandwich maker."

"I'm in a good mood."

"Oh, yeah?" He backed her toward the bed. "Why's that? Did you find that rich guy to wine and dine you?"

She fell back onto the mattress. "Sure did."

"Back in Grenada," he climbed over her, "not long after the first time we went out, I told myself that if we'd had more time, we would have meant more to each other. What do you think?"

"I think you were right." She stroked the back of his neck. "You mean a lot to me."

"I feel the same way about you. So, what do we do?"

"Enjoy the time we have together."

"What if I don't want to do that?"

"How about this?" She settled her gaze on him, and fuck, she was beautiful. He loved everything about her, from her shimmering complexion and that dimple next to her chin, to the mole on her calf that was such a perfect circle, it looked like a dot from a Sharpie. "I'll be your mistress."

He snorted. "Whatever."

"You don't think I'd make a good one?"

He supposed what he was proposing was a lot. It wasn't like he was the average man asking her to be his girlfriend. Everywhere they went, she would have a target on her back, and he wouldn't be able to sleep at night knowing he'd drawn her into that.

"Eija, women like you aren't mistresses." He kissed her neck. "Women who look like you, smell like you, sound like you, whose skin radiates like yours...you aren't mistresses." His lips grazed her shoulder. "You're wives. Queens. Conquerors." He nipped the tops of her breasts. "If you're going to be in my life, it won't be behind a curtain or creeping with me in the shadows. It'll be right next to me for the world to see."

When she didn't respond, he looked up.

"I want more, Eija. But," he added, when she started to protest, "I get it. It would be...complicated."

Even more complicated than she knew.

"Too much is wrong," she said. "Too much has happened. There's so much I haven't..."

"Told me?" he asked.

"Yes."

"Tell me now."

"I can't. It's too late. I should have told you sooner, but I didn't know how you'd react. How you'd feel."

"Eija, what is it? Tell me."

Her palm warmed the side of his face, and he leaned into it. "Dom, I'm falling for you..."

She'd said it.

He couldn't believe she'd said it.

Eija the flirt, and Eija the woman who would have taken Mr. Blond home if he hadn't shown up, and then he would have had to have Mr. Blond assassinated.

"...but I wish we'd never met."

It stung.

He understood what she meant, but it stung.

Between kisses, they undressed each other in the moonlight. Head buried between her legs, he devoured her until she came, twice, then spread them and entered her slowly. As he pushed his hips into hers, her ankles locked at the base of his spine, he kissed her like it would be the last time the universe allowed him a taste of Eija.

She turned over, and he entered from behind, tongue tracing the shell of her ear, teeth nipping at her earlobe.

He moved inside her until she came, and he followed not long after, dick jerking and spilling, his lips grazing the back of her neck and the apex of her spine, over and over.

When they were both spent, wrapped through and around each other, she took his hand and pressed her lips to the center of his palm.

"I hope, one day, you'll forgive me," she whispered.

He didn't ask her what for.

Chapter Twenty-Two

Twenty-four hours until
Dostavka-Koronatsiya

Dom hadn't picked a wife. He hadn't even thought about picking a wife. Some days, *most* days, he forgot about the whole thing. The only time he remembered was when Yuri brought it up. It was simple—he didn't want one of *them*.

He wanted *her*.

But they'd made an agreement, and no matter how much he wanted her, for this to work, Eija would have to want him too.

Yuri, Ekaterina, and Pavel all stood over him in Yuri's office, watching and waiting for his answer.

"Fine, I'll marry Leah."

Yuri grinned, his face porcelain on the verge of cracking. Pavel remained expressionless. Ekaterina's smirk was the closest she'd come to a smile out of fear of wrinkles and fine lines. They were all over the woman's face, anyhow. She might as well had expressed herself over the years.

"I'll finalize the preparations." Yuri headed for the door. Just before he exited, he looked back. "Now, my son, is she out of your system?"

Eija would never be out of his system. A small part of him hoped tomorrow went differently—for her to accept them trying to be together in *some* form. They were too good together. Chemistry like this only happened once, maybe twice in a person's life. Eija was the right person at the wrong time, and when it was all said and done, no matter what, he believed she'd learn to trust him again after tomorrow.

Yuri sighed, shook his head, and Pavel tailed him as the two men left, the door shutting behind them.

"I thought you should know that tomorrow will be Miss K's last day with us," Ekaterina said, turning to Dom.

He shot to his feet. "Why?"

"Yuri's reassigning her to another family within the brotherhood."

"Why?"

She gave him a knowing look. "Dominik, sweetheart, your eyes follow her wherever she goes. Your heart then joins the pursuit. Personally, I don't want to see her go. I like her quite a bit."

"I thought your decisions were your husband's," he said, harsher than intended.

"In public," she replied, matching his coarseness. "But you

don't get to be the wife of a man like Yuri Sokolov by lying down and turning over. It's why I knew, before he said anything to me, that Miss K was the woman from Grenada."

So Yuri *had* orchestrated his reunion with Eija. He wanted to thank the man...while driving a knife through his chest.

"He says it's because having her around will make you more agreeable. That he always has the option of threatening her life." Ekaterina smoothed her hand over his head. "Dominik, I've known you since you were a little boy. Since you were Yuri's secret. In some ways, his shame. Regardless, you were a sweet boy, and it was hard not to show you extra attention knowing you carried my husband's blood. I adore you. You know that. But, if it were up to me, I still wouldn't pick Eija to be your bride."

He tugged his head away.

"Son, as long as she's around, you'll never see straight," Ekaterina added. "And, when you step into your role, you'll need to look forward, over your shoulder, and behind. The person at your side must either be strong or dispensable. Think about someone hurting Leah, and then think about someone slitting Eija's throat."

Leah didn't deserve to be hurt for her association with him either, but the thought of someone touching Eija...

"You understand?"

He nodded. "Yes."

"Say your goodbyes tonight," she said, headed for the door. "And make them count."

* * *

Colin paced the apartment's front room, one hand in his hair. Leave it to him to pick the worst time to unravel. It was the night before the ceremony. There was nothing else to do. Nothing else they could do. The objective was to get Dominik alone, subdue him, and then Interpol would arrive to discreetly carry him out of the building through the back of the venue's north exit. Colin had asked her, dozens of times, how she planned to get Dominik alone, and each time Eija had told him she'd figure something out.

Little did he know...

Eija steeled her nerves and readjusted herself on the sofa. "This is our best chance. We both know he'll be there."

"Something doesn't feel right." Colin's gaze fell to the rapid rise and fall of her stomach, the soothing rise and fall of her hand. "You're scared too."

"Yes, but how many of these have I done scared? Completed while scared? I need this, Colin. This is mine. Dominik Sokolov...is mine."

In more ways than one.

In more ways than five.

Colin crouched in front of her. "Things are different now. Nana, she has no one else. You might think she wouldn't know or understand if you," he swallowed, "got hurt, but I beg to differ."

Eija let her head fall. "I know."

"Did Yuri threaten you? Are you required to be there?

You're hiding something from me, and we both know how terrible you are at that when it comes to me. Exhibit A."

He pointed to the spot Dom had found that first night at her apartment.

The knife wound.

"I won't fuck this up. Not again. But, if something *does* happen to me—"

"E, shut up."

The door behind them opened, and April entered with two paper grocery bags in her hands. She'd, shockingly, fit right into her faux domesticated role, and the way she and Colin looked at each other, Eija was certain he no longer slept on the sofa.

"Eija, I went to your place first, and there was a man outside the door," April said. "He was on the phone. Spoke Russian. Tall, low cut, gray eyes. Fine as hell."

Colin's brows lowered.

"Did he ask you anything?" Eija asked. "Did he say what he wanted?"

April set the bags on the countertop. "No, he seemed preoccupied."

"Could be related to the event tomorrow."

"Why's he *there*, though?"

"I don't know, but I have to go. As usual," Eija let her gaze fall a second time, "I have to go."

She quickly finalized the details with Colin and hurried from the apartment. Seconds after the door closed behind her, she heard Dom's voice.

"Eija?"

She rushed over, grabbed his hand, and pulled him in the opposite direction, toward the elevator bay.

He glanced back. "Were you just coming out of that apartment?"

"Yes."

"Why were you there? Do you know the couple who lives there?"

The elevator doors opened, but he didn't get on.

"Eija, do you know them?"

There was something in his voice, in his tone. Had he made April and Colin? Did she, after getting this far, just blow her cover?

"Are you accusing me of something?" she asked, needing a moment to scramble for a plausible answer. One she could remember should she have to repeat it while being tortured.

"No." The doors slid together, but he stopped them with his arm. "Should I be?"

"In case you haven't noticed," she flailed her arms in no particular direction, "when I'm not with you or Nikolai, I'm alone. I met the wife downstairs in the lobby not too long ago, and I'm hoping to make a friend. When you're finally...married, I'd like to be able to get over you. What other way to do that than talk shit about you over wine and cheesy romance films?"

He glanced back toward the apartment.

"Why are you on this floor anyhow?" she interrogated. "Were you going through floors looking for me?"

"There was an issue. Since I live in the building, I volunteered to personally take care of it."

First, his mother not being Ekaterina and the fact that he lived in the building, which was how he was able to get to her apartment so quickly.

"You know what? That makes sense. Plus, I'm just now realizing that I didn't know where you lived."

After one more glance behind him, he stepped into the elevator. "I've never taken you to my place because of some shit that happened there, but I want you there now. If this really is our last time together, I want it to be in my bed."

Dom she could dupe about the real reason he'd caught her leaving Colin and April's. Colin would take one look at her and know this man was Dom, and that she'd known he was Dom all along.

"Your father wants me at the ceremony tomorrow. I have to get myself together."

"I already hired a personal stylist and a make-up artist," he said, and she felt herself get warm all over. "That natural hair stylist whose page you follow? Her plane's touching down at Sheremetyevo within the hour."

"For who?" She touched her chest. "Me?"

"Yes, you. Eija, whatever's supposed to happen tomorrow, with me or whoever, in my eyes, you'll still be mine. You'll always be mine. I'll be damned if you're not going to be the most beautiful woman in the room."

The last word was barely out of his mouth before she pounced on him, his arms reflexively reaching out to catch her as she climbed his body. He braced her against the elevator wall, the metal cool against her back, while her tongue explored his mouth and her teeth sank into his bottom lip.

The pain stole a rough hiss from his throat, and he grabbed a fistful of her hair. One yank and her neck arched, bared for him to drag his tongue up the column of her throat.

She didn't hear when the elevator doors opened. All she knew was, at some point, they arrived at his place, the layout identical to hers but the decor much darker. It was all her mind took in before she was wrapped up in Dom again—scent, taste, touch. The sound of his moans mixed with hers.

"We don't need the bedroom," she said, her voice so harsh, she hoped he didn't mistake her desire for anger.

He set her on her feet, pressed her face-first against the floor to ceiling living room windows, and pulled down her top, her breasts spilling out. Then she was naked from the waist down and he was inside her, and it was like they'd never made love before this.

Everything was an erotic sensation—the weight of him stretching the tight walls of her body. His fingers clamped around her wrists. The roughness of his jeans against the backs of her legs. The slap of their bodies coming together. Yet, as much as she loved the feeling of the cool glass kissing her breasts, she wanted to see him as he came. Watch the color in his eyes as they eclipsed.

When he pulled out, she stepped away and turned around. He squeezed his rock hard length with one hand, stroking, pausing at the head before starting again. She spread her legs wider at the same time he dropped to one knee, and she didn't bother holding back cries of pleasure as his tongue took her to the brink of ecstasy then pushed her off the edge.

Before she could wilt, he picked her up and drove into her body again.

If he glanced away, she grunted.

If he turned his head or tried to look down that way men did, as if needing visual confirmation they were indeed fucking, she gripped his chin and brought his gaze back up to hers.

When he came, it was with his eyes on hers, his pupils stretching to their fullest, and a grimace on his face that smoothed with each second he returned from bliss.

"Shower?" he asked, chest heaving.

She nodded.

After their shower, she draped herself in one of his shirts. He told her to get comfortable and that he would be back, and he returned with takeout, dessert, and drinks that they ate seated around the coffee table.

"Know what tonight feels like?" he asked. "You know how prisoners get to have their favorite meal the night before the needle?"

She shook her head, laughing. "You're getting married. It's not a death sentence."

"Maybe." He shrugged. "It wouldn't be if I was marrying you."

To break the awkward silence that followed that statement, she crawled over to her purse, grabbed his mother's necklace, and handed it to him. "Here you go. It's beautiful, but your mother meant too much to you. I can't keep it."

His thumb slid over the pendant and his mouth opened as if to reply, but nothing came. Instead, he stood, headed down the hallway toward his bedroom, and came back with a slender gift box that he sat on the tabletop in front of her.

"This better not be a ring," she joked.

She removed the lid, and inside sat a gorgeous golden necklace. Two interlocking rings formed the pendant, diamonds circling them in a *pavé* setting so that no matter which way she turned it, it would always catch the light.

"The rings interlock," she looked up at him, "to symbolize us."

"No matter where you go in the world," he smiled, eyes downcast and mouth soft, "never forget me."

"I don't need this to remember you."

"Can I?"

She nodded and held it out.

He draped it over her head and latched it behind her neck, the rings falling to the middle of her chest. Would he snatch the necklace from her neck after tomorrow? Would she let him?

"If I'd known we were exchanging 'last day together' gifts, I would have gotten you something."

He kissed the top of her head. "I have everything I need right here."

"Are you sure?"

"I'm sure."

"So if I wanted to ride you wearing only this necklace..."

Five minutes later, she was doing just that in his bedroom, their silhouettes forming dark shapes on the wall. The night sky outside, the moonlight bathing him from head to toe, and the way she lost herself looking into his eyes was more than enough to send her over the edge.

She came on top of him, and he maneuvered her onto her back, drove into her with a few more pumps, and came with their fingers interlocked, like the rings, above her head.

* * *

Colin pressed his back against the corridor wall and waited until the elevator doors closed to release the painful breath he held. He loved Eija. Having grown up as an only child, she felt like the only sister he'd ever known. They hadn't gotten along well in the beginning—both their heads hadn't been able to fit in the same room—but that didn't last long. She went from partner to family almost overnight.

Yet, as much as he loved her, he didn't understand her. He didn't understand why, all of a sudden, she was allowing men to sabotage everything Interpol had worked on over the last several years. First, her fixation on Andrei in Grenada and now this—literally sleeping with the enemy.

In the past two years alone, she'd made three major mistakes. This one he couldn't see Randy forgiving if he found out.

Colin placed a hand on his stomach where a gnawing feeling had grown ever since the beginning of the op. It hadn't made sense; why hadn't Dominik Sokolov showed up yet? Everything had pointed to the Bratva prince having made an appearance, yet each time they asked, Eija said he was a no-show.

Overlooking Dominik was one thing, but fucking the man? Fucking one of the most sought after criminals in the world? Their target?

When he confronted her, he hoped she told him the truth. He hoped she gave him a reason she'd fucked up *this badly* that at least toed the line between justifiable and catastrophe. If she couldn't, he'd do everything in his power to convince her to retire.

He walked back to the apartment, slouched against the door, and dragged his fingers through his hair.

"Eija, why the fuck did you do this?"

The door handle rattled, and he stepped away just as April opened it.

"Everything okay?" she asked.

"No," he answered. "Change of plans."

Chapter Twenty-Three

Dostavka

Dom entered the elegant dining hall and felt the stirrings of tension in his bones. It filtered through the fabric of his tuxedo, tingled in his fingers, and made his heart pound its way up his throat. He grabbed a flute of champagne from a passing tray and downed it in one gulp, hoping it removed some of the edge.

A piano solo of *Moonlight Sonata* created the musical ambiance, the pianist part of the larger chamber orchestra in one corner of the room. Chandeliers, ceiling lights, and flickering candles set inside lanterns combined to give the room a moody glow. Instead of the event planner's theme of young love and new beginnings, this felt like the prelude to a massacre.

Yuri touched his shoulder, and he flinched.

Concern drew Yuri's brows to the middle of his forehead. "Something wrong, my son?"

Dom searched for another glass. "Not really."

"Well, pull yourself together. She's here."

The orchestra started up, a rendition of Bach's *Prelude in C Major*.

Dom faced the door.

And stopped breathing.

Blue and brown. All he saw was blue and brown.

Royal blue draped Eija's silhouette. Her gown tumbled to the floor in waves with a ruffled slit up the middle, giving him a sultry glimpse of her legs. It was one-shouldered with a small knot on the shoulder, and where blue ended, her skin began, like some sort of tropical, exotic, erotic border. Then there was her graceful neck where the necklace, his necklace, sparkled.

That hair he loved so much was swept to one side and held in place by diamond-studded combs. Her mouth, lips soft and sweet and fresh in his memory from the night before, was accentuated by a deep red tint.

"Doesn't she look beautiful?" Yuri asked. "See how the room fell silent when she entered?"

His eyes darted to Leah, who stood next to Eija. Her dress was pink...or something.

Leah spotted them and headed over, her elbow hooked with Ale Strinati's. Dom kept his gaze on Eija until she looked up. When she did, she smiled and gave him a small wave. He covered his heart with one hand, and she lowered her eyes before turning away.

"Dominik Sokolov." Leah's father extended a hand, and Dom absent-mindedly shook it. Eija had walked to the left, and he'd assumed she was going to her table, but he didn't see where she'd gone.

"Hi, Dominik," Leah greeted. "Mr. Sokolov's *son*. Papa gave me the news last night. I'm honored to be welcomed into your family."

He suppressed a smile, recalling the London predicament in Eija's suite. "Hi. How are you doing tonight?"

"To be honest," she pressed her palm against her stomach, "I'm a little nervous. What about you?"

Where the hell could Eija have gone? There was no missing her in that dress. Not underneath these lights.

"Shall we proceed with the ceremony?" Yuri asked.

Dom found her in the back corner near the kitchen, and his blood flashed hot. Mori had roped her into a conversation, and whatever he'd just told her made her laugh out loud.

"Dominik?" Leah called.

Another server passed by, and Dom downed a second glass of champagne, eyes stuck on Mori and Eija. Mori could be charming when he wanted to be, and Eija *thought* she was single, but if Mori didn't step away from her, fuck a relationship with the Yakuza.

He mumbled a quick, "Excuse me," and headed in their direction. It didn't matter anymore. No one was going to tell him he wasn't going to be with the woman he wanted to be with. He was done entertaining antiquated, chauvinistic bullshit. All he wanted, the only thing he wanted, was Eija.

She spotted him walking over and discreetly shook her head.

He didn't stop.

"Dom," she scurried forward to meet him, "what are you doing? You're supposed to be back—"

His mouth landed hard on hers, squelching her protests. Not long after, she gave in, lips parting, and wrapped her fingers around his forearms. He cupped the back of her head, both of them ignoring the gasps and murmurs.

This.

This confidence in her kiss, Eija's quiet moans, their bodies gently pressed together. It was all he'd wanted. It was everything he wanted.

One minute, he was kissing her.

The next, he was underneath collapsed tables.

Chapter Twenty-Four

Dom's ears rang. Through the ringing, he heard yelling. Screams. Bloodcurdling screams. Smoke billowed everywhere, black diffusing into gray, and when he inhaled, he welcomed a lungful of concrete dust.

He unfolded his body from underneath the tables and was hit, in the face, by carnage. An entire section of the event hall was missing. Fire had erupted in two corners of the room. Bodies were facedown on the floor, in pools of blood, some moving and others still. Some were in pieces.

Ale had his arms wrapped around Leah and both appeared to be safe. Neither Ekaterina nor Yuri were near the spots where he had last seen them.

He looked around.

Or Eija.

"Eija?" He scanned the room for blue. "Eija, where are you?"

A groan sounded behind him.

He turned to find her trapped underneath an assortment of tables, several bent completely in half. Her dress had torn at the shoulder. Spots of blood and dust covered her face.

"I'm going to pull you out, okay?" he told her, the tables too tangled to move. "Do you feel stuck to anything? Trapped underneath any pieces?"

Despite her predicament, her voice remained calm. "I don't think so."

He tucked his hands under her underarms and pulled. She released a scream, and he immediately stopped.

"Eija, where are you hurt?"

"My leg," she coughed, "was folded in a weird position. Go again."

The ringing in his ears was subsiding, but the screams had grown. Now that some of the dust and smoke had cleared, faces could be seen. The living searching for the dead. The living *finding* the dead.

Dom pulled again.

Eija clamped her jaw shut until he had her freed from the tables. He helped her up to stand, but when she tried to put weight on her left leg, she faltered.

They both looked down at the same time.

A metal rod had gone straight through her calf.

"I need to get you to a hospital," he said, shouting to cut through the moans and wails. "Hold on to me."

She shook her head. "No. We can't."

"Eija, I don't have time for—"

"Look."

Gunshots broke through the screaming. A group of at least a dozen, all wearing army fatigues and black masks, stormed into the venue. He pulled the piece from his hip and found the nearest wall for them to use for cover.

"The South exit," Eija said. "If we can get through that way, we'll be fine."

"How do you know?" He raised his gun and picked off two from the masked group.

"We have no other choice."

"I don't have nearly enough ammo for us to cut through this shit."

As though summoned, Pavel appeared, holding a pistol in one hand and a rifle in the other. Dom reached out and Pavel handed him the rifle. The pistol, he gave to Eija. She waved away Dom's protest, checked the clip on the gun, and returned to leaning back against his side without missing a beat.

He'd wondered why she'd visited the couple the other day, and the reason she'd given him for stopping by had been plausible until six seconds ago.

"Pavel, you see that door?" she asked, pointing. "Think you can get me and Dom over there?"

Pavel nodded. "Yes, Miss K."

"Dom?" She looked up at him. "I'll need one of your arms to hold me up, but the other...I'll need you to shoot. Can you do that for me?"

He'd never been more confused and turned on at the same time in his life.

"Yeah."

"Now, I have a pistol." She checked the safety on the gun. "Dom has a rifle and Pavel, you have a semi-automatic. That means the three of us should be able to get to that door," she ticked her head, "which will get us to the South exit. Are we in agreement?"

For a man not used to taking orders—at least, outside of his orders here in Moscow—Dom found it hard not to automatically fall in line with each word Eija spoke.

"We're in agreement," he and Pavel replied.

"Good, then." She pulled back the hammer on the pistol. "Let's move, gentlemen."

They used columns, walls, and fallen furniture as shields, staying close to the edge of the room. Dom kept one arm around Eija, *both* her feet off the floor, and Pavel covered the rest of their semicircle. Mori and his men had joined in returning fire, pushing the masked intruders back. The rest of the Bratva in attendance had activated. Judging from the gaping hole in one part of the venue, it was where the blast had occurred. The last Dom remembered, Ekaterina had been close to that area just before the explosion.

He, Pavel, and Eija pushed through the South exit door into an empty corridor.

Eija motioned to him. "Dom. Pain. Help."

He extended his rifle in Pavel's direction. In the process of lifting Eija into his arms, he swiped the back of her injured calf. Blood covered the entire limb. If she didn't get help soon, she would lose her leg.

She tucked something inside his jacket pocket.

"What'd you just give me?" he asked.

"I...fucked up." She lowered her face to his shoulder and squeezed tight. "Even now...it's the wrong exit."

"Eija, pick up your head. You're going to be okay, baby. Just breathe." He kissed whatever spots on her head he could reach. "I've got you. Nothing's going to happen."

"You don't understand. The plan...was...the north."

"The north?"

"North exit."

Pavel fired off rounds as they passed an adjacent hallway.

"I...betrayed," she added.

"Who, baby? Who'd you betray?"

"Everybody."

They came to the door.

Pavel went through first, and Dom followed before Pavel could give the all clear. Whatever was out there, they'd have to handle it. Eija needed help, and that was worth a few bullets.

He'd been expecting hired guns, not a fleet of armored vehicles and men in uniform with guns aimed in their direction. At the helm of the arch was one-half of the couple from the apartment—the redheaded man. And, seeing him now, Dom realized he'd seen the man's face somewhere else before but couldn't yet remember where.

Had they asked Eija about him?

Was that why today had gone the way it had?

"Dominik Sokolov," the redhead said, through a megaphone, "get down on the ground."

Dom shook his head. "She needs medical attention."

"Put the girl down and get down on the ground. The quicker you do so, the quicker she'll be able to get that medical attention." The man's tone changed from authoritative to pleading. "*Please.*"

"Eija?" He shook her until her eyes opened. "Eija, I have to do what they say or you'll die, okay? But I'll find you, baby. I promise I'll find you. I love you. Hold on for me. Can you do that?"

She nodded.

He kissed the top of her head and set her down. A team of three medics shoved their way between the human perimeter and rushed over to her.

"On the ground, Sokolov," the redhead repeated.

Dom did as he was told. He searched to see if Pavel had escaped, but a hard hit from the butt of a gun nearly cracked open his skull.

"Stop it!" Eija screamed. "Don't hit him! He's fucking complying!"

A medic placed an oxygen mask over her nose and mouth.

The redhead glared at her. "I'll fucking deal with you later. The South exit? Really? And I said put your hands behind your head, Sokolov."

Dom complied, but the man's days were marked. The

redhead had no idea who the fuck he was messing with or *what* the fuck he'd stepped in. By the time he found out, it would be too late.

The redhead swiped the gun again, this time knocking Dom clean out.

Chapter Twenty-Five

The sun could have risen and fallen at least a dozen times since the redhead and his band of merry men had tossed him in this cell—Dom wouldn't know. There were no windows, nothing he could use to etch lines on the walls. He didn't know where he was, where Eija was, but it had required a flight and a host of knockout drugs.

Where'd they tossed him definitely wasn't a Danish or Swedish prison. There, he'd have bedsheets. A desk. Soft lighting and IKEA furnishings. Here, the walls were all cinderblock, the bars reinforced steel. The outside of the toilet was more soiled than what went inside it, and urine-colored water came from a sputtering faucet they expected him to use to wash his face and brush his teeth.

He looked up when a shadow appeared just outside the cell bars. Every day since his confinement, it had been the redhead asking questions. Through the questions, he'd learned that Ekaterina had died from injuries sustained in the blast. Mikhail, in an attempt to shield her, had suffered critical injuries and had been hospitalized. Yuri's status was unknown—bodies were still being identified. Whenever he'd asked about Eija, the redhead had rewarded him with his head being smashed into a tabletop or a trip down the hall to an even grungier torture room. They'd tried everything from waterboarding to starvation to breaking his left wrist, but he'd taken an oath not to reveal his country's secrets.

"You are one tough son of a bitch," the shadowy figure said.

He momentarily ignored him, deciding the cracked mirror above the sink was more worthy of his attention.

The cell door slid open, and the man stepped inside. Dom switched from lying to sitting on sheets filled with straw and rocks they'd attempted to pass off as a mattress.

"Why the fuck was Interpol at the ceremony?" he asked.

"Cool it, Dom. I'm still your superior officer."

"Interpol works *for* the CIA on this one, not *with* them. I thought they understood that." Dom held up his wrist cast. "And you took your fucking time getting here."

Randy grated out a sigh. "We both know you wouldn't have talked. And I didn't even know you were here until two hours ago when I got the call that we'd apprehended 'Dominik Sokolov' in Moscow."

It was odd how his mind could recall everything except the actual explosion. He remembered Eija's lips on his and her fingers on his forearms, but there was no memory of an actual sound. Of any bright spots of light or Eija being torn from his arms. When he closed his eyes, it was all screaming. The smell of burned flesh lived in his nostrils.

"Yuri's the rat," Dom said. All the "free time" he'd accumulated while imprisoned had led him to the conclusion. "There's no snitch in the Bratva. *Yuri* was the snitch. I think he orchestrated the attack."

"To escape the Bratva and leave everything squarely on his son's shoulders," Randy said, pacing and picking at his bottom lip. "Apparently, he's been setting it up that way for years. That's what I was researching when I got the call that you were here. As of right now, Yuri's clean. I could argue until my tongue bleeds about everything he's had a hand in, for years, but I'd have no proof to back it up."

Dom snorted in disbelief. The sly motherfucker always had a trick up his sleeve. The only reason Yuri had come for him when was six, "rescued" him from strange men and starving nights was because of this; Yuri had wanted out of the Bratva and needed a different neck in offering when the world's counterintelligence and law enforcement agencies came swinging the hatchet.

One afternoon during his first year at Stanford, Randy had stopped him after class. Before that day, he hadn't known his mother and aunt had grown up with an older brother. Neither his mother nor Nasrin had ever spoken about Randy "Rahman" Almas, the golden child.

After confirming with Nasrin that Randy was who he'd said

he was, he'd granted Randy the meeting he'd requested. During that meeting, they'd talked about Yuri.

"Are our covers intact?" Dom asked.

"Solid." Randy stopped pacing and stuffed his hands in his pockets. "Dominik Sokolov still has an Interpol Red Notice. I'm still head of a task force on the Russian mafia. Only me, you, and a few others know we're from the agency."

"The redhead, what's his name?"

"Dom, he was just doing his job. As *his* superior, real or fake, I'll talk to him."

"And say what? Not to rough up your late sister's kid? Your ex-partner's son?"

Randy pressed his lips together and passed his fingers through his hair. "Look, my orders weren't to detain you. Favreau did that on his own. I told you not to get cornered. Shit, we put you in the same building as him. You were supposed to be keeping an eye out. What happened? Did you get distracted?"

Like a motherfucker.

Distracted wasn't the word. When he was with Eija, he forgot he had a job to do. The odds of her still feeling the same way about him if she found out he worked for the Central Intelligence Agency were slim to none. He'd lied to her since the day they met. There was only so much forgiveness one person could extend. When he'd told her he was Bratva, he'd wanted to go one step further, but that would have been too much information at once.

He stood, stretching his arms behind his head. It wasn't his first time in a jail cell, but he was ready to get the hell up out of this one.

"What about Nikolai?" he asked.

"Safe. We got the message from your coffee cup dead-drop in London."

"And the nanny? Is she...all right?"

"Eija?"

"Both she and Pavel were with me when I was arrested. She was hurt. Did she live?"

"Well, first of all," Randy began, "Pavel's fine."

"I know *he's* fine. Even if we don't get Yuri, he sure as fuck will. That Pitbull's teeth sank into Yuri's ass a long time ago, and he's not about to let up now."

Pavel had been Yuri's righthand man for the better part of a decade, and he'd been an informant for even longer. The Bratva was responsible for the death of Pavel's parents, cousins, uncle, and aunt, so Pavel had made it his mission to destroy as much of the organization as he could. His ultimate goal was to go Frank Castle on Yuri and his men.

"As for Eija," Randy continued, "she's on suspension."

"From her domestic duties? Why? Nikolai isn't even—"

"She's not a nanny."

Dom's wrist throbbed. "Then what is she?"

"Understand this wasn't my call," Randy said, easing into an explanation Dom could already tell he wouldn't like. "David and Linda wanted to work Sokolov from multiple angles. The man used to be one of us, and he's slippery as fuck. Eija is an *insanely talented* recruit."

David Smatters and Linda Vincent were their liaisons back at the agency and members of the select few who were privy to the entire Sokolov undercover operation. If their names had come up in the same sentence as Eija's...

"Who is she, Randy?"

"She's one of Linda's," he confessed. "At least, she used to be. Linda had Eija working light Bratva duty back in D.C., and Eija's primary focus, at the time, was Bratva cells in the US. Somehow, she found out that Yuri had a son. And, if you think Pavel's a Pitbull, Eija's a fucking Rottweiler. So, a few years ago, Linda sent Eija to me at Interpol to...refocus her attention. Eija's main purpose was to ID you. If she did before the dostavka, then we'd know we had to pull you out."

Dom stared at his uncle, speechless for a moment.

"Oh," Randy squeezed the bridge of his nose, eyes shutting, "and she's okay. Colin rushed her straight from the scene into surgery. He can be an ass, but he loves Eija. She wouldn't have died that day with him there."

Colin, Dom realized, was the redhead in Grenada who Eija had slipped the note with her name written on it. *Colin,* he'd address later.

"She's my handler," he half-said, half-asked. "You sent me a handler without telling either of us."

A lot of things could have been avoided had they both been clued in. Things Dom honestly wasn't sure he would have preferred to not have happened.

"Eija's a tracker," Randy went on. "She's good, Dominik. I'm telling you. She's a chameleon."

"So, her specialty is adapting to environments."

Lying about who she was.

But she hadn't been lying with him. To do that, she would have had to know who *he* was...unless she'd assumed she was seducing the Bratva prince.

Still, it wasn't possible to fake the smiles she'd given him. The laughs and the way she looked when she came. The joy on her face during the treasure hunt. After the attack, she'd directed him to the "wrong" exit. That meant, until the very end, she'd tried to protect him. That couldn't be faked.

He didn't know what he'd do with himself if it could.

"Dominik, your situation was a little different because you actually *are* Yuri's son," Randy said, leaning back against the bars. "If you'd come on your own to join the agency, Yuri would have tracked you the entire way. You wanted to take him down and, as a valuable asset, we started building your cover when you were nineteen. That made you both easy and difficult to identify, all contingent upon whether someone found out Yuri had knocked up an Iranian girl from California."

Dom was so stunned, he couldn't figure out whether he had a right to be upset. Who'd lied to whom? He'd told Eija his name was Andrei and that he was Bratva. He'd never mentioned the CIA. Therefore, his two lies appeared to cancel out her one. That meant he had to find a way to apologize. He had to see her again, to do more than apologize. Their personas might have been fake, but his attraction to her was real. If he'd fallen in love with a snake...

"Wait," he snapped his fingers, "why is she suspended, though? For finding me?"

Randy clicked his tongue. "Well, Eija violated protocol in a major way. April, the officer you saw with Favreau, wasn't initially supposed to go to Moscow, but Colin and Eija pulled her on last minute."

"And?"

"They brought her to secure the kid."

Dom's mouth filled with cotton. *"What* kid?"

"Look, like I said, Eija's one of the best we've seen in years. I respect her, really. But she's more like one of the guys than a... Suzy Homemaker, if you will. The difference is, you and I can't get pregnant."

"Randy, spare me the chauvinistic bullshit that nearly left my mother, your sister, homeless."

Randy held up his hands in defeat. "You're right, you're right. Anyway, she met some guy in Grenada. Andrei...something or the other. They hooked up and, I'm assuming, the condom broke. "

"Andrei?"

"April went as the first line of security for the kid, but she had an entire team on standby. The baby's name is Shiloh Grace Barrett, code name *Nana.* I've met her a couple of times, when she was still a newborn. Cute, *cute* little girl. And, let me tell you, it was like they were hiding Sasha Obama in Afghanistan."

"Shiloh Grace...Barrett?"

"Eija's last name. The father, Andrei, he's not in the picture."

That no longer appeared to be the case.

"She asked me to take her off the Sokolov project. At least, going undercover. Truthfully, she'd been asking for months."

"And you said?"

"We needed her, Dom." Randy slapped a cell bar. "When I found out about the kid, I asked her to make sure the baby didn't change our plans to get inside the penthouse."

"*What?*"

"No one else could go under. No one. So, after Eija hounded me for weeks and weeks about letting April take her spot, I told her to find a caregiver for her daughter or...or she'd lose everything I could take from her. Pension, severance. Fuck, her self-esteem. I'm not proud of it, but this came all the way from the top. My hands were tied."

Dom made a fist to send a sharp flash of pain through his injured wrist. If nothing else, the pain was just enough to stop him from stepping forward and driving his uncle's head through the bars.

Eija, it appeared, also had multiple secrets, but that second one...

He didn't know how he was still on his feet. Now he knew why the resort had given him the brush off when he'd called to talk to her. He'd assumed she'd asked them to screen his calls after he'd skipped out, and he felt like shit knowing he'd given up trying to find her. Had he tried harder, he would have known. He would have been there. Neither CIA officer nor Bratva Dominik were the type to skip out on a woman who...

Shit.

And he'd seen it, times where she'd seemed distracted. Where she'd go from smiling to depressed and back. Times where she'd looked at him as if seeing someone else.

The morning of their flight to London, she'd been completely out of sorts. Had it been because she'd had to leave Shiloh in Russia while she spent the week in London with someone else's kid? Then she'd gone to London with Shiloh's father, who she couldn't tell he had a baby without risking her daughter's future.

Shiloh Grace *Barrett*.

At least for now.

"Where is she now?" Dom asked, taking a seat. He *needed* to sit.

"Here. We're in Lyon, just outside Interpol headquarters."

"I need her address, and the clothes I had on. Specifically, my tuxedo jacket."

Randy laughed, but when he realized Dom was serious, his laughs turned into a series of coughs.

"Dom, I can't give you that information."

"You saw me with Eija in London at the Japanese restaurant. Didn't we look...cozy?"

Randy shrugged. "Yeah, but Eija's pretty easy to get along with."

Dom shot him a look.

"That's not a sexual reference. She's an amazing person,

even when she's disobeying a direct order. I really do care about her."

"Randy, get me her information. See it as recompense for threatening to put your family on the street, just like your parents did." When Randy raised an eyebrow, he added, "I was in Grenada. If a man named Andrei, who Eija met in Grenada, is Shiloh's father, then that's *my* little girl. Shiloh's your great-niece."

"Colin, get out."

Eija limped around her flat, picking toys up off the floor where she'd been playing with Shiloh before Colin arrived. Shiloh had just discovered she could crawl and *then* hold on to things. Add an injured leg, and chasing her daughter around was more effective than physical therapy at getting her back to full strength.

Colin bounced Shiloh on his knee on the living room sofa. "You haven't talked to me since Moscow."

"I've been busy."

"Talk to me now."

She whirled around. "And say what? What, Colin? What do you want me to say?"

"That you compromised our op, fucked the enemy, and lied to me. I knew you'd take him to the wrong exit. I fucking *knew* it."

Eija rolled her eyes and continued to Shiloh's toy box.

"You threw everything away for a penis, E," he pressed. "You really think Dominik Sokolov, of all people, cares about you? Because he carried you like a knight and gave you a little forehead kiss? He's a piece of shit, like his father, and he only cares about himself."

No, she didn't *think* Dom cared about her.

She *knew* he loved her.

Those three words had fucked her over, repeating so much through her mind, she couldn't look at her daughter without hearing them. They appeared in her dreams, kissed her cheek in the shower, and left indentations in the empty pillow next to her head.

"Right now, E, I don't know who you are. Maybe you should go back to pre-Andrei, Eija. Stock up on dick."

"Fuck you, Colin." She set narrowed eyes on him, grateful her daughter would remember none of this conversation by the time she learned to talk. "I've played along with that whole 'Eija is a cum bucket' shit from you assholes for long enough. You and your dick ran through half of the level-one analyst floor, yet nobody's given you a reputation. Hell, you made April, who's way too damn good for you, fall for you, and then you cheated on her. *You're* a piece of shit, your damn self. Tell me, Colin, how many people at work have I slept with?"

His lips parted.

"None," she answered. "Outside of Dom, how many times have I had sex while *actively* on the job?"

"Well—"

"None." Eija flipped up a finger with each name. "Tatiana, Raisa, Yuli, Carmen, Obi, Drea, Aimée...shall I go on?"

"No. I get your point."

"My *point* is this. You say you love me, I'm your best friend, whatever. Yet, you talk about me like I mean nothing to you. Like I could never mean anything to anyone."

He lowered his gaze to Shiloh, who'd fallen asleep back against his chest. Shiloh looked so much like her father, she wondered how Colin hadn't put the remaining piece of the mystery together. Hopefully, they'd allowed Dom to at least keep his clothes. As a condition of her suspension, Randy had prohibited her from stepping foot inside the building, so she didn't know what was happening to him.

"I'm sorry," Colin said, meeting her eyes. "You're right. I do love you, and I've been a huge fucking dick to you. I'm really, truly sorry. It's just...Eija, why him?"

Her lip twitched.

A fifty-pound weight dropped onto her chest.

It made little sense to keep hiding it. Everything else was out in the open.

"Dominik Sokolov was in Grenada. Our intel wasn't wrong."

Colin lay Shiloh on his stomach. "What are you talking about?"

"Andrei, Colin. Andrei Falcone is Dominik Sokolov. He was using the name Andrei because he was trying to fly under the radar. I didn't find out until that first day I spotted him at the penthouse, and Yuri introduced him to me as Dominik."

287

Colin's eyes went wide, his mouth even wider. "What?"

"I'd still planned to carry out everything, as agreed. At first." She went over and sat next to him. "But then he turned out to be the same guy. He was just as funny, just as sweet. The more time I spent with him, the more I realized I couldn't set Shiloh's father up to die."

"You looked for him, E. Even after she was born."

"I wanted her to know him. I," she studied her daughter's adorable sleeping face, "didn't want to assume that because of our short time together, he wouldn't want to know he had a kid."

"Does he know now?"

"I left a note in his jacket pocket."

"E," Colin slowly shook his head, "we stripped him as soon as he got here. He doesn't know."

"Is he alive?"

He didn't answer right away.

"Colin."

"Yeah. Yeah, he's alive."

Even if she asked, Colin wouldn't tell her all what they'd done to Dom. Especially not now that he knew what he knew. From his tight expression, she could tell he understood her conflict, but he didn't appear to agree with it.

Whatever.

It was in the past now.

She was on suspension. Maybe she'd quit altogether. Go back to the States, reconcile with her sister, and introduce Alecia to her niece. Get a desk job. It wasn't appealing, but for Shiloh, she would do anything.

The first time she'd seen that little face, those round eyes and pink lips, she'd been awestruck. Never in a million years would she have ever thought she'd be a mother. Randy had backed her into a wall the size of a tidal wave, but with no family in France, she'd wanted her baby nearby.

"I don't agree with a lot of this," Colin prefaced, "but Sokolov, at least, deserves to know he has a daughter. Especially," he looked down, "one as beautiful as my goddaughter. I'll pull some strings and get you in to talk to him."

His phone chimed.

A few seconds after he raised it to his ear, he started arguing with the person on the other end.

"You can't...how...Randy, that's bull—" Colin lowered the phone and brought it around to his face. "He hung up on me."

"What'd he want?" Eija asked, lifting Shiloh into her arms.

"They're thinking about letting Dominik walk in exchange for his cooperation on bringing Yuri down. How? It's not like we have lawyers negotiating shit."

Eija hid her relief. "*Randy* is?"

"Yeah."

"You won't win that fight."

Colin shot to his feet. "I'm going down there to see what's really going on. I'll call you when I find out. And I'll call you about the other thing too. Dominik's where he belongs, but at least Shiloh will be able to meet her father."

He gave her a quick hug and bolted out the door.

She took a deep breath and maneuvered until she was on her feet, Shiloh tucked in her arms. At least now, she would no longer have to sneak down to Colin and April's for only a few hours with her daughter. She would no longer have to sleep with one eye open in the nursery at their Moscow apartment in the event Yuri came looking, or be showered with guilt over the fact that she'd taken her *infant daughter* on an op. It was the last thing she'd wanted to do, but what would she be able to offer her child without a career?

"Well, Shi, I guess we'll go to bed at," she glanced at the clock on the stove, "eight today. Maybe you'll sleep through the night, hmm?"

Dominik appeared in the front room from the hallway. And somehow, she'd expected it. Felt it. The minute Colin said they could release him, she'd hoped he'd end up here. She just hadn't expected tonight.

Bruises created morbid artwork on his face in hues of black, purple, and red. A cast had been molded around his left wrist. Though covered in blood and wrinkled, he filled out his tux. Colin hadn't starved him, at least.

He took a step forward, and it looked like it pained him so badly, she stopped him.

"Let's talk in my room." She held up a hand. "I'm assuming you already know which one that is."

He turned and waited for her to walk ahead of him before he followed.

She set Shiloh in the middle of her bed and sat along the edge. Dom gingerly lowered next to her. A gorgeous pair they were, Miss Bruised and Mr. Battered.

Much needed silence passed between them. He deserved

this moment to stare at Shiloh, to get his thoughts together. It was one thing to find out she'd been spying on him—if he was here, he knew. It was another thing, entirely, to find out he had a baby.

"I got your note." He patted his jacket. "And the picture."

"Since I didn't get yours in Grenada, I had to put this one somewhere you would definitely find it. I had the stylist stitch in that little pocket just before you left."

He reached out and tentatively stroked Shiloh's pinky with a fingertip. "When we were in London and you said there was something it was too late to tell me, was it her?"

"Yes."

"For what it's worth, no matter when you'd told me, it wouldn't have been bad news."

She reached for his face, and he sucked in a breath before her fingers made contact.

"You're not going to ask me how I'm here right now?" he asked.

"No."

"You could be harboring a fugitive, Eija."

"Who also happens to be my daughter's father."

The whites of his eyes glistened. "I...I don't even know what to say. She's so damn cute."

"She looks like you."

"I noticed."

Eija stood. "Are you hungry? Did you eat?"

She turned to leave, but he grabbed her hand.

"Eija, wait. I need to ask you something."

She returned to her spot on the bed, the space still warm, and prepared herself. She'd been preparing herself for this moment ever since she found out she was pregnant. In Grenada, she'd hounded him until they finally fell into bed together. In Moscow, it had taken a while for them to sleep together, but he *had* caught her in the middle of going home with another man she'd met at a pub. She wouldn't have actually gone home with "Wesley Langstaff," but Dom didn't know that.

"Do you know someone named Linda Vincent?" he asked.

"Dom, I won't be offended if you want to take a DNA tes— wait, what?"

"I'm not worried about if she's mine, Eija," he said. "But, Linda Vincent. She's CIA, and the one who sent you to work with Randy Almas."

Eija glanced at Shiloh. "I don't know who these people are."

"My mother was Aani Almas, Randy's sister. I know Linda and David. And Randy doesn't work for Interpol. Not officially. I guess, in a way, neither do you."

She remained quiet, one eye on her daughter.

"I've been with the agency since I graduated," he continued, and she kept her expression blank, though pure shock rocked her on the inside. "Randy's my uncle."

Next to them, Shiloh stirred, stretched, and yawned. Her eyes opened, and when she noticed Dom, she graced him with an enormous smile before her eyes closed again.

"Damn. I felt that." His hand went to his chest. "Can I hold her? Or would I wake her up, you think?"

"Even if she wakes up," she gently scooped Shiloh from the mattress and set her in Dom's arms, "it's to meet her father."

"Daddy," he said, trying to find a comfortable position for both his wrist and daughter. "I want her to know me as 'Daddy.'"

Eija remained quiet, but she couldn't rein in the smile on her lips.

"At ease, Miss *Barrett.*" He smiled back. "I'm telling the truth."

"So, no venture capital?" she asked.

"I really am Yuri's son. I invested my trust fund in risky star-tups, hoping for failure because I didn't want Yuri's blood money. It backfired."

"And your mother's related to Randy, you said? Actually, hold that thought. I'll be right back."

It pained her to look at him, so she left to get her First Aid kit. Now, she preferred the shorter hair. She couldn't imagine seeing those dark, beautiful locks in the same condition Vasily's had been in.

He continued his story while she patched him up. Even if he'd just gotten her to blow her cover, he was Shiloh's father. She couldn't have him sitting across from her in pain.

"Randy's birth name is Rahman, and my mother met Yuri through Randy. It was one incidental meeting but, apparently, it was all it took. Yuri's whole back story? Fabricated. A story created by the agency. Yuri and Randy were partners working covert intelligence back when the USSR still existed. It was Yuri's idea to infiltrate the Bratva, take it down from the inside.

By then, the CIA had already theorized that the Brotherhood would rise into power after the Russians ousted Gorbachev. The goal was to monitor nuclear technology. Given Yuri's ties to the country, he spearheaded the project, going undercover as *Krestniy Otets*. Pakhan. Boss. Then, he went rogue."

"And where do you come in?"

"My mother didn't know Yuri had gone rogue. When they 'met up' again in California, she got pregnant. My grandparents tossed her out when they found out, so she went to live with my aunt. Aunt Nasrin was ten years older than my mother, and my grandparents had already kicked her out years before for liking girls, weed, and converting to atheism. Somehow, Yuri found out my mother was pregnant and went to California promising to reconcile. He then brought her to Russia and sold her to get rid of her existence."

"With a baby in her belly."

"Yep. She was still," Dom's jaw pulsed, "useful in that industry. Some men preferred a pregnant woman for the night. Then, she had the baby, and Yuri found out it was a boy. His only son. That part was true, him looking for us and finding us when I was six."

"So your mother wasn't an escort?"

"Nope." He brushed a reticent kiss over the top of Shiloh's head. "She wanted to go to medical school. In the beginning, so did I, but Randy found me at Stanford and told me who he was. He's even older than Aunt Nasrin, so I'd never heard of him before that day. After meeting with him, I decided I'd go to the CIA. I'm, honestly, not much different from Pavel."

Eija cocked her head to the side. "Pavel?"

"He's one of ours. An informant. The Bratva killed his *entire* family."

"Pavel's disposition makes sense." The quiet ones were often the most terrifying. "But yours, I wondered about. I didn't peg you as someone who could sell women without blinking."

Later, when she was alone, she'd scream her relief.

"By the way, what does your camp want with him?" Dom asked.

The longer he held Shiloh, the more comfortable he grew with her. Eija was grateful he hadn't put her through the whole "she's not my kid" ringer. Between the leg surgery and roller-coaster past couple of weeks, she wasn't sure she would have been able to handle it.

"Yuri obtained information that could be potentially damaging to three major counterintelligence agencies, if not more," she explained. "We don't know what he plans to do with it. All we know is that the CIA, MI6, and DGSE want the information retrieved and destroyed. My speciality," she splayed her fingers across her chest, "is espionage. I work primarily with organized crime units infiltrating their sects to dismantle the regimes from the inside. We've targeted and taken down parts of La Cosa Nostra, the Irish, the Albanians, and major drug organizations in South and Central America. Usually, we can disable their supply chains, reroute shipments... things like that. It helps keep a great deal of product, whether its drugs, weapons, or humans, out of the wrong hands. This time, with Yuri, is the first time we've had such a major threat to global security."

He stared at her.

"What?"

"It makes sense now how you went from Miss K to Miss *Komandir* in an instant at the ceremony. I'd already had my eyes on Favreau and the other officer—"

"April. She came on to ensure Shiloh's protection."

"It never crossed my mind you could be working with them."

"Well, for now, I'm suspended," she said. "Though, if we'd crossed paths at the agency before this, Shiloh would have been like seven by now."

No matter how she'd met Dom, as long as they'd gotten to know each other, she believed they would have ended up in the same place.

He laughed, and it was nice to see that smile again.

"I'm reading between the lines," she began, "and I'm hearing that my actual job was securing your cover."

It took him a moment to answer. Shiloh cooed in her sleep, and it had him completely enraptured.

"Randy said you're a Rottweiler," he replied. "You found out Yuri had a son despite the agency's, and Yuri's, best efforts to bury my existence."

"So, what was it? If I ID'd you, they'd pull you?"

"Yes. And you did. But you didn't turn me in."

"Because I liked you."

"And now?"

Now, he was sitting across from her holding their daughter, and he wanted Shiloh to know him as "Daddy."

Eija slapped her hands on her thighs, stood, and wobbled a little before she found her balance. "Well, since I'm not truly harboring a fugitive, how about I get you something to eat?"

He eyed her, and his face flashed with a question she hoped he didn't ask.

"Can I put her to bed?" he asked instead.

"Of course."

She'd already made macaroni pie, baked chicken, and coleslaw for dinner, so she reheated a plate for him and set it on her barely used four-person dining table. When he entered the front room, it was without his jacket, and she got the feeling he'd kept the shirt on because things underneath were worse than what was on his face.

He pulled out the chair and carefully took a seat.

She set a fork next to his plate. "I don't have vodka, but I do have wine."

"Water's fine."

"I don't have men's clothes here, either," she said, pouring him a glass. "But I can wash those for you. I'm good at getting out bloodstains."

"Like that knife wound?"

"About that." She raised her shirt. "Not a knife wound. I didn't really get that big with Shiloh, but she still gave me a couple of stretch marks. I didn't want you to feel them and start asking questions."

He used the hem of her shirt to draw her closer. "Every time we made love," he traced the marks with his thumb, "it was in the dark, or you kept your top on. I didn't notice until now."

"Eat, Dom. I'll get you whatever you need to take a shower. Leave your clothes on my bed. You can strip all the way down."

"I don't—"

"You can strip all the way down," she reiterated. "It's okay. I know what my division does. I know how it operates. I won't judge you and, if you don't want me to, I won't touch you."

"Why wouldn't I want you to?"

"If it's painful."

While he ate, she set out a towel, toothbrush, and extra gauze and bandages. Then she worked on his clothes while he showered, scrubbing them before tossing them in the washing machine. She didn't want to think about how many designer labels she'd destroyed with her practical laundering skills, but she wanted the bloodstains gone. The bruises, the evidence of what they'd done to him, would linger for a while, so she'd control what she could control.

She heard when he left the bathroom, saw when he passed the bedroom door, a towel wrapped around his lower half. Shiloh's bedroom camera showed him doing what Eija had done every night she could—watch Shiloh sleep.

He returned to the bedroom, and she kept her eyes glued to the TV. It was another crime show, in French with English subtitles. If she looked at him, she'd stare at his injuries.

The bed sank with his weight.

The covers shifted as he slipped beneath them.

"What's this one about?" he asked, once settled.

"Women who are deadly," she said. "It's one of my favorites."

"Why, because you're deadly with a handgun?"

She peeked and found the covers drawn up to his waist. His bruises looked like tattoos, and she wanted to punch Colin in his fucking face. Was it right that this pissed her off when Vasily had been put through the same thing?

No, it wasn't.

But she didn't have a child with Vasily. She wasn't in love with Vasily. So, right now, fairness didn't matter.

"I'm good with a rifle, a shotgun, and a semi-automatic." She mimed taking a shot. "You name it, I've fired it."

"Eija?"

"Hmm?"

"I want to be in her life."

She went to him, and he folded her into his chest from behind. He smelled like her soap, and those knots only Dom could give formed in her belly.

"I want to be in your life too." He kissed her neck, behind her ear, the back of her head. "If that works for you. We've...lied about a lot of shit, but I don't think we lied about how we felt. Unless I'm wrong, but you'd have a hard time convincing me of that with how you've treated me since I got here."

"I didn't lie about how I felt about you."

"You're just not ready to tell me exactly how that is."

"I'm...working on it."

"Okay." He pointed to TV. "Now, this woman poisoned her husband."

"Nope, Mabel likes to get her hands dirty," Eija said. "She strangled him."

A few minutes later, the narrator revealed Mabel had actually set the family car on fire with her husband, still alive, inside.

Dom bristled. "Damn."

Laughing, Eija burrowed further into his body.

Chapter Twenty-Six

A crash woke Eija up out of her sleep.

It only took her a second to orient herself and identify what it was—the silk ficus tree she kept by the front door falling to the ground. With force. She'd tripped over the thing several times herself, but Colin had gotten it for her as a gift. As he popped by from time to time, she kept it until she could come up with a plausible excuse for its unfortunate disappearance.

Last night came rushing back, and she searched the space next to her to find it empty.

Dom.

"Dom, you okay?" she called out, rubbing her eye with the back of her hand. "The light switch is on the wall close to the TV. If you can't find that, the lamp on the left end table is a touch lamp."

Silence.

"Dom?"

He appeared in the doorway, holding Shiloh with one arm. "I was actually looking for the kitchen light."

"The kitchen's nowhere near that plant."

"I learned I was a father *yesterday* and still got up to make my daughter's bottle so her mother could sleep."

Eija left the bed and walked past him to the kitchen to turn on the light. Once her eyes adjusted to the flood of brightness, she spotted powder sprinkled on the butcher block countertop, an uncovered can of baby formula, several jars of baby food, and a box of baby oatmeal cereal. The pantry door was wide open.

"All of this and you didn't find a single light? Not even the stove or pantry light?"

"I've done more complicated things in the dark. I don't know why I couldn't accomplish this. And you," he tickled Shiloh's belly, "didn't even help."

Shiloh chewed on her fingers.

"Did she give you the 'you're useless' face?" Eija asked, leveling a scoop of formula. When she'd finally told Randy about her pregnancy, he'd looked at her like she'd told him the baby was his from his sperm diffusing into her because they'd stood next to each other on the elevator. He'd asked if a baby would interfere with their Sokolov operation, and when she'd tried to answer, he'd responded with, "It better not," before storming off.

After she'd realized she'd have no one to watch Shiloh, she'd gone back to him several times, meeting a higher wall with each attempt. So, as a precaution, she never breastfed. She hadn't wanted her daughter to become used to or reliant upon something she might not be able to provide.

"It was more like a 'look at this idiot' face." Dom gave Shiloh's belly another tickle that drew a tiny smile from her cheek. "Give me time, Shi. Daddy'll figure it out."

Eija finished making the bottle and handed it over.

"I test it on the back of my hand, right?" he asked.

"Just hold the bottle up like this," she raised her arm, "and let a few drops fall onto your tongue."

He did as instructed.

And gagged.

"That's what baby formula tastes like?"

"For future reference," Eija pointed to the bottle warmer on the other side of the counter, "I keep water warmed for middle of the night feedings."

"So you made me taste that for nothing?"

"Not for nothing. For my own amusement." She tipped her chin at Shiloh. "Heads up. She's three seconds away from a meltdown if you keep dangling that bottle in front of her without handing it over."

Dom barely extended the bottle in Shiloh's direction before she grabbed it and brought the nipple up to her mouth. She'd only started holding bottles without help about a month ago, but the way she leaned back against him with it tipped up, one leg splayed, she looked like she'd been feeding herself from birth.

Even Dom's smile was a mirror image of Shiloh's. Her grandmother used to say that the more a child came out looking like their father, the more the mother hated him while she was pregnant, so she must have loathed Dom.

Part of her had been upset with him for disappearing, but she'd been more disgusted with herself. Getting pregnant without being able to contact the "sperm donor" had only made her feel like all the names she'd been called within the agency for doing the same thing, to a much lesser extent, as her male colleagues.

Eija glanced at the clock on the stove. It wasn't even six yet.

"Are you hungry?" she asked.

"Yes, but," Dom handed Shiloh to her, "let me feed you for a change. You ladies hang out."

"Don't make borscht." She walked to the sofa, sat, and Shiloh leaned back against her chest, the bottle already half-empty. "I never took to borscht."

"For breakfast?"

It felt like mere seconds between him grabbing flour from the pantry and then calling her over to the dining table. At some point, she'd fallen asleep.

"Shi got tired after she ate, so she's taking a nap." He filled a mug next to a stack of pancakes with black coffee. "I'm guessing you take no cream in your coffee if you worked for the agency?"

She headed over. "And about a pinch of sugar."

While they ate, she used one ear to listen for Shiloh waking up. The other, she used to listen for the door. The Sokolov operation wasn't over. They hadn't yet discussed the siege at Dostavka-Koronatsiya with either of their teams, although she suspected she'd be kept out of the loop because of her suspension.

After breakfast, they turned to the door.

She sighed. "Nothing yet."

"Yet being the key word," he said. "Don't worry. I'm not going anywhere before then."

They came three days later, and it was three full days of her watching Dom and Shiloh fall into their own little routine. His bruises looked better. Not perfect, but better. Whenever she was close enough, Shiloh touched them. Studied them. And Eija wondered what went through her mind when she did. One day, hopefully, she'd know this man was her father...if, in her own way, she didn't already.

Four hard knocks echoed against the front door. Dom gave his daughter a kiss on top of her head and went to open it.

Linda and Randy entered the flat. Bringing up the rear, looking both upset and contrite, was Colin. Eija sent Dom a look, silently asking him not to look smug, but it was too late.

Linda took a seat on the loveseat across from the sofa, her Audrey Hepburn replica pixie cut as golden as the sun's rays that cascaded off the wavy locks. Square, black metal frames sat low on her nose.

Randy sat next to her.

Colin looked like he hadn't caught a decent night's rest in weeks, but Eija could tell only because of how long she'd known him. To the untrained eye, he was handsome as usual and well put-together in his dark gray suit. Joining the DGSE in France and then Interpol had been an act of rebellion against his family's wealth, but he carried the air of old money with him wherever he went.

"Hi, little one," Linda cooed. "Oh my, she's adorable. She looks just like Dominik."

"I see it now," Randy said, studying Shiloh. "I don't know how I didn't see it before."

Colin waved a hand. "Can we get to the point of this and wrap it up?"

"Colin, we all know you don't like being wrong." Eija met his eyes. "You were wrong about Dom. So was I. Get over it and let's move on."

Shiloh crawled over to Randy, used his pant leg to hoist herself up, and then looked, expectantly, up at him. Picking up on the nonverbal hint, he set her on his lap, and she busied herself with the pattern on his tie.

"Obviously, you know why we're here," Linda said. "Yuri's still missing. As of right now, the rumor around the Bratva is that Dominik Sokolov's being held in a prison at an undisclosed location by a group of Americans. According to Pavel, they're mobilizing to find and retrieve the Bratva prince. Ironically, just like when Gorbachev was ousted, it's unclear who's in charge, so there's been some chaos."

"You can't take him back to headquarters," Eija said. Reading between the lines was a necessity in this line of work. "And, if his cover's still intact, that means he can get back into the penthouse."

Linda's head bobbed in agreement. "Yes. There's an old

Soviet prison in Krasnodar. The plan is, we'll be transporting him there, but Bratva will intercept the convoy."

Dom asked, "Have they narrowed down any leads on what group Yuri hired to attack us in Moscow?"

"No," Randy offered. "But Pavel said because of the contentious history the Bratva's had with the Chechens, ever since the theatre hostage crisis back in '02, they've already targeted two major figureheads in the Chechen mafia. What's left of it, anyhow."

Eija looked at Dom, who was already looking at her. "When does Dom leave?" she asked.

"We'll transport him underground tonight, get him back to Russia," Randy said. "Then, in three days, we'll take him on the convoy to Krasnodar."

"They want you to go too," Colin added. "A room full of Bratva, Yakuza, Irish mafia, you name it, saw Dom leave with you. Your name's come up several times since the event. Virtually everyone, except me, apparently, knew you and Dom were hooking up, so they're concerned you're not only a weakness and distraction, but involved in Yuri's death somehow. Being American."

"We want to put you in the U.S. Embassy," Linda explained. "You'll say you went there after the attack seeking refuge, and you've been hiding out. Dom, as the new head of the Brotherhood, will go there to retrieve you. You think he's taking you to safety, but he's looking for a head to chop off."

Dom scrubbed his chin, eyes unfocused. "If I target you for

questioning or worse, then it solidifies that nobody's safe in the course of the inquiry."

"It shows I'm not a weakness," Eija concluded.

Dom winked. "Even though you are."

Colin rolled his eyes.

"And it also shows he's prepared to take the helm," Randy finished. "Yuri planned this expecting Dom to take the fall. Right now, Dom has. If Dom returns to the Bratva, the turtle might poke his head from his shell."

Eija gestured to Shiloh, who'd crawled from Randy's lap to Linda's. "But, as you can see, I have obligations. Priceless obligations."

"You have a sister," Linda said. "Alecia Baker. According to her last tax return, she lives in Richmond with her husband and two dependents."

Eija masked her surprise. The last time she'd snooped on her sister, there'd only been Alecia Baker, Ulysses Baker III, and their daughter, Analeigh Rose. Analeigh was now around eight or nine, and she'd only met her niece three times—her birth and their grandparents' funerals. She'd only shown up at Analeigh's birth because Alecia had begged.

"I do have a sister," Eija said, nodding slowly. "But we're not exactly close. You can't be suggesting she become Shiloh's temporary caregiver. You're asking me to leave behind my baby. Again."

Linda's voice jumped an octave. "The plan is too delicate, Eija. You can't just go missing. We need you back in the penthouse. These are the sacrifices we have to make in this field. You're not the only person who's had to make hard decisions."

"Watch how you talk to Eija," Dom warned.

"You still answer to us, Dominik."

"When it comes to those two right there," Dom pointed to Shiloh and Eija, "I don't answer to anybody but God."

Randy rotated his shoulders. A hard sigh flared his nostrils. "Nephew, Linda's right. The Bratva's like a fucking hair trigger. The puzzle's been jumbled, and now we're attempting to put it back together. We can't do that by hiding pieces."

Shiloh discovered Linda's earring, and Linda gently pried the golden hoop from Shiloh's small fingers.

"Eija, Shiloh will be safer with your sister," Linda insisted. "No one knows your sister's associated with you. Think about it. Going in there with Dom, that's for Shiloh too. David's son grew up without a father and I'm sure, had David the opportunity, he'd go back and make different choices."

Colin snorted.

Eija cut him a look.

"That wasn't for you, E." Colin looked over at Dom. "Sokolov, I didn't make you. Nothing about you screamed 'CIA' or any other intelligence agency. You're Yuri Sokolov's biological son. You have his...ways in your genes. I don't see why no one else feels like we're opening a can that'll only ooze worms."

"Do you have a father?" Dom asked him.

Colin sucked his teeth. "Don't we all?"

"Could you kill him? Because I can kill mine. I can pull the trigger without blinking."

"But you won't," Linda interjected. "We need Yuri alive. That's years of intel. Years of inside information. He's too valuable."

Eija held up a hand. "How do you intend for me to just leave my *infant* with my estranged sister?"

"A cover story." Linda switched Shiloh to her other arm. "You were injured and you'll be out of commission for a while. The only next of kin we found was her, and we need her to take Shiloh in while you recuperate."

Eija waved away the suggestion. "She won't do it. She'll ask to see me."

"We need you, Eija."

Eija looked at Dom.

Shiloh was his daughter too.

He shook his head, but then he shrugged. "Look, I won't tell you what to do. I'd rather she stay with us both. Since it can't be us, then you. If not you, I'd rather her be with friends of mine. Friends who I trust. I don't know your sister, so I can't advocate for her with my daughter."

"But you *will* need me at the penthouse."

He cracked a smile. "I'll always need you."

Colin clenched his jaw so tight, it clicked.

Eija stared at Shiloh, who was still trying to get to Linda's earrings. It was either stay behind and risk Dom's life, possibly Shiloh's as well, or leave Shiloh behind.

Again.

Over the course of the past year, her priorities had changed. First, they'd changed for Shiloh. Now, they revolved around

Shiloh and the man she couldn't accept not being part of their lives.

"I have conditions," she said. "If we don't find Yuri, or at least a ping his general location by the time my baby girl gets to nine months, kill Miss K and pull me out. Point blank. The second...Dom, you said you have friends you trust."

"In Sweden."

"Can they keep her safe?"

"Safer than the pope."

"Then, I'd rather Shiloh stay with them. It's too risky with my sister. Alecia and I will reconcile on different terms."

Shiloh fussed until Linda set her back on the floor. Then, she crawled over to Dom, pulled herself up using the fabric of his pajama pants, and set the same expectant eyes on him. He picked her up, and she lowered her head to his shoulder.

"Nine months old," Linda agreed. "You have my word."

Eija stood, hands shaking, and headed to the nursery. As though he'd been right on her heels, Dom's presence shadowed her from behind.

"Eija, you okay?"

She moved about the room but couldn't focus.

"You don't have to go," he added.

"Your friends," she stopped, faced him, "what all do they do?"

"It would be easier to tell you what they don't."

"Which is?"

"Give up."

Her tongue moved over her lips, and stinging in the middle

of the bottom lip was the only telltale sign she'd been nibbling on them at some point.

"One of them, I helped out not too long ago," Dom explained. "I took care of his pregnant wife while he was...detained."

"Incarcerated?"

"More like abducted. They have a baby. A son. Mikey's older than Shi by about eight months or so, but she'll be okay with them. *If* she goes with them."

"Sending Shiloh to stay with your friends is me protecting my daughter," Eija said. Recited. She needed to hear it as much as she needed to say it. "Me coming with you is me protecting her father. Dom," she wrapped her fingers around his cast, "I heard what you said in Moscow just before we got separated. You're important to me too."

He squinted one eye. "I don't recall saying *that* in Moscow. I'm pretty sure I used different words."

"Dom," she let a few breaths pass and waited for her heartbeat to calm down, "there's something about you. Something about me when I'm with you. That something makes me understand all the sappy love songs and poems and romantic comedies, and it's been that way since that very first date. You say you want to be in me and your daughter's life? Well, I want you in our lives too. I want, when all of this is over, to go with you to that tropical paradise with Rihanna."

A smile spread across his face. "You'd share me with Rihanna?"

"Get it right. I'd share Rihanna with you."

"Ah. Of course."

"Do you understand?" she asked. "I did my best, but I hope what you heard, through all of that fumbling, is that I love you. Jesus, I love you, Dominik."

When she'd imagined using those words for the first time, she'd pictured a sword going through her chest. Drowning. A major explosion tearing her to bits. Strangely, it was all of that, but as soon as the sensation eased, she wanted it back.

His smile grew. "I did."

"If, after a month, there's nothing, I'll exit the op."

"And I'll come join you when I'm done."

"Even if you can't—"

"I will."

She folded her fingers into fists and pressed them into her hips, avoiding his eyes. Sometimes, like now, he spoke to her through his eyes, and what they said was far more than she could ever articulate.

"Okay, then. Come on, Shi. Let Mommy and Daddy help you pack."

Chapter Twenty-Seven

Dom kept his head down in the back of the van as the convoy ambled along. Pavel had assured them that the Bratva would intercept him along the Kuban River. Linda and Randy hadn't explained to those involved in the transport that he was *supposed* to be taken, needing this to "remain several levels above top secret." All that meant was they wanted to absolve themselves of any guilt if and when lives were lost in the process.

He'd talked to Eija right before they started on the journey. She'd met his friends who lived in Sweden, and it had eased her mind to know Shiloh would be in more than capable hands.

The van rolled to a stop.

Next came voices.

Muffled gunfire rose into the air. Shouts and commands, in English and Russian, mixed with the gunfire. The van was bulletproof all the way up through the windows, so he didn't worry about any shells penetrating the exterior.

Metal scraped the van's back door, and he heard what sounded like chains falling. Then, the doors opened, and led by Pavel were six Bratva, their guns aimed at the van opening.

Pavel tucked away his gun and made quick work of releasing the cuffs and manacles. The Bratva then formed a perimeter around Dom, just like he'd watched them do for Yuri time and time again, and escorted him to a waiting car. With loyalty like this, it was easy to see how Yuri had swayed.

They helped him into an SUV and sped away. When they were about a half hour away from the scene, a man he recognized as Liev pumped a fist.

"The prince lives!"

The other men, all except for Pavel, roared in excitement. Pavel remained silent, head down. Dom gripped his shoulder and nodded, but he didn't look up.

"You have heard what happened to your father?" Liev asked.

Dom nodded.

"And Ekaterina?"

"Yes." Her loss actually did bring him a rush of grief. "How is Nikolai?"

"Safe," Pavel said. "We won't be bringing him back to the penthouse."

The men murmured their agreement.

Dom gave Pavel's shoulder another squeeze. Pavel might not have wanted Nikolai to know the truth about his paternity, but that hadn't stopped him from doing everything he could to look out for his son.

"I need to make a stop," Dom said. "At the U.S. Embassy."

The men exchanged quizzical looks.

"The nanny's involved, and I'll get the truth out of her. One way or the other."

* * *

Eija sold the act of a helpless nanny, overwhelmed with gratitude that her employer had come looking for her. She'd changed into a plain white T-shirt and long cotton pants as though the embassy had given her whatever clothes on hand they'd had for her to wear.

On cue, she'd brought tears to her eyes, and Dom had rubbed her back and spoken with gentle words all the way back to the SUV. Once they were inside, it was a different story.

"Hey!" Eija tugged on the rope that kept her hands fastened behind her back. "What are you doing?"

Dom studied her through narrowed eyes. "You know who killed Yuri."

"What? How would I know that?"

They'd switched the vehicles so that only he, Pavel, and two Bratva rode with Eija. The others took the initial SUV in the event they were being followed.

He leaned forward, inches from her face. "Because I know who you work for. Didn't you think I'd figure it out? Toss a little bit of pussy my way, and I'd fall to my knees?"

Her pupils dilated, and her bottom lip disappeared into her mouth, and he gave a slight shake of his head. Now was not the time or the place. Seeing Eija tied up was like role play, and it fucked with his head too, but an SUV full of men would smell a wet woman from the first drip.

"What could I possibly know?" she asked.

He leaned back. "I aim to find out."

"Please, I swear. I don't know anything. What can I do? How can I make you believe me?"

Now, she was stumbling into fantasy territory.

Liev, grinning, grabbed his dick. "Sir, I don't mean to be forward, but maybe you should hear her out. Maybe she can persuade us all."

"You think with your dick often, Liev?" he growled. "Can I trust that, if you are questioned about the Bratva, all you'd need to be offered to talk is a whiff of pussy?"

Liev's smile fell. "No, sir. This is not the case."

"See that it's not."

They arrived at the penthouse, and he ordered them to lock Eija in a room off Yuri's study so he could monitor her. It was where Yuri had hidden women if Ekaterina dropped in for an unannounced visit, already furnished with a bed and the crystal chandelier that dangled above it.

Apparently, it was all Yuri had needed for his trysts.

Eija fought the entire way, the men thankfully missing the hardness of her nipples.

They strapped her, by the wrists, to the bedposts. When they left, he left with them, but he was back already, standing in the doorway. She watched him through hooded eyelids, chest pitching high.

They hadn't touched each other in Lyon. There, Shiloh had been the priority, and they'd both been nursing fresh injuries. Now, he was looking at Eija Barrett, the mother of his child. The woman who'd compromised a years-long operation.

For *him*.

"I promise I know nothing," she whispered.

He left the room and returned with a pair of scissors and more rope, which he used to strap her to the bottom bedposts by the ankles.

"Please, Mr. Sokolov. I had nothing to do with this."

"I don't trust you, Miss K." He snipped off her panties and wasn't at all surprised to see just how wet all this had made her. "You arrived here around the same time as I did. I also learned that you were in Grenada at the same time as I was. Rumor is," he slid two fingers along her slit, "we even have a kid together."

Each pass of his fingers made her eyelids flutter.

"Please..."

"Please, what?"

"I'll do anything you want."

He cut the shirt down the middle, the halves falling to both sides. Her nipples were so firm, they *looked* like they ached. To help soothe them, he bent and sucked one into his mouth.

She nearly flew through the ceiling.

"Something wrong?" he asked, lips brushing her nipple. "You seem...agitated."

"I just," she swallowed, "want to give you what you want."

"Is that right? And what do you think I want?"

She cried out when his mouth and tongue found the other nipple. While he sucked, he stroked her clit, and the way her thighs clenched, he could tell she wanted to squeeze them together.

Too bad.

"Quiet, Miss K. I don't want the rest of the house to hear what I'm doing to you. What would they think of me?"

"That you're a wicked man," she hissed.

"Wicked?" He kissed his way down her body. "What else?"

"Dom, please. I can't be quiet."

"What'd you just call me?" He sank his teeth into her inner thigh. "What's my name?"

Goosebumps flashed over her skin. "I'm sorry, *Mr. Sokolov.*"

"You don't tell me what to do with your body. You don't tell me what you can or can't handle."

His head disappeared between her legs, and she tried to pull away, but the restraints kept her locked in.

Her moans became gasps.

Then cries.

She writhed and bucked.

Pleaded.

When he took her to the edge and stopped, multiple times, with only the tip of his tongue pressed lightly against her clit, she prayed.

When he finally let her climax, her body arched into a bow, and he kept going until she nearly jerked a post from the bolts that attached it to the bed frame.

He sucked the taste of her into his mouth from his bottom lip. "You still say you know nothing?"

"Even if I did, why would I tell you?"

"Oh, is that right?" He undressed and then stood naked along the edge of the bed. "So, you *want* me to give you a reason to tell me?"

"I'm...not sure."

"Tell me what you want, Miss K. Is this," he motioned to his dick, "what you want?"

"Yes."

"Are you sure?"

She nodded. "Please."

He removed the restraints but tied her up again, hitching her up against the bedpost, stomach first and her body slightly bent. He grabbed her chin and turned her head to slip his tongue into her mouth as he pushed his way into her body.

"Tell me what I want to hear, Miss K."

She whimpered with each surge forward, and he held her hips steady with both hands.

"Miss K," he bit her neck, her earlobe, "answer me."

"You," she said, winded. "I want you."

He'd asked her to tell him what he wanted to hear as Mr. Sokolov, but now she was speaking to Dom. Her Dom. And it made him even harder.

"I love you," she said, and that it was nearly inaudible made it more salient. "When all of this is over, I just want you."

An orgasm shot from him like molten lava, so strong he had to hold her against him to absorb some of the sensation. It covered him from head to toe, activating every nerve fiber. He kissed her any and everywhere, then held her until their heart-beats returned to normal.

Eija fell limp against him.

He untied her and helped her into bed, where they drifted off to sleep.

Hours later, he emerged from the suite. Another Bratva, Zurik, met him on the stairs.

"Did she talk, sir?" Zurik asked.

Dom shook his head. "Not yet. Whoever she works for trained her well. I suspect I'll be back up to try again several more times. *Several* more times."

Chapter Twenty-Eight

Eija stared at the monitor screen in front of her, scouring the images she'd taken in Yuri's office for the millionth time. Dom was out, staying authentic to his role of trying to find who'd orchestrated the attack. Pavel had switched out the computer in Yuri's office with one supplied by Colin, and when Dom wasn't around, the study door remained locked. Because he didn't trust anyone but Pavel to watch over her, she locked herself inside the office whenever he needed to take Pavel with him. If she needed him, she had a phone. If she couldn't get to a phone, she had a gun.

The office and her "cell" were soundproofed, so she freely moved between rooms. She and Dom hardly saw each other during the day, but he came to her at night. He came *with* her every night.

His friends in Sweden, a team of elite soldiers with families of their own—one of them was a blade-wielding madman responsible for a fair share of Dom's scars, and she didn't know how that screamed *friend*—sent videos and images of Shiloh, who looked happy in each one. Two more weeks and Shiloh would be back in her arms.

"What *are* these?" Eija rotated the images, rotated her head. "They're schematics, but for what?"

Her grandfather had been an enigmatologist who'd loved puzzles until the day he died. After retirement, he'd joined senior puzzle and chess tournaments, winning a few. He'd religiously watched detective crime shows, which was why she loved them so much. He was also the reason she'd chosen to go into covert work. What bigger mysteries were there to solve than those which could level entire cities? Result in biological warfare? In her opinion, there was no greater puzzle than the mind of a human being, especially those in positions of power.

An alert on the screen showed Dom entering the penthouse. He was with Pavel and Liev, but Pavel remained behind while Liev followed Dom up the stairs. At the top of the stairs, he glanced at a painting on the wall, a portrait of Tchaikovsky, letting her know they were headed to the office.

She closed out the images, went to the private room, and "cowered" on the bed.

The study door opened.

Several footsteps later, Dominik appeared in the private room without a suit jacket. Blood splatters turned his white collared shirt into a Jackson Pollock. She knew it was Dominik from the look in his eyes, and she never asked him what he did whenever he left. They did what had to be done to get results.

Liev entered behind him.

Eija pulled the covers up to her chin. Dom had left enough bruises on her neck from his biting and sucking for the marks to look like injuries from afar. However, the ones on her breasts and ass would give everyone a more accurate idea of what they'd been up to.

"Still nothing, hmm?" Liev asked. "You don't appear to be bloody and swollen enough for me. What kind of torture have you been using, sir?" Liev looked over at Dominik. "I think it might be the kind she likes."

Dominik's gaze moved slowly from Eija to Liev.

"I can take a turn, hmm?" Liev went on. "Maybe she'll sing on my cock."

It was such a precise cut to the neck, a surgeon could have done it.

Dominik twisted the knife before pulling it from Liev's throat. Liev, gasping, fell to the floor, eyes open, and they remained that way until he stopped twitching.

"He asked too many questions." Dominik shrugged off his shirt, used it to wipe the blade, and tossed them both at Liev's head. "I would have asked Pavel to handle it, but this one felt personal."

Eija stared at the lifeless body.

Dom strode over, sat on the bed, and rubbed the sole of her foot with his thumb. "You okay?"

"Colin thinks Yuri, most likely, hasn't left Russia," she

slowly began. "They cross-referenced flight manifests with his name and demographics. So far, they've found nothing. If he's left, he hasn't done it by plane, train, boat, or...hell, diving gear."

"And what do you think?"

"I think he hasn't *yet*. He's waiting for something. I'm guessing it's a buyer for whatever those plans will, eventually, show me."

He looked around. "You okay locked up in here?"

"I'm keeping busy. Plus, a friend comes in here at night to play with me."

"And how's your calf?"

She lowered the sheet. It was nowhere near gruesome on the outside, but she had suffered some nerve damage. It would make for an interesting story one day. She'd tell Shiloh once she was old enough.

"It's not bad, right?" she asked.

He fingered the scar's marbling. "What'd you think, you'd come out looking like the monster Frankenstein built? You're gorgeous, Eija. Scars and all."

"Frankenstein? Oh, baby," she leaned forward and gave him a quick kiss, "you and that Nietzsche-quoting brain of yours."

She hurried back to the computer, hopping over Liev's body. As she moved the images around, he watched from over her shoulder. It took close to an hour, so he went from watching over her shoulder to pacing until she ended up on his lap, his hands kneading her hips. She had no idea how she'd survived working any other way before then.

"Dom, tell me what the Soviet atomic bomb project is."

"You're assuming I know."

She looked at him over her shoulder.

"Well," he sighed, "it was basically Stalin's response to The Manhattan Project when Soviet spies discovered the U.S. was developing nuclear weapons. The secret cities here in Russia? They're where the Soviet Union did much of its nuclear testing. The effects are still felt to this day in the surrounding areas."

"God, I love you." She positioned herself so they could both see the screen. "We were wrong. Yuri didn't steal information from foreign countries. These are part of a set of notes on nuclear fission. Nuclear weapons. I thought we were looking for military weapons. Maybe a design schematic for a gunship or an unmanned fighter jet. Not, dare I say it, weapons of mass destruction. Why the hell would he want this?"

"Maybe he wants it, but he doesn't intend to use it," Dom said, fingers moving to her spinal column. "Having this information is still powerful. Can you imagine what countries would pay for it?"

Realization hit them both at the same time.

"That's why they did the Dostavka-Koronatsiya so soon," she said, too shocked to feel betrayed. "Yuri still had years left in him, but he needed to be pulled out. Think about it, Dom. Who would this information benefit the most?"

Dom let his head hang, shook it. "Us."

"Exactly. And the only price, in my opinion, Yuri would accept for this information is his freedom. Linda, David...they helped him do all of this. They created an entire fake op, a fake task force, to retrieve Yuri. It's like she said; that's years of intel.

Yuri's too valuable. It's the real reason Linda sent me to work with Randy. She was afraid I'd figure it out. Shifting my focus to you took the heat off Yuri. Even if I'd sent your information in, they wouldn't have done shit with it but throw me another bone. I wouldn't be surprised if Randy has no clue."

Dom called Pavel up to the room, clued him in, and the stoic man somehow went even more stoic. He didn't have to speak for them to know, in his eyes, that there was no way Pavel would let Yuri get anywhere near safety.

"We still don't know where he is," Dom said, helping her to her feet. "And, if we're going based on the theory that Randy doesn't know what Linda and David are up to, they won't leave him alone and risk me calling him without them running interference."

Eija paced the room, mind going so fast her mouth could barely keep up. "The human brain likes comfort. It creates comfort using familiarity—patterns, rituals, rhythms. Predictability. Yuri had to lie low somewhere he felt safe. Somewhere familiar. Pavel, you know Yuri better than any of us. Say he had only two weeks to live. Where would he go?"

"Home," Pavel said. "Astrakhan. It's where his grandparents are from."

"We used to go down there all the time," Dom added. "He'd walk around the city, dredge up memories."

Astrakhan was southern, like the regional dialect they'd picked up on, which meant Yuri had likely orchestrated the attack at the dostavka-koronatsiya outside of Linda and David's knowledge. He'd wrapped himself in the comforts of home, right down to the contract killers he'd hired to go after his only son, knowing Dom would handle them. But he'd needed to sell the lie of a snitch.

Yuri didn't love Dominik. Like any narcissistic parent, Dominik was an accessory. A prop. A means to an end.

Eija drew in and released a sigh that pained her lungs. "Yuri has a buyer. He's lying low from the CIA, reneging on his agreement. Someone with more money, power, or influence wants those plans."

Pavel handed her a gun that she tucked under her shirt.

"Call Linda," Dom said. "Tell her we 'know' Yuri's in Astrakhan. They'll arrange an immediate flight out." He turned to Pavel. "Eija's walking out of here with us, so I need you to clear a path. Ludmila, Manya...all the staff, they stay unharmed, but if anyone takes a shot—"

"I've got it." Pavel readied a shotgun. "It would be my pleasure."

Chapter Twenty-Nine

Eija, Dom, and Pavel touched down in Astrakhan a little under three hours later with Colin, Linda, and Randy. On the way, Randy had gotten in touch with Interpol, and Linda had coordinated with the local police. Anyone who matched Yuri's description was to be stopped and detained, no questions asked.

A few minutes after landing, they received an alert that someone fitting Yuri's description was outside the airport, so they'd had to organize a strategy for preventing him from boarding his flight on the go.

It didn't take long.

Less than a half hour later, Eija found herself staring at Yuri waiting in line to get to the front desk. She'd expected him to be in the business lounge, having grown used to living life in the lap of luxury, but he wore no designer labels. Instead, a baseball cap covered his always-perfectly-cut silver hair, and the man wore *gray cargo pants* and a *T-shirt*. He even had a backpack slung over his shoulder. Had they not been looking for him, she was sure they would have never guessed *this* was Yuri Sokolov.

"I've got eyes on the king," Eija said.

Dom groaned in her ear. "Don't call him that."

"If you're the prince, that makes him the king."

Yuri finished at the check-in desk, thanked the woman standing behind it with a smile, and started off. Eija couldn't tell the last time she'd spoken to someone at a check-in desk. If she ever ran late for a flight only to realize she'd forgotten her phone, she'd have to skip the entire trip.

He weaved through the crowd, headed toward his gate, in her direction. A local uniformed officer stepped from the crowd and followed.

"Can somebody call him off?" Eija asked.

It was too late by the time she asked.

The officer wasn't being nearly as discreet as he thought he was. Yuri never took more than three steps without looking over his shoulder, an expert at evaluating his surroundings to exploit and slip through any tiny cracks he discovered.

Yuri picked up his pace.

Colin stepped between Yuri and the officer to redirect the officer's attention.

Eija cocked the hammer on her gun and stepped from her hiding spot just as gunshots echoed through the terminal.

Chaos ensued.

People sprinted and dashed in all directions, screaming. They bumped into her, creating a moving blur, blocking her path to Yuri. Then she saw the officer on the ground, prone and unmoving. Colin was kneeling next to him, red dots dripping to the floor, but his back faced her, so she couldn't see where he'd been hit.

"Colin?" She stepped through and around bodies, heading in his direction. "Colin, talk to me, babe."

"I'm okay, E," he said, and she quickly assessed his voice through the speaker. "He hit the vest. Looks like he's one of Yuri's. And I don't mind when *you* call me babe."

The officer taking a shot at Colin meant Yuri had been one step ahead of them—again. He'd known they were coming the minute Linda contacted local police.

At the far end of the terminal, two more uniformed officers lay on the ground. Pavel stood over them, his firearm in his right hand.

"Miss K..." Hard steel cooled Eija's temple. "I didn't expect to run into you all the way down here."

She held up her hands. The gunshot had cleared the terminal, except for the check-in staff, who'd taken cover behind their desks. Without the sea of bodies, she had a direct line of sight to Dom approaching them, gun raised. Randy approached from Dom's left while Linda went to check on Colin. Colin shoved her away and stood, turning his attention to where everyone else's had fallen.

"I like to travel," Eija said. "And I heard the farther south you go in Russia, the better the weather. No frozen eyelashes."

Yuri laughed. "I did always like you."

"How do you think this is going to play out?" Dom questioned. "You can't possibly think we're just going to let you walk."

Yuri's gaze flashed first to Randy, then Linda. "You can't kill me. Your bosses here made that clear."

"I don't have to kill you when I shoot you," Dom said. "And you know I can make this shot."

"You also know, the minute you pull that trigger, I'll move Miss K in the path of your bullet. You wouldn't be able to survive accidentally killing the love of your life."

Dom made no move to lower the gun.

"It's Barrett, by the way," Eija said. "Eija Barrett. You don't really have to call me Miss K anymore."

Another laugh rumbled against her back from deep in Yuri's chest. She caught Dom's gaze and silently conveyed what they both knew needed to happen. Her calf was sore, but it wasn't a broken bone. She wasn't a helpless damsel in distress. She could get herself out of this situation with the right timing. Being trigger-happy wasn't the right timing.

Colin raised his weapon.

"Old friend, you look like all of your years," Randy taunted. "I guess it was the expensive haircuts and clothes keeping you up?"

"And you look like her," Yuri said. "Anya. It's funny how someone who grew up in such a religious household so easily spread her legs for me. That woman never did a single good thing for me."

"It's *Aani*," Randy corrected.

Dom's forearm flexed.

Eija narrowed her eyes. Yuri was a shit-talker, and he'd been a shit-talker longer than the last five minutes. He was obviously trying to get under their skin, get them to pull the trigger so he could use a bullet in her skull as a distraction.

Dom might not have cared about Yuri the way a son cared for his father, but it would have never been easy to hear that sentence leave Yuri's mouth. Once this was over, she'd remind him, every day, that it didn't matter; he was a good, great, and amazing part of her and Shiloh's lives.

Fuck Yuri Sokolov.

"Put them down," Eija instructed. "He's right. You shoot, and I'm dead."

Yuri wouldn't risk his own life by shooting her. Not with his freedom and, quite possibly, billions on the line.

Dom and Colin stayed the course.

Randy dropped his weapon and laid a hand on Dom's forearm. "Come on, Dom. Do what Eija says."

Dom tightened his grip.

Eija turned to Colin. "Colin, help me out here. Drop it. It's the only way right now. He made us. We have to accept that."

"Do what she says, *Colin*," Yuri goaded. "This here is a smart woman. Hell, I might take her with me. Would you like that, Miss Barrett?"

"That depends. Where are we going, Fiji?"

"After, perhaps. I have a stop to make first."

Dom's jaw clenched, turning his face into granite. She saw him trying to read her, read the situation.

"Baby," she softened her voice, "please *lower* the *gun*."

335

Dom's arm slowly fell.

She breathed a sigh of relief.

Then, in one movement, she slipped out of Yuri's hold, pushing the nozzle of his gun up toward the ceiling.

A single shot rang out.

By the time Yuri realized he no longer had his human shield, she already had a gun on him.

"Set it down or die, Yuri," she instructed.

With both hands in the air, Yuri set the gun on the floor. Before he could fully right himself, three shots whizzed by, but by the time she heard them, Yuri was already on his back.

The smell of gunpowder exploded like a cloud.

A smaller pistol fell from his fingers.

Two of the shots had come from Dom, but if Dom hadn't taken the opportunity—she noticed Pavel tucking away his gun —Yuri still wouldn't have lived through the standoff.

Linda hurried over to Yuri, speaking rapidly into her phone, but no paramedic on Earth could save him.

Linda and David had compromised an entire team of officers, Randy included. They'd kept them out of the loop, sending them in on dummy missions. Yuri was responsible for the deaths of thousands.

As far as Eija was concerned, they'd intercepted him taking the nuclear plans to his mysterious buyer. They'd done their part. Her objective had been to prevent it from getting into the wrong hands. Dom's had been to take Yuri down. Pavel was a lone wolf, and even he'd gotten a slice of revenge pie.

Linda's scream echoed throughout the terminal. "Son of a bitch! Sokolov, do you know what you just did?"

Dom didn't spare her a glance, staring at his father as though expecting Yuri to rise from the dead only to be killed again.

"Randy, cuff him."

Eija's head snapped around. "Excuse me?"

"He disobeyed a direct order. Randy, I said cuff him before I have someone else, who won't be as gentle, handle your damn nephew."

"This is bullshit." Eija stood in front of Dom, arms outstretched. "Yuri had a gun in an ankle holster."

"We'll never know now if he was going to use it, will we?"

Dom handed over his gun and held his wrists out in front of him. Randy slapped on the metal bracelets.

"You assholes went full *Smokin' Aces* on us, playing with our fucking lives," Eija said, on the brink of snapping and shooting Linda herself. "You expected Dom to yield when he saw Yuri was about to shoot the mother of his child?"

Allegedly.

Her coded message to Dom had been to let him know Yuri had a "lower gun," which had brushed her ankle when Yuri crept up behind her. Whether or not he'd reached for it, Dom would have shot him. Pavel would have shot him. Colin would have shot him. Yuri was lucky he hadn't gone out like Scarface.

Randy pulled her into an embrace. "I'll take care of this, Eija."

"Can I say goodbye?" she asked.

"It won't be goodbye."

She nodded and covered her mouth, swallowing a cry as she faced Dom.

He bent.

She rose onto her toes and wrapped her fingers around the back of his neck. Their lips came together, her tongue slipping into his mouth, tasting every nook to hold her over until she saw him again. There was no way in hell she wouldn't see him again.

"Come on." Linda walked over and grabbed Dom by the cuffs. "Enough of that. You don't get to fuck my entire operation and then expect to go fuck."

Interpol taped off the scene.

Colin walked up behind Eija and wrapped an arm around her shoulders. His other hand cradled his lower abdomen.

"You should get that looked at," she said.

He groaned. "It's a minor flesh wound. Plus, I'm ready to go home and see my girl."

They headed for the exit, Pavel silently trailing them.

"April took you back?"

"It's a conditional offer. We're in a trial period."

She eyed him.

"I'll be good! You've inspired me with your love story."

"Whatever." She gently elbowed him. "But, I think I might be done with this. Think I'll retire early and be a stay-at-home mom until Shiloh starts school."

"What'll you do after that?"

She shrugged. "Who the hell knows?"

But she wouldn't be doing it alone.

* * *

Randy squeezed his forehead and studied Dominik through the car's rearview mirror. Next to him in the passenger seat, Linda chatted with David on the phone.

He didn't know what they were going to do with his nephew. It wasn't as if Dominik could go into Yuri's mind and reveal the secrets they'd lost with Yuri's death. But the way Linda made it seem, and from the information she relayed to David, it was like she believed Dominik had obtained confidential information from his time undercover. She was treating Dominik like he was truly the Bratva's successor.

They flew back to Moscow right after the terminal incident. The entire way, Dominik didn't speak. All he'd done was stare at Eija with unmistakable awe.

At the airport, they separated.

Linda didn't want to wait to get Dominik stateside for interrogation, which was probably her biggest weakness. Since he'd known Linda, she'd always been impulsive.

"Randy!"

"Shit!" He stepped hard on the brake pedal seconds before he would have slammed into the back of a large truck.

Linda glared at him. "Where's your head?"

"Sorry." He shoved his fingers through his hair and took another glance in the backseat. *Today,* Linda's impulsivity would be her downfall.

She spun around in her seat. "Where'd he go?"

He checked the backseat as though it was his first time looking. "Fuck! How'd he get out of the cuffs?"

A smile clawed at his cheek, but he pushed it back.

Eija.

She snatched the handcuffs key from his pocket.

No wonder that last kiss had been especially sloppy. No wonder Dom didn't say a single word on the flight. She'd slipped the key into his mouth.

"Randy, I swear to God if you had anything to do with this." Linda scrolled through her phone. "He can't hide. Doesn't matter where he goes; I'll find his ass."

Randy tightened his grip on the steering wheel and allowed the smile to bloom on the side of his face Linda couldn't see.

Chapter Thirty

Six months later

"Shi?" Eija walked through the house, down the hallway, picking up toys like a trail of breadcrumbs. "Sweetheart, Mommy's going to teach you the clean-up song."

It had been around six months since she'd last heard anything from or about Dominik. Colin, now in a steady relationship with April, returned to French intelligence. He still sent her coded messages, and the last one seemed to indicate that he and April had finally agreed to move in together—this time, without the cold feet.

Pavel took Nikolai into his custody and fell off the face of the map, which was precisely what Pavel had wanted.

Linda, David, and Randy spent hours interrogating her

about Dom's location, but she had no idea where he was. They never discussed where he'd go if they'd had to split up, and it was that plausible deniability—and a little training—that helped her pass polygraph after polygraph.

Eventually, they left her alone.

Without her knowing, before the Yuri incident and before he found out about Shiloh, Dom set up an offshore account for her to access in the event he'd gone through with the arranged marriage.

The first time she did, she'd only expected enough money to tide them over for about a year or so. Get them set up in their new spot. However, when the bank manager gave her the balance, she realized "venture capital" meant more than she'd expected.

This was "change your life" money.

"Leave the country and start over" money.

So, she did. She retired from the agency and moved to Panama City with her baby girl.

Six months had felt like six years, all because she didn't know if Dom was okay. It was hard to believe he'd willingly stay away as long as he had.

Maybe something had happened to him. Maybe Linda and David indeed had him locked up somewhere. Some variation of those fearful thoughts kept her awake for hours every night.

"Shi? Baby, where are you?"

Shiloh hadn't gone from crawling to walking. She'd gone from crawling to Usain Bolt.

She found her daughter in the living room, staring out at the backyard through the French doors that led to the patio. When Shiloh heard her approach, she looked up, but then she turned back to the doors and pointed.

"Dada."

Eija crouched next to her. "You want to go upstairs and look at more pictures of Daddy?"

"Dada," Shiloh repeated.

Then she took off toward the doors.

"Wait, baby—"

"It's okay. I've got her."

Eija froze.

Had he always been this beautiful?

In six months, he'd managed to grow out a good deal of his hair. Now that there was no further threat of a torture-style interrogation, she was fine with it being longer again. He also seemed taller, which could have been because he was holding Shiloh in his left arm. It was also possible she was emphasizing his most attractive traits because she'd missed him.

Shiloh grabbed his face. "Dada."

"We look at pictures of you," Eija said, voice shaking. "Every night. She knows your face."

He placed a loud smack on Shiloh's cheek, teasing out a screaming giggle. "Eija, why are you all the way over there when you should be," he tapped his chest, "right here?"

"I'm afraid I'll walk right through you."

"You won't, baby." He extended his right arm. "I'm finally here."

She walked over and wrapped her arms around his waist.

"Yes, you are. And, now that you're here," she smacked his hard stomach, "six months, Dom? Do you know all the ways you died in my mind in six months with zero contact? One of them involved a very agitated Silverback gorilla."

He laughed, stroking her back. "I know. I'm sorry. I had to lie low for a while, but this was as long as I could last. I missed my girls."

She stepped back and motioned around. "You like it?"

"Very nice." He nodded. "Your husband bought you this house?"

"Yes, he did."

"So you ended up finding yourself that rich guy, huh?"

Satisfied with the reunion, Shiloh wiggled until Dom set her on the floor. Then she walked off, in search of something more interesting than her parents, and Dom pulled Eija back to his chest. Eija raised her chin, and he dropped a kiss on her mouth.

Then another.

And another.

Until she was the one giggling.

"Remember the friends I told you about?" He locked his arms behind her back and gently swayed her from side to side. "One of them hooked me up with a favor. A couple of them."

"He's the one who sent the bank information?" she asked.

He graced her lips with another kiss. "Mm-hmm. He also manipulated our information in government databases so that, if we're spotted anywhere on camera, facial recognition won't link back to us."

"What, he gave us longer chins or something?"

"I don't know. Maybe."

"By the way, he sent me something else along with the banking information."

"Did you sign it?"

She wrinkled her nose. "Only because I was feeling emotional. You owe me a ring. Right now, I'm your 'almost' wife."

"The ring's being made as we speak."

"I'm guessing we're not Mr. and Mrs. Sokolov?"

He grinned. "Inside, we're still Dom and Eija. Out there, we're...Andrei and Emerald Falcone."

Eija laughed so hard she had to hold on to him to remain upright.

"You okay with that?" he asked.

"I am. I'm more than okay with it."

"God, I missed you." He kissed her forehead, her nose. "I love you, Eija."

"I love you too, Dom."

Saying it was so easy now.

So wonderful now.

"So," he glanced over her head at where Shiloh played, "what do you want to do now that I'm here?"

She stepped away from him. "No."

"No?"

"One's more than enough for now." He reached for her, but she backed away, squealing. "No, Dom. You won't get me to give you a baby."

"How about we at least try? Remind me how they're made again?"

Each time he reached for her, she shrieked and stole away from his grasp until he was chasing her around the house. Once again interested in her parents, Shiloh joined in, screaming and giggling as Dom chased them both.

Epilogue

Eija turned a padded yellow envelope over and over in her hands. It had been addressed to the Falcones in Panama, but she didn't recognize the return address.

"Dom?" She walked into the house and headed up the stairs to their bedroom. "Baby, you up?"

Just as she entered the bedroom, he stepped from the bathroom, a towel around his waist and steam billowing behind him. His hair graced the tips of his shoulders, wavy from the shower.

"What's that?" he asked.

"It's addressed to the Falcones. It's from Australia."

He smiled. "It's Pavel."

"Pavel? How do you know?"

"Is it from 'Frank Castle'?"

She nodded.

"It's Pavel." He took the folder, tore it open, and pulled out a sheet of paper. On it, in scratchy handwriting, were the words "Please watch," with a link printed underneath.

Eija's heart warmed over. "That's Niko's handwriting. I hope they're doing well. Do you think this is him checking in?"

It would be nice to see their faces.

Both their faces.

Dom pulled up the link and cast it to the TV. Then he sat on the bed and pulled her to him, lips falling onto her slightly protruding stomach.

The link turned out to be a video.

Of Leah.

In London.

"Where should I put myself?" Leah said, unaware she was being recorded via a camera hidden in Lyu's replacement collar. *"Where do you think she'd like me?"*

"She?" Dom asked.

Eija remained quiet.

Leah's eyes brightened. *"I know."*

She stripped off her clothes and slipped into the bed in Eija's hotel room at the Havre. Lyu hopped up onto the mattress and curled up next to her.

"So, when she comes in, I'll be like..." Leah opened her arms. *"Too much? You're right. I'll get under the covers and then just,"* she mimed letting the sheets fall, *"keep them low and pretend I was covering up."*

Lyu meowed.

The door rattled.

Leah pushed Lyu under the covers.

Eija clipped off the video.

Dom, holding back a grin, cleared his throat. "Well, then."

"Guess you were right." She cocked her head to the side. "Damn. If she'd shown up *before* what happened on the bridge..."

"Then...what?" he asked, brow raised.

"Then," she shrugged, "she'd have shown up before what happened on the bridge. Why? What'd you think I was going to say?"

She tried to step away, but he dragged her back and toppled her onto the bed. In the process, he'd removed the towel.

"I told you what would happen if you kept fucking around," he warned. "Open up."

She let her legs fall open.

He dipped his tongue between them, and her eyes rolled to the back of her head.

Right.

Pussy monster.

Thank you for reading.

xoxo

K. Alex

Acknowledgments

Special Thanks to:

Rudi_Design

WritePath Editing

Continue the Series

Moonlight Retribution
Book 2 of the International Mafia Series

* * *

When they realized they were sitting close together on a park bench, staring at each other as though no one else existed—and dozens of other people did—they separated. He focused on the ice cream, and she looked down at the skirt of her dress, fingers gripping the edge of the wooden seat.

"How'd I do?" she asked, peering at him from the corner of her eye.

"Well," the bulb in his throat bobbed, "you're only half right."

"What did I get wrong?"

"You never answered what it is you think I want from you."

Zaraia flicked her wrist. "Oh, that's easy. Sex."

"No."

"No?"

"Zee, asking you to sleep with me in exchange for helping you didn't even cross my mind."

Which was unfortunate. Even if she did wind up saying no, had he asked, she would at least have had to consider the odds. Right now, they were about seventy-thirty in favor of their hot, sweaty, naked bodies sliding over and against each other.

Attraction was a sneaky, *sneaky* bitch.

"When I look at you, I don't think something as trivial as fuck-buddy," he said. "That's not a role I would ever ask a woman like you to have in my life."

"What role would you have me play, then? Confidante? Co-conspirator?" She lowered her lashes. "Girlfriend?"

"None of the above. Then again, maybe that last one, but that's not what I was going to ask, either."

She grabbed his bicep—his thick, solid bicep—and tried to shake him into revealing the question but ended up pulling herself closer to him.

"Ask me anyhow. You've got my interest all piqued."

"Fine." He faced her again, setting the ice cream cup on the bench seat. "But only to put you out of your misery."

"Thank you. It's all I ask."

"Zaraia," he took her left hand, "will you marry me?"

Books by K. Alex Walker

International Mafia

Prince of The Brotherhood

Moonlight Retribution

Knight for a Queen

Myths, Legends, and Monsters Anthology Series

The Gatekeeper

Elias The Wicked

The Girl in the Mountains

Jonah's Ghost

The Game of Love

The Game of Love

The Game of Love - Sequel

Angels and Assassins

The Wolf

The Protector

A Fighting Chance

The Anarchist

The Dark Knight

The Shadow

The Darkest Knight

Hidden In The Shadows

<u>The Boys from Chapel Hill</u>

Seducing The Boss

No Feelings Allowed

Breaking the Code

<u>Kismet</u>

Fated

The Woman He Wanted

About the Author

Don't forget to leave a review!

I'm a creative creature from the Caribbean who likes animals, Star Wars, quirky humor, and any kind of media that deals with people finding love in an otherwise impossible time.

Connect With Me:

Mailing List:
Text BOOKADDICT to 66866!

Blog - http://www.kalexwalker.com
Website - http://www.kalexwrites.com
Amazon - amazon.com/k-alex-walker
Instagram - instagram.com/kalexwrites
Facebook - facebook.com/mskalexwalker
Bookbub - bookbub.com/authors/k-alex-walker

Looking for exclusive stories, updates, giveaways, one on ones, and more? How about writing a book *with* me?

Join me on Patreon!

facebook.com/kalexwalker
instagram.com/kalexwrites

Made in the USA
Monee, IL
01 October 2023

43776449R00215